> Usually, the mother-to-be prepares the guy... She makes a romantic dinner, wears a special dress. She says, "Honey, you better sit down because I've got something to tell you."

But Remy had accidentally heard the news—and from the very man who was apparently going to give his child a name!

Jayne was watching his face. She'd probably thought he'd gone crazy. Maybe he had. And maybe he had a right to.

He was going to be a father!

All his life, Remy had ruminated on how his own father had deserted him. He'd planned his fatherhood, too, thinking he'd teach *his* son how to trap crawfish, crack open oysters and run trotlines through the bayou waters.... Oh, countless times, he'd imagined hearing he'd made a woman pregnant.

But he never once imagined the woman would be named Jayne Wright.

Dear Reader,

Ever wonder what it would be like to meet not one but *four* fabulous handsome hunks? Well, you're about to find out! Four of the most fearless, strong and sexy men are brought to their knees by the undeniable power of love—in this month's special VALENTINE'S MEN.

Meet Remy Lafitte in *The Bounty Hunter's Baby* by Jule McBride.

In 1993, Jule McBride's debut novel received the *Romantic Times* Reviewer's Choice Award for "best first series romance." Ever since, the author has continued to pen heartwarming love stories that have met with strong reviews and made repeated appearances on romance bestseller lists. Says Jule, "To me, New Orleans conjures a million sensual images—music spilling onto steamy streets and meandering waterways curling around moss-hung trees—but one of those images has always been Remy Lafitte, my bad-boy bounty hunter. As soft on the inside as he is tough on the outside, I hope readers will love him!"

We don't want you to miss out on any of these sexy guys, so be sure to check out *all* the titles in our special VALENTINE'S MEN.

Regards,

Debra Matteucci
Senior Editor & Editorial Coordinator
Harlequin Books
300 East 42nd Street
New York, New York 10017

THE BOUNTY HUNTER'S BABY

JULE McBRIDE

Harlequin Books

TORONTO • NEW YORK • LONDON
AMSTERDAM • PARIS • SYDNEY • HAMBURG
STOCKHOLM • ATHENS • TOKYO • MILAN
MADRID • WARSAW • BUDAPEST • AUCKLAND

For the Pratt family, especially Aunt Judy who shares my
soft spot for books and big cities

ISBN 0-373-16617-6

THE BOUNTY HUNTER'S BABY

Prologue

Four and a Half Months Ago

Remy Lafitte gasped. "Mind repeating that, *chère?*" The man had plenty of muscles to spare, but he didn't move a one. He remained sprawled in the swivel chair in his dimly lit bail bondsman's shack, with one of his dusty black alligator-skin boots propped on the desk, next to a half-empty bottle of whiskey. The other was on the floor beside a radio tuned to soft jazz. After a moment, Remy absently touched the flimsy brim of his bush-style hat, as if he wasn't quite sure whether or not he was in the presence of a lady.

"I'd very much like to initiate an intimate sexual encounter with you, Mr. Lafitte," Jayne Wright repeated primly. She knew her choice of words was strange, but she didn't want the man to think she was confusing sex with really making love.

When he said nothing, Jayne became a tad queasy. Everything seemed blurrier. Was it because she was about to faint, or because she'd removed her glasses for vanity's sake? *Just remember, Jayne, you're taking this bull by the horns,* she thought shakily.

Of course, she knew less than zilch about the rules governing one-night stands, but as a lawyer, she possessed highly honed negotiating skills. She simply couldn't fathom why Remy Lafitte wasn't responding. Although her glasses were hidden in her shoulder bag, Jayne anxiously tapped the bridge of her nose with her index finger, as if to afix them more firmly to her face. She'd been so convinced that Remy would rise immediately, stride toward her and...

Instead, his silver eyes narrowed to a squint while hers drifted over him. His wavy black hair was pulled back in a queue, his jaw was dark with stubble, and his denim shirt hung open. His tanned fingers nestled in his chest hairs, just touching a red crawfish tattoo that had been etched on his well-developed left pectoral, right over his heart. If Jayne hadn't known he was a bounty hunter, she never would have guessed just which side of the law he was on.

"Well?" Jayne's resolve was wavering as much as her voice, but she glanced pointedly past Remy toward the back room, which contained an iron-framed single bed.

For the past two hours, she'd wended her way beneath the ornate, wrought-iron balconies of the French Quarter, and all the while a great weight had seemed to press down on her chest. Neon signs advertising raw oysters and spiced shrimp had pulsed in rhythmic time with the zydeco music that spilled from honky-tonks onto the old flagstone streets, and Jayne had felt sure she'd suffocate from the intoxicating scents of martinis and magnolias.

As she walked, she'd kept thinking of Remy in terms such as "specimen" and "experiment," and she'd tried to forget that this evening in early October was hardly the first time she'd surreptitiously haunted the man's neighborhood. She'd tried to forget how he'd affected her when she first saw him, too—making her breath catch and her eyes widen with the shock of recognition, as if he were an old lover she hadn't seen for years.

Now she realized that the steamy, sultry New Orleans night had gone to her head and made her lose her mind.

"Look here, *chère* . . ." Remy's drawl seemed to come straight from the depths of the deepest bayou in the Delta. Vowels curled around consonants slowly, the way southern Louisiana waterways meandered around moss-hung cypress trees.

"Yes?" Jayne croaked.

"I'm still not sure I heard you right."

Had she misinterpreted Remy's flirtation? Jayne swallowed around the lump in her throat. "I do believe you heard me correctly."

For a whole year—ever since she'd moved to New Orleans to start a practice with her college and law school chum, Parker—this bounty hunter, whom her firm frequently employed, had led her on mercilessly. Or was that just wishful thinking? Two warm spots of color heated her cheeks. How could she save face now? "Well," she managed to say, "that's *certainly* not the only reason I came."

"Sugar, pardon my saying so—" Remy's mouth quirked "—but if your second reason's anything like your first, I sure can't wait to hear it."

"I need you to track down one of my missing clients." Ignoring the perspiration beading on her upper lip, Jayne squared her shoulders regally and crossed the room, hoping Remy couldn't see her mortified expression in the darkness. When she placed the case file on his desk, her fingers trembled. *Don't let him notice,* she prayed. *Oh, please, don't let him notice.* She'd never propositioned a man in her life, and if she could just leave this awful shack without dying from embarrassment, she swore she never would again.

"The name of the client is Judas Sweeny. He's due in court tomorrow on a mugging charge, and his mother hired me to defend him."

"Dreadlocks and a mustache." Remy nodded. "Folks call him Smoothtalk."

Remy's drawl could send shivers of longing down any woman's spine—and did. At the sound and in spite of the heat, chills spread over Jayne's skin. Instead of looking over the case file the way he was supposed to, Remy looked *her* over—from head to toe, and without apology.

Fortunately, everything about Jayne's person—from her single strand of pearls to her impeccable gray suit and matching pumps—indicated that she meant business. She wore only a hint of makeup, and her recalcitrant shoulder-length wheat-colored curls had been forced into submission with a blow dryer, then twirled into a tidy French twist.

But had she actually marched into a bail bondsman's shack near the wharves and offered herself bodily to a bounty hunter? She wanted nothing more than to pivot and run. It felt as if one of her migraines were coming on, and her fingers itched to release the pins from her tightly bound hair. She wished she'd worn her glasses, too. Squinting at Remy, she cleared her throat a full three times before she finally found her voice. "You'll find my client?"

Remy merely shook a cigarette from a pack on the desk, snapped open a square silver lighter and lit it. After a moment, his tongue darted out and he touched the tip, removing a fleck of tobacco. As much as Jayne wanted to give him her usual lecture on secondhand smoke, she refrained. She'd known about his nasty habits—smoking was only one of many—before she so brazenly approached him.

"Now, let me get this straight..." Remy tilted his head and shot her a lopsided grin, his teeth flashing white in the room's dimness. "Did you really just storm into my office and say you wanted, er... a roll in the hay?"

"I did not say that!" She added candor and an off-color vocabulary to the list of his vices. When Remy blew out a sigh, the obvious relief in it made her face turn crimson. Catching her necklace between her fingers, she nervously toyed with the pearls. "An... encounter," she said weakly. "That was my exact terminology."

"Well, I'll be damned," Remy said.

A second later, his throaty chuckle filled the room, and Jayne decided she'd give everything she possessed—her law practice, the trust fund, and her membership in the Daughters of the American Revolution—to take back these last few, humiliating moments of her life. As a dull ache of desperation settled deep inside her, she assured herself it was due to wounded pride, not a broken heart. *Just thank your lucky stars he's rejecting you, Jayne.* After all, Remy Lafitte wasn't the sort of man with whom she should be seen. At least not in broad daylight.

Nevertheless, he made desire stir at the core of her in a way she'd never imagined, much less actually felt. He could be so powerfully quiet and so watchfully still. Those silvery eyes were dangerously perceptive—the eyes of a man who made his living by tracking down criminals.

"Ms. Wright—" Remy stubbed out his cigarette after he had taken exactly five puffs "—what in the world's gotten into you?"

Jayne made a strangled sound. "I thought you would be pleased," she said tightly.

Remy's ensuing belly laugh was so resonant that she felt it vibrate inside her bone marrow.

"Surely I'm not the first woman to suggest a one-night stand," Jayne continued, in the most casual tone she could muster. "I just assumed a man like you was glad when such requests are filed." *Did I really say "filed"?* Pure panic made her knees buckle. "I may be unclear as to protocol," she added quickly, "but I *was* serious." She lifted her chin a prideful notch.

Remy caught the brim of his bush hat between his thumb and finger, then tossed the hat on his desk. He ran a flattened palm over his head, slicking back his hair, then shook his head, as if he didn't know whether to laugh or cry. "You're filing a request?"

Of course, the phrase was funny-sounding, but every time Jayne encountered Remy she became tongue-tied. Her heart thudding, she watched him rise and circle his desk silently.

"*Chère,* your, er... protocol *is* a little strange."

In spite of all that had transpired, Jayne sure hoped he'd wrap those strong arms around her now.

Instead, he leaned against the desk and said, "Why tonight?"

She crossed her arms and widened her stance with a practiced courtroom air, each nuance of her body language calculated to communicate self-confidence. "You often flirt with me. Isn't that correct?"

"Aw, darlin'..." Remy stared at her, slack-jawed. "I'm a flirt by nature."

"Oh!" she gasped. As soon as the word was out, she clamped a hand over her mouth.

"Not that I don't think you're real..." Remy's voice trailed off.

"I'm sorry," Jayne rambled defensively, "but isn't this all your fault? I mean, you began this, shall we say, flirtation." *Why can't I quit using moronic phrases like "shall we say"? Oh, Jayne, he's a man, not a judge and jury.* "I've, er...worked sixteen-hour days ever since I can remember. Then, on my way here, to discuss Judas..." She sounded so darn stiff! Remy had called Judas by his street name. "Er...*Smoothtalk* Sweeny...I suddenly realized that it's my..." She paused, feeling scarcely capable of saying it. "My thirtieth birthday."

Remy looked at her as if she were foaming at the mouth. "So the lady lawyer decided she wanted me for her birthday?"

That was pretty much the story, but something in Remy's eyes told her not to admit it. The rest of him—his lazy voice and his powerful body—continued to convince her that he'd be a wonderful lover. And how could she live a day past thirty without knowing what that meant? She was so tired of being a plain Jayne.

"Bring a cake for me to jump out of, *chère?*"

"No." She tossed Remy a quick smile, as if his rejection didn't concern her in the least. "I brought a condom."

He gaped at her. "A condom?"

Unfortunately, he put the emphasis on the word *a,* and she gawked at him, not knowing what to think. She'd had sex with two men during the time she was in law school at the University of Virginia. Neither had required more than one. "This was a big mistake," she said levelly.

Remy studied her with the penetrating gaze that had brought her here in the first place. His head tilted, his silver eyes narrowed above his high cheekbones, and his bow-shaped lips parted in what might become a smile. Her insides turned to mush.

"Oh, heavens, darlin'..." he said warily.

This time the endearment stung. *Darlin', sugar, chère*—he'd called her all those names, and she'd been fool enough to think they meant something special.

Swiftly he crossed the remaining space between them and brushed her forehead, as if a lock of hair had fallen. Not that it had. Her French twist was rolled as taut as a drum. "Ms. Wright..."

"Jayne," she squeaked. "Under the circumstances, you may feel free to call me Jayne."

Remy looked thoroughly exasperated. And up closer, in spite of her blurry vision, his eyes looked as silver as the lucky lining said to be inside rain clouds. But he was going to turn her down. She was positive he'd been with a number of women, so why not her? Without warning, her arm shot upward and her fingers curled around his biceps. She dug her manicured nails deep into his skin, which seemed marginally more dignified than saying please outright.

"Ms. Wright...er, Jayne...I—" Remy stopped cold and glanced toward where she clutched at his muscle.

"What's wrong with me?" she wailed. It was thoroughly embarrassing to ask, but she had to know. She had six sisters—all younger than she. Not only were they all married, but all had recently announced their first pregnancies.

"Nothing's wrong with you, Jayne," Remy said. "Why, I'd like nothing more than to show you the best lovin' available this side of the Mason-Dixon line, but..."

"You would?" she gasped. Too late, the word *but* registered. She wanted to kill herself, or him—which didn't matter. "Never mind, it's...er, it's okay."

"Aw, hell," Remy muttered.

He grabbed her waist so fast that her feet left the floor. In an instant, her breasts were crushed against his rock-hard chest and the man was raining hot, wet kisses up and down the column of her neck.

Jayne locked her knees so that she wouldn't fall and sighed softly. Darkness invaded her consciousness, and when she opened her eyes, pin-size white dots sparkled in the air like fairy dust. The more she blinked them away, the giddier she felt. But she *had* to keep remembering that it would take more than a kiss to make a prince out of Remy.

"This is only for one night." Her husky voice remained so formal that she might have been a princess just given a night's reprieve from the castle. "You can never call me."

Remy's lips stilled on her skin, and she knew she'd take back the words a thousand times—if only Remy would kiss her again.

"Why's that, *chère?*"

"We are entirely ill-suited."

"Yeah?"

"You're a bounty hunter," she whispered, as if that explained everything.

He resumed nibbling her earlobe. Between bites, he whispered, "And you're a big-time lady lawyer in Orleans Parish. You've got your own firm, and your partner, Parker Bradford, has political aspirations."

"That is correct," she gasped. *Good.* She'd so feared he wouldn't understand. How could she have explained that she hailed from the Wrights of old Virginia? They'd voyaged to the colonies on the *Mayflower* and fought in the American Revolution and then the Civil War—on both sides. The current generation wouldn't take kindly to Jayne's having a hard-loving, hard-drinking, bounty-hunter boyfriend. Jayne moaned softly, each touch of Remy's tongue making her melt.

"Well, Jayne..." Remy blew on the trail of wet spots he'd left on her neck. "By morning, I guarantee it'll be you—not me—who comes back asking for seconds."

Unable to believe the audacity of the man, Jayne hoarsely said, "I am in complete control of myself."

"Not for long, *chère*," he assured. And then his lips descended hungrily on hers.

Chapter One

"Happy Valentine's Day!" someone shouted.

"And Mardi Gras!"

"And wedding!" Lynn Seward yelled breathlessly.

"Wedding?" a costumed cupid called from the center of the cobbled street. "Who said wedding?" The masked, shirtless reveler wore white boxer shorts printed with red hearts, and his skin was painted gold from head to foot. As he leaped beneath the street lamp like a ballet dancer, the feathers of his gold wings ruffled in the breeze. Suddenly he stood stock-still and struck a statuesque pose, his muscular chest gleaming dramatically in the New Orleans twilight. Then the cupid gracefully readied his bow and shot a long golden arrow straight toward Parker Bradford's distant upstairs veranda—and right at Jayne Wright's heart.

Thankfully, the arrow was rubber-tipped. It sailed over Parker's usually pristine lawn, which was now littered with lost masks and party hats, then shot through the second-floor balcony's lacy, wrought-iron grillwork, grazed Jayne's stocking and whizzed through the open French doors behind her, into Parker's study.

"So much for being lovestruck," Jayne whispered, glancing down just as her panty hose ran from her ankle to her knee.

Below her, Parker's assistant, Lynn Seward ducked beneath a limb of a banana tree, then moved toward the front door of Parker's Garden District mansion. "And don't you dare forget to throw me your bouquet, Jayne!" she continued. "Girl, you two are going to have the cutest little babies!"

"One, anyway," Jayne whispered. "And sooner than you think." Nervously she toyed with her pearl necklace, thinking she really should do something nice for Lynn. Ever since the wedding had been announced, Parker's assistant had become uncharacteristically friendly—cutting helpful hints from bridal magazines and encouraging Jayne to talk about her prenuptial jitters.

Still, she hoped Lynn didn't head to the veranda. Parker was hosting a party to celebrate both the wedding and Mardi Gras, and Jayne had come outside to escape the crowd.

Not that she had. The streets below were thronged with tourists and locals. Some were costumed, many guzzled hurricanes or carried cups overflowing with Mardi Gras beads and doubloons. All were leaving the Endymion parade. In the distance, Jayne could still see the krewe's final float—an extravagant feathered confection pulled by two mammoth swans—passing by on Saint Charles Avenue.

"Congrats, Jayne!"

"Thanks!" Jayne leaned over the veranda rail and mustered a jaunty wave just as her own assistant, Celeste

Beauregard, ducked under the banana tree, supported by two dapperly dressed silver-haired men.

One was a fiftyish business associate of Parker's named Hal Knowles. The other was Boyd Laney, a forty-something new junior partner in Jayne's and Parker's law firm. Jayne smiled, knowing she'd been right to hire Boyd. Although the man had been accused of embezzling when he was in his thirties—and the charge had later caused other firms to discriminate against him—nothing had ever stuck. Since a man was innocent until proven guilty, at least according to Jayne's code of ethics, she'd felt obliged to hire Boyd. So far he was working out just fine.

"Your husband-to-be's a real fine catch, Jayne!" Boyd shouted, threading his fingers through his silver hair, then waving a final time before entering the house.

"You're marrying money, at any rate."

This time the voice came from the interior of Parker's study. *How long has* he *been standing here?* Jayne wondered, her palms turning slick with sweat. And had he overheard her whispered remark about the pregnancy?

She tried to force herself to turn around, but she simply couldn't bring herself to face him—not yet. *Lord, this man's in my blood like an illness,* she thought shakily. For four and a half months, she'd self-medicated with a killer work schedule and a whirlwind of business-related activity—until she'd finally gone into what she hoped was a full remission.

But now, at nothing more than the soft sound of that seductive drawl, all her symptoms returned—the cold sweats, the nervous stomach, the heart flutters. Not to mention the headache pangs. Her list of ailments was so long that Marcus Welby could have aired on the networks again—with her as the lone patient.

Jayne mentally counted to ten—hoping she was mistaken about the identity of the man behind her, praying he'd leave. When he didn't, she very slowly turned around.

Sure enough, she was face-to-face with the last person on earth she ever wanted to see again—the father of her baby.

"Remy," she said.

"Jayne."

Somehow she'd expected something more explosive to happen. She looked him square in the eye, willing herself to forget that steamy night when she'd so shamelessly propositioned him. Just recalling the impassioned way he'd kissed her—as if it were all his idea, as if he didn't view her as a pity case who'd come knocking on his door—she felt her cheeks burn with shame.

Remy had never called her, of course. Not even when he'd returned her client, Smoothtalk Sweeny, to the county lockup. No, Remy had avoided her—until now.

He must know I'm pregnant.

At the mere thought, a headache pain boinged above her left eye. Ignoring it, she set her jaw determinedly. She pulled on a mental mask that hid her features as surely as the actual masks worn by the Mardi Gras revelers—making her face expressionless, unreadable, safe.

Judging by Remy's friendly demeanor, Jayne decided that he remained blissfully unaware of the baby. He was carrying the stray golden arrow, though—and the fact that Cupid had struck both her and Remy with a single blow was unnerving.

Feeling embarrassed, she glanced away from him—only to frown again. Because the office of the law firm was directly on the main parade route, Boyd Laney had been preparing a legal case in the study at Parker's home. From here, it looked as if Parker's safe were open a crack. Chastising herself for not fully trusting Boyd, Jayne squinted into the study—until she realized that Remy was watching her and she forgot the safe entirely.

He smiled. "So, how've you been?"

"Fine."

His eyes narrowed, as if he found her tone off-putting. Roughly shoving the arrow into his back jeans pocket, he said, "This thing damn near killed me."

"Maybe next time," Jayne offered.

Remy raised a bushy eyebrow. "What's your problem?"

That she was pregnant and still couldn't get Remy off her mind. A pack of cigarettes peeked from the frayed pocket of his flannel shirt, and he was wearing cowboy boots. His hair cascaded over a brown suede jacket that had a gaping rip in the shoulder, and he was carrying a bottle of Dom Perignon—but no glass. As rakish as he looked, Jayne felt wistful.

"Guess it's been awhile since you've seen me, *chère*." Remy's playful drawl hinted that she'd been staring at him—and loving every inch of what she saw.

"Not long enough."

He chuckled softly and moseyed over, leaning his elbows on the veranda rail and wedging the toe of a boot into an ironwork curlicue. "Why the show of temper?"

Because four and half months ago I told you to stay out of my life. Now she had to get rid of him before he realized she was pregnant. Nevertheless, against all her better judgment, Jayne surrendered to vanity, removing her eyeglasses and slipping them into the pocket of her suit jacket. She shrugged as if her testiness had nothing to do with him. "What are you doing here, anyway?"

"Parker invited me." He flashed her a quick grin. "As you know, it's hard to turn down a man of Parker's ... stature."

"Are you implying I'm marrying Parker for his money?"

Remy stared at her. "Mind telling me what I did wrong?"

"You said you wouldn't call me," Jayne returned nervously, as if a day, rather than four and a half months, had gone by. She casually buttoned her gray blazer over her abdomen. After all, Remy had eyes like a hawk—and a right to know about his child. She felt so guilty that she almost blurted out the news. But surely a man like Remy wouldn't *want* to know.

"I *haven't* called, Jayne." Remy was wearing the bemused expression that graced his features each time he saw her—as if she were some strange curiosity he'd found in one of the voodoo shops in the French Quarter. The smile that ghosted over his lips broadened to a grin. "Given your engagement, I figured you'd feel safe from the likes of me."

She smiled back wryly. Her body could be rigged with a high-security system of alarms and locks and bars—and she still wouldn't be safe. Because Remy didn't pose a threat. It was *she* who couldn't be trusted. Fifty wedding anniversaries down the road, she could imagine herself sneaking away from Parker and forcing herself on Remy.

Finally Remy said, "Well, I've been meaning to congratulate you since I read about your engagement in the *Times-Picayune*." He took a lazy swig of champagne, then proffered the bottle, raising an eyebrow in an unspoken question.

She wanted to say that even before she became pregnant with his child, the mere thought of alcohol had made her queasy. "Don't you think Dom Perignon deserves to be drunk from glasses?"

"Speaking of glasses, you don't have to remove yours for my sake."

Jayne tamped down a flush. Was she that transparent? Five minutes around Remy, and she was sure cellophane hid her insides from the world, rather than good old-fashioned skin. Had he also guessed how many lonely nights she'd lain awake thinking about him? She finally said, "I didn't."

He shrugged. "Why, I was just hoping you'd keep undressing."

If he thought that would rattle her cage, he had another think coming. "Surely not in front of you."

"I've seen you lusciously naked," he returned in a stage whisper. "In fact, I've still got one of your shoes."

Her heart thudded dully, and she could hear the blood whirring in her ears. For days after Remy had made love to her—the phrase *sexual encounter* hardly summed up what had taken place—Jayne hadn't needed her missing shoe. She'd walked on water and floated on air. She'd known she couldn't see him again, but she'd bought a red strapless evening gown that she'd never have the nerve to wear. Because the impulse purchase still hung between two gray suits, she thought of Remy each time she opened her closet.

Silently, until dawn, Remy had shown her the ways of love. She'd expected ravishment, never suspecting that his touch would be so gentle. There'd been more emotion in his fingertips than Jayne imagined she'd find in most men's whole bodies. She'd longed for Remy from the first moment she saw him, but that night he'd become her prince, and the run-down bondsman's shack had become their castle. As the hours wore on, she'd realized she wanted to stay with Remy forever. Right up until he'd rolled onto his back and snored so loudly that he could have raised the dead.

She'd stared at him for a full hour, trying to imagine what common ground they might share, what they might find to talk about. Giving up, she'd donned her clothes, almost as quickly as Remy had divested her of them. But she'd found only one shoe; she'd shoved it into her pocketbook when she went to catch a cab. Not that it mattered. She owned four pairs of gray pumps exactly like the ones she'd worn that night.

Jayne realized Remy was scrutinizing her. Her heart pounding, she gripped the veranda rail and haughtily lifted her chin. "Must you make veiled references to the past?"

"Darlin', it wasn't all that veiled." Remy chuckled. "The only thing that's going to be veiled is you."

She emitted a short sigh.

"Jayne, can't you take a joke?"

"What I take is responsibility for my actions." When she realized her words carried the self-righteous ring of a proclamation, her knees turned rubbery.

Remy said, "What do you mean by that?"

"Not everyone carouses around downtown, lives easy and takes a new lover every day of the week." She said it calmly, as if his reprehensible lifestyle weren't worth a second thought.

"Jayne, I'm lucky—" Remy suddenly threw his head back and laughed "—but I ain't *that* lucky."

Jayne forced herself to look bored. Even though the tension underlying their exchange had lifted with his laughter, she still had to get rid of him—or escape herself. He could never realize they'd made a baby together. No one could.

"You and Parker..." Remy shook his head. "I never would have guessed."

"We've attended functions together for years, and we began a law practice together," she reminded him.

Remy's mouth quirked. "How romantic."

"I hardly need your permission to marry the man I love," Jayne volleyed back.

Remy shrugged. "Well, I hope Parker wins the election."

Jayne did, too. In November, a seat had opened up in the Louisiana House of Representatives, and Parker had decided to run. Because he'd been representing the tenants of the mismanaged Carrollton Riverside apartment complex, his profile was at an all-time high. The much-publicized case, which Parker had agreed to take free of charge, was still pending. The election was to take place next Wednesday, the day after their marriage. If Parker won, it would be the beginning of a political career that could take the newlyweds all the way to Washington.

The moment Parker was officially on the ballot, he'd proposed. And when Jayne told him she was pregnant, he'd said the offer still held. No questions asked. Even though the public would eventually realize that she'd been pregnant when he married her, he loved her and wanted to claim the child as his own.

Thinking about how selfless Parker was—taking on the Carrollton Riverside apartment case and agreeing to father another man's child—Jayne's heart swelled with emotion. "Parker's a good man," she found herself saying.

Remy chuckled. "Personally, I never took a woman to a 'function.'"

"No," she returned dryly, "You take them all straight to bed."

"Only when they ask," Remy countered.

Jayne's pulse surged, and her heart missed a beat. Why couldn't she simply remain civil until the man left? Maybe she could—but his glances kept insinuating that he satisfied her more than Parker could. "I'm in love with Parker."

"Who says you aren't?"

Jayne was sure Remy assumed he was more of a man than her fiancé. Maybe he was, but Jayne wasn't going to let him get away with thinking it. "Parker and I have a great relationship. I'm definitely not marrying him for his money."

Remy smiled. "You'd be just as happy with a poverty-stricken bounty hunter from the bayou?"

Her eyes dared him. "Is that some sort of proposal?"

"Hell, no."

There was a long, explosive silence.

Finally Remy said, "C'mon, we barely even know each other."

"That didn't stop you last October."

He gaped at her. "Are you mad at me for not calling you?"

"Of course not." She winced, wishing she hadn't said it quite so quickly. Defensive tension bristled inside her. "I'm perfectly happy with my life." *It sounds like a bald-faced lie, Jayne,* she thought, watching Remy's lips thin by degrees. Her mind raced. "Parker's...everything a woman could want...and more."

Remy's eyebrows raised. "So, he's all right in bed?"

She guessed she'd been trying to communicate that subtly, so that Remy would never guess the baby she carried was his. But how had the conversation gotten so completely out of control? If she didn't know better, she'd think that Remy was jealous of Parker. "Did you go to a special school?'' she inquired, knowing full well how juvenile she sounded. ''One with whole courses in how to ask inappropriate questions?''

''Sugar, we spent one real long night together. As a past fling...well, I just wanted to make sure you were...'' All at once, Remy laughed again—in a way that was flirtatious, infectious and kind.

Jayne swallowed hard. ''That I was what?''

His fool eyes were sparkling. Against his bronzed skin, they looked like silver fish leaping in dark waters. ''Taken care of, darlin'.''

The directness of the comment made her insides shake like jelly. *Just thank your lucky stars you didn't tell him about the baby, Jayne.* It would have gotten him out of her life, since men like Remy probably didn't propose in such circumstances. But in the worst-case scenario, he *would have* proposed. Now, the Quarter's consummate bad boy would be hosting a party in his bail bondsman's shack. Maybe men with scars, tattoos and an overabundance of facial hair would be drinking straight from bottles and roughly inquiring about Remy's expertise in the bedroom....

Without warning, Jayne's knees buckled, and she slumped over the veranda rail. When Remy's palm settled at the small of her back, she nearly jumped out of her own skin.

''You okay, Jayne?''

No. The warmth of Remy's fingers seeped right through her clothes, somehow reminding her that she and Parker had never actually gotten more intimate than a French kiss. Parker was too much of an old-school Southern gentleman. ''Parker truly is just wonderful,'' she murmured.

"I think the lady protests too much," Remy teased. He leaned so close to her ear that his silken lips touched the lobe, and then he whispered, "Does that mean you won't give me a kiss goodbye, for old times' sake, *chère?*"

Jayne gazed into his eyes. Those gray depths were utterly mesmerizing. Thoughtfully she twined her fingers through her pearls. "Well, I guess maybe we could..."

Remy winced. "Jayne, you're engaged."

Enraged was more like it! He'd merely been toying with her again, and it was a sore reminder that she'd misinterpreted his gestures in the past—seeing heartfelt desire where there was only meaningless flirtation. For once, she wished she could catch him off guard. Maybe she *would* tell him about their baby.

"You're getting married," Remy said warily.

"Not until Fat Tuesday," she said.

And then Jayne flung her arms around his neck and kissed him hard. Once their lips locked, he didn't exactly turn her down, either. In fact, he twirled her around and bent her spine right over the rail of the balcony. At the sudden movement, the run in her stocking shot from her knee to her panty line, and her pearl necklace looped over her shoulder.

Jayne felt so instantly revved up that she thought of race cars. Remy's tongue flickered inside her mouth, igniting sparks, and before she could so much as breathe, her pulse seemed to leap from zero to 260. The next thing she knew, her hair seemed to unroll and fly out beside her. And they were zooming around the racetrack at full throttle.

I just knew something explosive would happen, she thought, feeling faint. He was kissing her and she was kissing him back—and the voice inside her head now exclaimed, *You lovestruck woman, your fiancé is in the house!*

Jayne told herself to slam on the brakes and screech to a halt. When she realized she couldn't stop, she told herself to take a detour or a pit stop or to start waving a checkered flag. But how could she, when Remy was hers again? She could only shut her eyes and revel in his kiss. It was a jumble of warm, hazy impressions—solid muscles and leather, champagne and soap, tobacco and peppermints.

"Why, Jayne—" Remy released her abruptly and stepped back "—you sure are a wild one."

She chuckled and grasped his lapels playfully. She was hardly inclined to think in curse words, but she realized that an old suede coat smelled more manly than a brand-new suit—a *hell* of a lot more manly.

"You're getting *married*," Remy repeated.

At the sobering words, Jayne realized that everything was blurry. She fumbled in her suit pocket for her glasses, thinking this situation required some clarity. "Sharper focus," she mumbled under her breath.

But slipping on her spectacles didn't help.

Everything still seemed surreal.

She had kissed a man other than Parker at Parker's house. She was pregnant with Remy's child and Remy didn't know it. Parker knew Remy, since Remy did some work for the law firm, but Parker had no idea she was pregnant with Remy's child. If Parker ever found out, he'd never look her in the eye again—much less marry her. He naturally assumed the baby's father was an up-and-coming Ivy Leaguer, just like himself.

Jayne wanted to dive right off the balcony. She took the safer option and backed slowly toward Parker's study. Edging away from Remy, she flattened her palms against the air, as if she were a street mime touching an imaginary wall. "Please, Remy...just leave me alone, just..."

"I didn't *do* anything, Jayne."

But he had. The man's sheer existence was too much for her constitution. He could never fit into her world, and yet she was powerless to resist him. Of course, he wasn't exactly pursuing her, she admitted with horror.

"I know you didn't do anything, Remy..." Feeling giddy from his kiss, she raised a wobbly index finger and wagged it in his face, as threateningly as she could. "But if you would just...just kindly back away..."

"*Chère,* what in the world are you—?"

Jayne fled.

"I've been looking for you everywhere," Parker said cheerfully when Jayne collided with him on the stairs.

"Thank heavens you didn't find me!" Jayne blurted out in breathless panic. What had she just said? And how could she have kissed Remy?

She was incorrigible. Parker couldn't help it if he wasn't a Remy Lafitte. Parker was just a little more...cerebral. His wheat-colored hair had been styled at the best salon in Metairie, and his trendy sea green horn-rimmed glasses made his pupils appear doubly green. His columned Greek Revival–style mansion was a study in old-fashioned Southern grace. Any woman in her right mind would fall in love with him.

"Jayne?"

Jayne felt as if Remy were still kissing her. Her heart was pounding in her ears like a drumroll. Her skin felt boiling hot. "I believe I need to take a bit of air," she murmured.

The next thing she knew, she was running down the rest of the stairs as fast as her gray pumps could carry her. When she skidded to a halt at the front door, family faces swam before her eyes—her mother and the judge, her six sisters and their husbands. All the faces wore thin-lipped, pained expressions of understated Anglo-Saxon Protestant disapproval.

The pang above Jayne's left eye boinged to her right.

"They'll kill me...." she whispered to herself.

But she picked up her briefcase, slung the strap over her shoulder and flung open the door. Then she clenched her fists and crooked her arms and ran out into the night. After two blocks, she ran past the very same Cupid who had shot her in the leg and ruined her panty hose. That Cupid's love-tinged arrow had struck both her and Remy seemed like the worst kind of irony.

"Thanks a lot!" Jayne spit out murderously, without slowing her steps.

She ran as if she could outrace her own memory. With each step, she was running even farther away from that humiliating night four and a half months ago when she'd so brazenly entered the shack by the wharves. She ran until she thought her sides would split and her briefcase strap would break and her burning lungs would burst. And all the while she wondered where on God's green earth she was going—other than as far away from Remy Lafitte as she could get.

UPSTAIRS, a man stopped dead in his tracks and nervously threaded his fingers through his silver hair. Unable to believe his eyes, he stared deep inside the dark, empty recess of the open safe in Parker's study. Sure enough, the books—four small green cloth-bound ledgers—were gone.

"Who could have taken them?" he whispered. Earlier he'd gained access to the safe, just so that he could leave the books here. He could have sworn he'd locked it.

"Was Jayne all right?" a voice called, out in the hallway.

"Where was she going in such a hurry?" someone else asked.

Lynn Seward peeked inside the study. "What are you doing in here all alone?"

"Waiting for you." In spite of the circumstances, he surveyed Lynn—her shapely figure, slender neck and short blond bob. Casually he asked, "What's all the brouhaha about Jayne?"

Lynn shrugged. "She just bolted."

Celeste Beauregard appeared behind Lynn. "She grabbed her briefcase and ran out of the front door like the hounds of hell were on her heels."

"She took her briefcase?" he asked, imagining that his four ledger books were inside it.

Lynn nodded. "Care for a drink?"

He managed to say, "Maybe a martini."

"As dry as your sense of humour?" Lynn suggested.

He nodded.

"I'd better see if Parker knows what happened to Jayne," Celeste murmured in a concerned tone.

As soon as the women were gone, the man glanced inside Parker's safe again. Then he breezed through the French doors and leaned over the veranda rail. His eyes alit on a mop of red hair—then a tuft of black. "Speedo? Smiley?"

Two men looked up.

"Is Smoothtalk Sweeny with you?"

The men shook their heads. He guessed it didn't matter. "Could you do me a favor and come up here, boys?"

"What do you need, boss?"

To find Jayne Wright, he thought. And to retrieve those incriminating books.

Chapter Two

Thursday, February 15

The last person Remy wanted to see at ten in the morning was Parker Bradford, and he swore it was because Parker had plied him with too much expensive champagne the previous night. Convincing himself he had a hangover was definitely easier than admitting he'd lain awake until dawn thinking about the man's unpredictable fiancée.

When it didn't look as if Jayne were around, Remy sighed in relief. If she was in her office, she might charge into Parker's, rip open one of her starched white blouses with the Peter Pan collars, then bare her prim Maidenform bra. He could almost see the buttons scattering across the carpet. After that, she'd probably start kissing him or something even worse—and right in front of Parker. With Jayne, there was just no telling.

Lynn Seward swished into the office and left a file on Parker's desk. "Coffee, Remy?"

"No, thanks."

Parker's eyes followed Lynn as she exited the room; then he covered the phone's mouthpiece and nodded at the file. "I've a criminal for you to track, Lafitte. I'll be with you momentarily." Parker swung the receiver to his lips again. "I can't have you worrying, so let's do lunch, Hal. Why don't we meet at Antoine's?"

Remy frowned. Was Hal Knowles on the line? A few years ago, Remy had considered working at one of Knowles's sugar refineries on Bayou Lafourche—until he decided that something about the man made his skin crawl.

Reminding himself that Parker's business associates weren't his concern, Remy sprawled into a chair. The law firm of Bradford and Wright was located in an ultramodern high rise in the American sector of the city—a far cry from Remy's dimly lit space at the far end of the French Market. Like Jayne's, Parker's corner office was entirely of glass, with black lacquer furniture that looked stark against the plum-speckled gray carpeting.

Remy glanced over his shoulder, but he only saw Boyd Laney, who skulked past as if he were having a bad morning. Remy told himself he was watching for Jayne out of self-protective instinct. He just couldn't understand her. Ninety-nine percent of the time, the woman seemed prim, proper and refined. Exactly the type of woman an old-fashioned Southern guy might be sorely tempted to put on a pedestal—and marry. But then she went plumb wild, announced her secret libidinal desires and actually attacked.

Remy bit back a groan. Lord knew, he'd imagined making love to Jayne from the moment he laid eyes on her. How could he help it? Those trim suits kept her so well covered that a man was left with nothing but his wildest imagination. He just wished he could quit remembering how she'd looked that night four and a half months ago—her skin rosy, her hair golden, those arresting gray blue eyes the color of the sky on a summer morning deep in the bayou.

All at once, Remy felt as if he were trying to take deeper breaths than his chest would allow. Oh, there was just no denying his attraction. Sure, he'd expected Jayne to come around again. But she hadn't. And that bothered him. So did the realization that he'd been flirting with her. Since her arrival in town, he *had* made an awful lot of unnecessary visits to the law firm.

And their night together had been . . . perfect. He was a large, muscular man, but when Jayne Wright marched into his office and all but demanded he lie down with her, a newborn baby could have pushed him over with a feather.

He should have called her afterward.

But when she told him never to contact her, he'd been sure she meant it. He'd decided to abide her wishes, too. Mostly because she'd brought out the gentleman in him.

Last night, though, she'd snapped at him as if he were a criminal. During their exchange, he'd kept wondering what he'd done wrong, besides not call. He could have sworn she looked . . . almost guilty. Then, without warning, she'd done that complete about-face and kissed him. Explosively, too. Like a pressure cooker that had just blown. Glancing guiltily at Parker, Remy assured himself that he was just feeling sorry for Jayne. Heaven only knew what kind of environment had produced such a volatile woman.

But *he* knew.

Upper crust. Jayne was wealthy and well educated. It was just a crying shame that she was about to marry Parker Bradford, who was every bit as waspishly skittish as she. Right now, Parker was pacing self-consciously, looking as if he hadn't grown accustomed to his own skin in all the years he'd inhabited it. Parker, Remy decided, bothered him nearly as much as Hal Knowles.

Just be glad Jayne's getting married.

Rule-lovers like Jayne rarely suggested one-night stands, much less extramarital affairs. By the time Remy tracked down Parker's missing person, she'd probably be married to Parker. Not that Remy would be thinking about Jayne while he was gone, of course. If the case involved a hard-core felon, things could turn tough.

Parker hung up. "Sorry to keep you waiting."

"No problem."

Parker circled the desk and placed a folder in Remy's lap. As Remy opened it, he kept his gaze fixed on Parker's. "What's the charge?"

"Traffic violations."

"Traffic violations?" Remy chuckled in disbelief. "I don't do parking tickets. Get Buddy Wyatt."

Parker leaned against the desk. "Buddy's busy this morning. Besides, this case involves over three thousand dollars in outstanding fines."

Something wasn't right. Parker involved himself only in high-profile defense cases, such as the Carrollton Riverside case, which was getting him favorable press for fighting for tenants' rights. Riffling through the file, Remy saw that it was full of notes, with names and addresses of friends and family members. The usual. When his gaze landed on the subpoena, he groaned. This simply couldn't be happening.

But it was.

The firm of Bradford and Wright was actually hiring him to track down Jayne Wright.

His first impulse was to turn down the job. Then he imagined finding Jayne—and holding her for just one more heavenly night. He could almost feel her whispery breaths on his chest and her trembling fingers on his skin. Her delicacy made him feel strong. And her warm gaze made him feel as if he'd found something genuine in a world full of pretenders. *Forget it. The woman's marrying Parker.*

As if sensing reluctance, Parker doubled his standard fee.

"That's what I get for murder one," Remy countered.

"But this person has broken the law."

The file made a flapping sound as Remy shut it. "This *person*—" Remy squinted at Parker "—is featured almost daily in the Living section of the *Times-Picayune*. This *person* has been kissin' sweet little babies all over town to help you, her fiancé, win the election to the House of Representatives next week. Parker, this *person*—"

"I want this person back!" Parker pounded his fist on the desk for emphasis.

Remy sighed. "Parker, where I'm from, if your woman takes off, you go and haul her back yourself. You don't collect old parking tickets and then hire a professional tracker to—"

"Here." Parker extracted an envelope from his inner pocket and slapped it into Remy's hand.

Judging by the weight of it, Parker had anticipated an argument. Remy shook his head, hardly looking forward to his upcoming run-in with Parker's missing person. Their kissing encounters were rough enough. An arrest encounter could prove fatal.

Especially after last night. Remy didn't understand it, but he had gotten the distinct impression that Jayne would just as soon shoot him as look at him. "Well, I do guess Jayne'll be easier to track then your average felon."

"You'll have her back soon?"

Was it Remy's imagination, or did Parker sound downright scared? And why wasn't Parker going himself? Had Jayne called off her wedding? If so, Remy hoped the kiss they'd shared last night had absolutely nothing to do with it. At least that was what he told himself. Judging from how Jayne had lunged at him last night, she needed more than a man. She needed a husband.

"ASAP?" Parker said.

Remy shrugged. "I'll have her back by sundown."

JAYNE had been home less than ten seconds before she remembered why she'd left in the first place. Oh, she loved her large, picture-perfect family, all the siblings of which had arrived from various parts of the country for their father's sixty-eighth birthday, and she loved the old grand piano on which she'd play the birthday song after supper. She loved the Wright residence, too—an old white-columned plantation house that was nestled in the rolling hills near Charlottesville, Virginia. From the front windows, over the crest of a distant hill, Thomas Jefferson's home, Monticello, could be seen peeking through the now bare trees.

Still, hundreds of years of wealth and privilege had taken their toll on the Wrights. The family eccentricities were as harmless as they were obvious. Politics and the illustrious history of the Wright family were the only allowable subjects of conversation, for instance. The everyday cups and saucers were all over a century old and arranged in the cabinets according to pattern. And Helen Wright, Jayne's mother, possessed the common but unnerving quality of communicating in snappy clichés.

Then there was Jayne's father, the Honorable Judge Robert E. Lee Wright, who made no secret of the fact that he'd meant for all seven of the Wright girls to have been boys. All the daughters had received variations on boys' names, for this reason. Jayne's first name was actually

Roberta, after the judge, which meant he called her Robert. In the first grade she'd started using her middle name, Jayne.

Heaven knows, she thought, glancing around the table at the sea of gray suits, *I did rebel in my own small ways.* As upstanding as she was, Jayne was considered to be the family's renegade black sheep. Mostly because she didn't want to be called Robert.

Well, I'm a true black sheep now. She guiltily surveyed her pregnant sisters and tried to assure herself that Lafitte blood would liven up the Wright gene pool.

"Good to have you home, Robert." Her father's booming voice shook her from her reverie. He clapped Jayne on the shoulder as if she were his favorite old football buddy, and the fabric of her suit bunched beneath his huge, pawlike hand.

Her father had twice lost in bids for a Virginia senate seat, but he still ate, slept and breathed politics. Now that Jayne was engaged to Parker, who was running for office, she was back in the judge's good graces. She'd hoped her law degree would impress him, but all Judge Wright really wanted was a grandson.

Oh, Jayne, there's simply no way out of this marriage to Parker. Her younger sisters had all made good matches. Their husbands were actively campaigning for offices in six different states, and all her sisters were pregnant.

So am I. Jayne was suddenly glad her father's hand was on her shoulder, steadying her. She knew family history well enough to know that hers was the first out-of-wedlock pregnancy in the family since 1874. At the first sign of puberty, all Wright daughters were lectured on the unfortunate case of unwed mother Emily Anna Wright, who had "stained the family record" by becoming a "scarlet woman."

Jayne smiled wanly at her sisters and their husbands as her father seated her for supper, which had been served precisely at three since the judge's retirement. His birthday cake was already on the lace-covered table, positioned between two sterling-silver candelabra. Edwina, Paula, Christina, Antonia, Charlotte and Alexandra all beamed at Jayne.

"When's the baby due, Ed?"

Jayne winced at her father's tendency to address them using the boys' names he'd initially picked out for them. Everyone else in the family thought it was amusing.

Edwina chuckled and named her due date, then grinned at her husband. "The baby should be eating solid food by the time the Nebraska primaries roll around."

The judge chuckled. "And Charlie's due right before the November elections."

Charlotte nodded. "But if Antonia really has twins—" she looked at Antonia's husband "—Beck's going to be a shoo-in for the Oklahoma senate."

"Good going, Anthony," Judge Wright said agreeably. "Paul will deliver right on time, too." He nodded at Paula. "You always were the most punctual."

Because Wrights were never late, *punctual* meant *early.* "I sure hope so," Paula said with a heavy sigh. She was due in less than a month.

Alex giggled. "Jayne's going to be next," she said happily. "Right, Chris?"

Christina nodded.

Jayne nearly choked. Her own due date was June 23, not that she'd mention it. "Could be," she managed to trill.

Helen Wright usually remained silent during family gatherings, since the talk was often of politics, which she assured everyone was way over her head. Now she put in her two bits from the head of the table. "I hope all the babies are healthy and happy, and that you all win the elections, too. Still, it's not who wins or loses," she declared, "but how you play the game."

Jayne smiled at her mother. *Would any woman in her right mind announce her out-of-wedlock pregnancy to this family?* Helen Wright might smile kindly and say, "So it goes!" or "Nothing more surprising than a surprise!" But the judge would scream bloody murder.

"Well, we're all packed!" he exclaimed, as Ilsa—who had served the Wright family suppers from time immemorial—silently removed the serving plates and left the soup bowls. "Next thing we know, we'll all be in the Big Easy, seeing Parker win the election to the Louisiana House of Representatives." Judge Wright grinned, as if his life's work were now complete. "And, more importantly, to see the last of my beautiful daughters married off!"

Jayne's mother sipped from a heavy silver water goblet, then smiled pleasantly. "I didn't doubt it for one moment!"

Oh, yes, you did. Jayne winced. They'd all expected her to marry first. Everyone else had gone to the altar in the order of their ages. *If I don't marry Parker, I'm ruined.* Her gaze swept over the walls—panning the mounted family crest and landscapes that were bordered by carved and gilded frames. She tried to imagine Remy Lafitte standing in this room—and simply couldn't.

"Oh, Jayne, I just know your wedding's going to be as beautiful as ours," Edwina began. "Your announcement *was* somewhat hasty, but—"

"Now, Ed," her father said chidingly. "The six of you had long engagements. And you know Jayne's always had her own ideas about how to live her life."

"Well, you know what I say," her mother murmured sweetly. "There's just nothing more surprising than a good surprise." She surveyed Jayne for a long moment, her face full of a mother's love.

"Jayne, mother's ordered white roses, just like we had," Antonia said. "And she's decided on some lovely music...."

Political wife that she was, Helen Wright could plan a wedding overnight, from a thousand miles away, and with her eyes shut. Jayne had happily given her and her sisters carte blanche. The only stipulation had been that the marriage take place in New Orleans. Parker's father had a recurring ear infection that made travel difficult. The Wright women, of course, would be capable of travel no matter how pregnant they were. Since Fat Tuesday was usually a day for revelry, not weddings, Helen Wright had named that date and managed to secure Saint Louis Cathedral, in Jackson Square, for the high-society ceremony. Conveniently, the election was the following day.

While everyone but Jayne happily discussed the wedding, Ilsa removed the soup bowls and left the main course. Jayne didn't bother to look down to confirm the menu. Thursday meant roast beef, corn bread and stewed tomatoes, regardless of special occasions.

Jayne's heart sank. Yes, any deviation from the great menu of life would cause the family she loved a great deal of stress. It was one of many reasons Jayne couldn't tell Remy the truth he so deserved to hear.

The Wrights led calm, predictable lives. And that meant Jayne would marry Parker. She supposed her mother was the most flexible of the group. Still, if anyone in the family so much as applied a salad fork to a main course, it would be tantamount to revolution. One unified gasp would arise at the Wrights' table, as if the very social fabric of America had been threatened.

That was what Jayne was thinking when a fork actually did clatter to the well-oiled hardwood floor. She gasped along with everyone else and glanced up.

"Heavens to Betsy," her mother said.

Jayne shifted her weight on the needlepoint seat of her antique ladder-back chair and craned her neck around. A whimper escaped her lips. It simply could not be Remy Lafitte.

But it was.

He was leaning casually in the doorway, surveying the scene. In his black knit cap, black leather gloves, white T-shirt and worn brown suede jacket, he looked thoroughly out of place.

"Take anything you like." Judge Wright very calmly placed his raised fork on the table. "We will not resist. We're well insured, and I am only concerned about the welfare and protection of my family."

Her father thought Remy was a burglar! "Oh, Daddy," Jayne croaked, her heart beating wildly. "I know—er, I mean, I *sort* of know him, and he's..."

The ineffectual explanation came too late. Remy was already rambling into the room as if he owned it. He didn't stop moving until he was behind Jayne's chair.

Just when Jayne was sure matters couldn't get any worse, they did. The fool man said, "Hey, *chère*." Then he placed her missing gray pump on the lace tablecloth, right next to her bread plate. The toe was aimed directly at Judge Wright's birthday cake.

Remy's lazy grin said he knew exactly what kind of havoc he was wreaking. "I happened to be in the neighborhood and thought I'd return it." Remy nodded at the shoe, as if Jayne might not recall which item of clothing she'd lost.

"You know this man?" Judge Wright sounded appalled.

"She sure does, sir," Remy said.

A long silence ensued.

Jayne gaped at Remy, wondering which was more surprising—his presence, or the fact that she wasn't as furious as she should be. The devilish glint in his silver eyes seemed to dare her. "You came all the way from New Orleans to Charlottesville, just to deliver a shoe I lost somewhere?" She was pleased that she didn't sound the least bit rattled.

"Now, *that* would certainly be surprising," Jayne's mother interjected in a curious voice.

Remy shot Jayne an amused grin. "You didn't *lose* it."

The quick sweep of Jayne's gaze took in crystal, lace and sterling. In the blur of gray suits, she saw her father—who merely stared back at her as if she were a complete stranger.

"You left it," Remy continued. "At my place."

"That would be highly unusual," her mother commented.

Remy chuckled. "It was unusual, all right."

"All a great misunderstanding, I'm sure," Edwina murmured.

But it wasn't. And Jayne wondered if Remy had come to claim her. Making love with him had proved he had a poetic streak, and the symbol of the shoe *was* straight out of Cinderella. Maybe Remy had found out about the baby. Or maybe the kiss they'd shared last night had convinced him he couldn't let her marry Parker. All at once, her heart thudded and her breath caught. She tried to tell herself that it didn't matter—that Remy wasn't the man of her dreams, that he was merely her baby's biological father.

"Remy?" She choked out his name uncertainly.

"C'mon." He gently placed his hand beneath her elbow.

At the touch of his fingers, she remembered the pressure of his lips. He'd devoured her with his kisses—not just hungry for her, but starved. Parker's face wavered before her eyes like a mirage, and she cringed with guilt. "Where are you taking me?"

"New Orleans."

Gazing into Remy's eyes, Jayne decided not to worry about her family. Undoubtedly she'd been disowned when Remy waltzed across the threshold. When the shoe hit the table, she'd been erased from the will. If she stayed much longer, her father was going to deliver his usual line about not darkening the hallowed Wright doorstep. If anyone so much as *thought* she was pregnant with this man's child, she would be sent to live in Siberia, under any other name except Wright.

"New Orleans?" Feeling increasingly sure that Remy had come to claim her, she watched in horror as he reached behind himself and whipped out his handcuffs.

"Peaceably or otherwise."

Jayne's father wheezed as if a bone had gotten stuck in his throat.

Covering her husband's faux pas, Jayne's mother quickly said, "Jayne, perhaps your, er, *friend* would like to join us!"

Jayne heard another piece of silver cutlery clatter against bone china.

The next silence was so chilling that the room's temperature seemed to drop. Jayne could have sworn the air fogged and the windows frosted. When Ilsa appeared in the doorway, she froze, as if she'd just become an ice statue of herself. Jayne felt the cold so deep in her bones that not even Remy's eyes could melt her. "Excuse me, Remy?"

"I'm real sorry, Jayne," he said. "But I've got to arrest you."

"Excuse me?" she repeated.

"By the power invested in me by the state of Louisiana—" Remy reached in his back pocket, found a paper, unfolded it against his chest, then placed it on the table next to Jayne's gray pump "—you're being extradited to Orleans Parish, where you'll appear in court tomorrow at 10:00 a.m."

Jayne stared down. She'd examined hundreds of subpoenas during the course of her legal career, but certainly never one with her own name on it. She jerked her head in Remy's direction. "What's the meaning of this? What's the charge?"

"Traffic violations," her father said, reading the subpoena.

"Impossible!" Jayne exclaimed.

Remy's mouth quirked, as if he might smile, but his silver eyes looked steely. "All I really know," he said softly, "is that you very definitely have the right to remain silent."

Jayne's mother murmured softly to herself, running through her list of expressions and rejecting those that didn't make sense in this situation. "A penny saved is a penny earned" sure didn't work. Neither did "Love makes the world go round."

"I have the right to remain silent?" Jayne said shakily.

"If nothing else—" Remy's lips came so close that she was sure he was going to kiss her "—you can consider it a personal favor to me, Jayne."

Chapter Three

"Don't you know it's February?" Jayne screeched.

Remy sighed, gripped the handlebars and gave the motorcycle more gas. When he looked at Jayne in the sideview mirror, his eyes narrowed. Then it hit him, like a revelation. Driving badly was the least of Jayne's transgressions. She was guilty of something far more serious.

He knew guilt when he saw it—and he saw it just about every day of his life. People often lied to him while trying to protect friends and relatives who were on the lam. He'd learned to read emotions in facial features, the way a fortune-teller might glance at a palm and read the future. Jayne was watching him as if she'd wronged him personally. Each time she thought he wasn't aware, her eyes fixed on him intently. And then he'd catch her looking, and that blue gray gaze would trickle away like leaking ink. What was she hiding?

"February!" she shouted again.

He'd thought it would be warmer in Virginia. But instead of apologizing for renting a motorcycle instead of a car, he yelled over his shoulder, "Well, you know what a womanizer I am. All February means on my calendar is that I've flipped past the redhead to the brunette."

That silenced her. Could he help it if the day had gone awry? The Wright residence was the largest home he'd ever been inside. The White House, which he'd visited, didn't count. It was public. He'd sat at the end of the long driveway for nearly an hour, staring at the countless white columns along the porch. A uniformed woman had ushered him inside, and when he'd finally entered the dining room, its palatial splendor set his teeth on edge.

So had the cool challenge in Jayne's eyes. The more he'd looked at her—in that gray suit, with her hair in a tight bun—the more he'd wanted to see her all loosened up. He really had just meant to return her shoe. Placing it on the table had been unconscionable.

But one second inside that formal dining room had told Remy he'd never belong there—or in Jayne's life. Worse, the crowd at the table had represented the extended family he'd never had. And then, of course, Jayne's father had mistaken him for a thief.

Remy had stood behind Jayne's chair, feeling the age-old knife twisting in his gut. He'd thought of birthdays and Christmases spent alone with his mother on Bayou Mystique when he was just a kid. He'd longed for money to buy her the gifts his father should have given her. And he'd longed for the daddy who'd deserted them.

In a strange way, it was Georges LeJeure's fault that Remy was riding a motorcycle in the cold today. If not for him, Remy wouldn't have become a tracker of men. Because there was only one man Remy had always hoped to find—the father he'd never known.

Damn. When Remy's eyes caught Jayne's in the mirror again, she glanced away, but that shame-faced, hangdog expression was as easy to read as a newspaper headline. She kept expecting him to...accuse her of something? He sighed. What he wanted was to pull the pins from her bun and muss her hair beyond recognition. It sure didn't make a lick of sense. And he told himself he'd better ignore the impulse. But as he'd manhandled Jayne over the Persian runner in her parents' downstairs hallway—with her wrestling him all the way, like a riled-up gator—he'd wanted nothing more than to feel her arms and legs wrapped around him again. Even now, he kept imagining taking her back to New Orleans—and then beyond, until they were deep in the swamps, at his place on Bayou Mystique.

Remy pulled in front of the airport. As he unlocked one of her cuffs, he bit back an apology, reminding himself that he was merely doing his job. Sounding more formal than he intended, he said, "Please hop off and wait on the curb."

"You are *truly* despicable." Jayne hiked up the beige raincoat that she'd grabbed on their way outdoors, then swung her leg over the seat and charged toward the airport's electronic double doors. As he headed toward the outdoor car-rental stand, Remy could feel her eyes boring holes into his back. Not that he blamed her for being angry. He was hardly proud of how he'd behaved at her parents'.

While the attendant readied the papers for his signature, Remy stamped his feet against the cold. Then he turned in Jayne's direction—and his muscles tensed against the traitorous desire that rippled through him. Fury suited her. Even from here, he could see the passionate glint in her eyes. Her drab raincoat was rumpled beyond repair, the Peter Pan collar of her blouse fluttered against her pearls, and her cheeks were the same guilty pink as the collar's piping. Catching his gaze, Jayne lifted her chin a haughty notch and stared away pointedly.

"Sir?"

"Hmm?" Remy's eyes remained riveted on Jayne. Was it his imagination, or was she really hiding something?

"You need to sign."

Remy affixed his John Hancock to various dotted lines, retrieved his credit card, then ambled toward Jayne. He felt almost as guilty as she looked. "Sorry about the way I stormed into your folks'," he said gruffly. "I just—"

"I refuse to go peaceably," she interjected hotly. "I demand to know how you came up with these trumped-up charges, which—"

She stopped in midsentence, her eyes searching the air, as if for a word, and Remy squinted at her in concern. "You think I'm falsely arresting you?"

"Obviously."

"Why would—"

"I know you typed that subpoena yourself," Jayne said.

"Jayne..." How was he going to break the news that her own fiancé had handed him the subpoena? *You better calm her down first.* "Now, *chère,*" Remy said softly, "I really don't want to treat you like a criminal. That's the honest truth. Here, let's just take off these handcuffs."

She swung her arm behind herself. "Oh, no, you don't. I'm a criminal, remember?"

So she intended to play the martyr. "Jayne, please be reasonable."

She jerked her head in the direction of the doors. "Shall we enter, and consummate this ordeal?"

"Consummate?" he echoed. Her speech was getting stilted because she was flustered.

Raising her voice, she continued, "If we do not consummate, I may very well attack an innocent bystander."

Heads turned. Passersby gaped. If she was trying to embarrass him, she was doing a good job of it. He swiftly locked her free wrist in the handcuffs again, glared at her, then seated himself on a ledge beside an ashtray. Beneath his backside, the cement felt cold.

Jayne gaped at him. "Why are you sitting down?"

"I want a cigarette before I get on the plane. All my prisoners wait."

She squared her shoulders stoically. "Remy, do you mean to inform me that my law firm pays for you to sit around chain-smoking cigarettes?" Before he could respond, she continued, "And why should *I*, a nonsmoker, freeze because of your vile habit?"

"Because you have no legal choice?" he suggested.

In the silence that followed, he glanced around. Everyone was racing somewhere, and in some deep part of himself Remy wished he was taking Jayne anywhere other than to Parker. When two well-heeled women paused on the curb and pointed at Jayne, Remy could hardly believe what ensued. As he fished a smoke out of his jacket pocket and lit it, Jayne called, "Yes, I *am* a dangerous felon."

The two curious-looking women walked around Jayne in an exaggerated circle. Then the electronic doors whooshed open and they ran through. Remy took a drag from his cigarette, then exhaled a stream of smoke. "*Chère*, why don't you just sit down?"

"Next to you?"

"Why not?" Trying to ignore the tension between them, he playfully grabbed her hands.

She withdrew her fingers. "Parker is going to kill you."

"Parker won't do a thing."

"Sure he will." She sniffed as if she'd been crowned grand poobah of the temperance society. "And that smoke is making me positively ill."

"I never would have guessed." But why were such strong undercurrents flowing beneath their argument? Jayne might not approve of his smoking, but she was angry at *him*. Had been last night, too, so it had nothing to do with how he'd acted at her parents'. Thoughtfully Remy flicked his ash in the general direction of the ashtray. "My smoking didn't bother you four months ago."

She sent him a perplexed frown. "Did something happen four months ago?"

Somehow he'd expected her to be more adult. "If it did, I'm trying to forget."

She shrugged. "Well, a lot sure has happened since then."

He tried not to react, but his jealousy flared. "I'm well aware of your engagement, Jayne."

"That's not what I meant, Remy."

He ignored the cryptic comment and nodded toward a taxi driver who'd glanced in their direction. "Please keep your voice down."

"Do all your dangerous criminals go without protest?"

"Usually," he lied. "And according to the subpoena, you *do* owe three thousand dollars in outstanding fines."

"Three thousand dollars!" she blurted out. "Remy, I'm going to sue the pants off you for unlawful arrest."

He couldn't stop himself. He shot her a penetrating look and said, "You're that anxious to get my pants off me again?"

Color drained from her cheeks. Just as quickly, she recovered and groaned. "Believe me, right after I sue them off, you can have them back. Now, why did you fake the subpoena?"

Did she believe he'd falsified a subpoena in order to see her again? "Why would I present you with a forged subpoena, Jayne?" Her face turned beet red. "Jayne?"

"When Parker hears about this, you'll never work for us again."

"We'll discuss it in New Orleans."

With a sudden, relieved smile, she said, "I'm half owner of Bradford and Wright."

"So?"

"I hereby release you from any future employment with my law firm."

"Fire me all you want, but I'm finishing my cigarette."

Jayne merely shook her head. "Aren't you even worried about what Parker's going to do to you?"

Remy stabbed out his cigarette, which he now realized he'd smoked to the butt. "Jayne," he shot back, "Parker's the one who gave me the subpoena."

Pure disbelief rearranged Jayne's features. "Parker?" She barely choked out the word.

"Parker," Remy said.

HIS BACK AND SHOULDERS ached with tension. Staring at the speakerphone, he threaded his fingers through his silver hair. "You haven't found Jayne Wright yet, Speedo?"

"We're still looking, boss."

"Well, keep looking."

Where was Jayne? he wondered when Speedo hung up. And why had she left town less than a week before her wedding? Parker had offered various explanations for Jayne's disappearance, but it was obvious that she'd fled—and that her fiancé had no clue where she'd gone.

If she'd bolted due to an argument, then Parker never would have hired a professional tracker like Remy Lafitte to retrieve her.

Lafitte. That was the last thing he needed.

He sighed. Parker had fired Celeste, too. Parker claimed Jayne's assistant was doing shoddy work and casting aspersions on Lynn Seward's character. According to Parker, he simply couldn't abide competitive employees in a firm where teamwork was required. He'd said that firing Celeste was entirely unrelated to Jayne's disappearance. Well, maybe Celeste *had* missed some appointments and meetings—but the timing sure seemed odd....

Did Jayne have the books—or didn't she?

If she didn't, then why had she fled? The only explanation he hadn't considered was that she'd gotten a case of prenuptial jitters.

"No way," he whispered, rejecting that possibility once and for all.

"JAYNE..."

She chuckled. "I love how you say my name."

Remy grunted. "How's that?"

"Like it's a death threat."

Ten more minutes, Remy thought. Ten more minutes—and he'd drop Jayne at her fiancé's and say, "Nice knowing you, *chère*." It could have been sooner, but the cabbie—who'd spoken no English and was convinced they were tourists heading for the French Quarter—had insisted on dropping them right in the middle of Bourbon Street, near Dumaine.

Staring into the light drizzle, Remy decided nothing could be worse than the plane ride. Once they were seated, Jayne had told the stewardess she'd been arrested for holding a pregnant woman hostage. Where Jayne had come up with that one, Remy would never know. She'd refused food, saying she deserved only lukewarm water and stale bread. Then she'd informed him that she was utilizing her time in the air to plan another crime. Because of her traffic violations, he'd suggested she not drive her own getaway car.

"Your lips are moving."

He stared at her. "What?"

"You're talking to yourself, Remy."

He suddenly realized he'd been standing stock-still in the middle of Bourbon Street, replaying their conversations, and he forced himself to start walking. This whole thing was like an overlong joke that had long ago lost its punch. He winced. *Just ten more minutes.* At least he'd removed those ridiculous handcuffs.

"Lovely night," Jayne said pleasantly as they headed toward the American sector of the city.

Remy squinted against the drizzle. On their right, a tuba player ran past. On their left, a street mime juggled oranges beneath a street lamp while his partner held out a hat. "Just wonderful, darlin'."

"Come on in and check out Linda Lou!" a hawker cried.

Remy's mouth went bone-dry as he glanced at the many strip joints along the street. Even though Jayne lived in New Orleans, he couldn't help but want to protect her from some of the sights. He quickly turned off Bourbon Street and onto Saint Ann, which was quieter.

"Voodoo dolls." She halted in front of a shop called Madame Rochet's. "Maybe there's a doll in there with your name on it, Remy."

Chuckling softly, he caught her hand and pulled her away from the window. "I know just where you'd stick that first pin, too."

Her bubbly laughter was so warm and musical that he realized she probably had a good singing voice. He played piano—and was a sucker for women who could sing. He finally said, "You've really enjoyed getting a rise out of me, haven't you?"

"You can be fun to tease."

Remy glanced her way—and wound up staring. For the briefest instant, her eyes had looked so vulnerable and sweet, so soft and knowing...as if they were shining with the inner light of the world's best-kept secret.

All at once, he realized they were holding hands. He told himself he'd slid his fingers through hers because he could hold onto her better that way. After all, he had to get her back to Parker's one way or the other, didn't he?

When he gently disengaged their twined fingers, Jayne looked a little bereft. Then her face flooded with guilt. This was exactly the sort of thing that happened before she attacked. Or before he started kissing her like a demon. Remy gripped her elbow in a firm, businesslike manner and headed down the street again, colliding with a Lucky Dog hot dog stand in the process.

Jayne chuckled. "Maybe *I* should be manhandling *you.*"

Remy decided not to encourage conversation.

And yet the closer they got to Canal Street, the more the noise died down. And the more he started thinking about relinquishing her to Parker.

To hell with Parker.

Just as he squelched the thought, Remy caught that sheepish expression again. "Mind telling me why you look like the cat that swallowed the canary?"

Before Jayne could respond, his gaze darted away from her profile. He glanced over his shoulder casually. They were on a residential section of Orleans Street now, and it was empty. He didn't see anything but parked cars.

Jayne looked at him. "What is it?"

He shrugged. "Nothing." But things didn't feel right. The silence didn't *sound* right. And Remy had been a tracker far too long not to listen. *Keep walking. Don't pick up the pace but get ready.*

Suddenly he said, "Get down, *chère.*"

When Jayne didn't react, Remy grabbed the back of her raincoat and gently pushed her between two parked cars. He landed on top of her. She gasped, wriggling beneath him, trying to dislodge herself. "My glasses!"

She was lying on her side on the rain-slick pavement now, with one of his arms around her. His chest was pressed against her back, and water was seeping through his jeans. There wasn't much space, just a scant foot between car fenders. Mardi Gras beads and trinkets glistened against the curb.

Remy pressed a finger to Jayne's soft lips. Then he cocked his head and listened. From somewhere above, Ella Fitzgerald's voice floated down through an open window. She was singing "Let's Fall in Love." More distant still, car horns sounded in toots and blares, then fell silent.

"I've no idea what you think you're doing, Remy," Jayne whispered, "but a gentleman would help me retrieve my glasses."

"Please, Jayne," he whispered back.

"We know you've got Jayne Wright," someone called.

The voice was far away, and muted by the music, but the speaker was definitely a man with a New York accent. And he was on the street, rather than in an apartment.

A *pa-choo* sounded, then a whoosh of air.

A bullet hit a tire, Remy thought.

Jayne squirmed toward the curb. "This little joke of yours has gone too far. First you get me preg—"

"Get you what?" he whispered, still straining his ears in the direction from which the man's voice had come, hoping for a clue as to who was heading toward them.

"Er—arrested," Jayne said. "And now this. Would you kindly inform me of what's going on?"

"Somebody's shootin' at you," Remy drawled dryly. "But if it's any consolation, I'm starting to think I might kill you myself."

Chapter Four

"You must be mistaken," Jayne said tightly. *Or crazy.* Why, Remy had flung her onto the pavement bodily. If he only knew how close he could have come to hurting his own unborn child.

"Please be quiet," he whispered.

As Jayne's crablike fingers crawled frantically over the wet flagstones in search of her glasses, a strand of red, heart-shaped Mardi Gras beads snagged on her engagement ring. "You've really gone too far this time," Jayne muttered, shoving the beads into the pocket of her blazer. She didn't believe people were shooting at her any more than she believed Remy hadn't falsified that subpoena. She just hoped he hadn't done so because he'd found out about the baby.

But that would have a certain logic, she thought with dread. It was a lie of omission not to tell him she was pregnant. Because she'd lied, he'd taken it upon himself to track her down. Even if Remy knew nothing, there was still a cosmic, karmic rightness in the fact that he'd arrested her.

Her guilt feelings intensified, becoming utterly unbearable. Had all her secret sins and hidden lies really culminated in this wretched moment—when she was lying between two parked cars in a mud puddle? What she'd done was surely wrong, but was wanting a family a crime? She submerged her thoughts. Only Parker knew of her condition, and he'd never tell. She was merely projecting the worst. Feeling more confident, she said, "I really can't find my glasses."

"They won't do you any good unless you're alive, Jayne."

She stretched an arm far beneath one of the cars—it was an old Monte Carlo—and as she swept her hand to and fro across the pavement, her nose bumped the exhaust pipe. "Would you kindly release me, Remy?"

The man didn't budge. One of his huge hands was in the last place on earth Jayne wanted it to be—wedged between her abdomen and the street. Even worse, her behind had settled in the cradle of Remy's lap, and the contact was quite disturbing. Fortunately, her raincoat provided protective padding and also kept her suit from becoming unduly soiled. "Please," she repeated.

Silently Remy scooted upward. The hand that wasn't beneath her belly slid from her shoulder to her hip and rested protectively on her vanishing waistline. *Your baby's tough-guy daddy thinks you're in trouble, Jayne, and he intends to rescue you. Oh, kiddo, I've got to tell him about you.* The thought made her heart ache. Remy's breath fanned across her cheek, warming her skin.

"On the count of three," he whispered. "Run toward Burgundy Street."

"Not without my glasses." Her stage whisper was calculated to point out the foolishness of what he was suggesting. "Drats," she said when her fingers hit something hard. "It's just a rock."

"Hand it over."

Jayne proffered the stone. "Be my guest, caveman. Do you intend to brain our supposed attackers?"

His silver eyes were a scant inch away—and glaring. "If anyone's chasing me, Remy, they would have attacked by now."

"They haven't figured out where we are yet."

Jayne sighed and wriggled farther beneath the Monte Carlo. She'd heard a man yelling something, but surely it hadn't been her name. "My glasses."

Just as she snatched them from the pavement, Remy began manhandling her out of her raincoat. She struggled to keep it, since the temperature was hovering around fifty.

"It's tan," Remy whispered insistently. "It'll be harder to spot your suit in the dark."

"It's a Burberry!"

While wrestling Remy for possession of her best outerwear, Jayne found her footing. She rose to her haunches just in the nick of time, saving her skirt from muddy peril just as Remy whisked away the coat, rolled it into a ball and tossed it beneath the Monte Carlo.

"Someone *is* trying to kill you," he said.

"My work schedule doesn't permit much socializing," she whispered back crossly. "So, if I haven't had time to make friends, how could I have made enemies?"

"Remember, run to Burgundy." Remy shifted his weight and crouched in front of her. "One..."

Jayne wedged herself sideways, planted her hands on either car fender and got ready to push off. Was she really going to humor Remy by making a run for it? She wanted to tell him that gym class had been right up there next to prom night when it came to her small failures in life. Numerical analysis and cross-examination were her forte, not sprints. Realizing her glasses were clutched in her fist, she started to put them on. Then she glanced at Remy, changed her mind and slid the specs into her blazer pocket.

"Two..."

She started to protest, but he grabbed her hand. His palm was so dry and warm and strong....

"Three!" As Remy yanked her to her feet, he pitched the rock with a long, circular swing of his arm. Above, a streetlight shattered, and everything went dark. Glass rained down like hail.

Jayne kept pace—until she heard pounding footsteps other than hers and Remy's. Coming to a dead halt, she gawked over her shoulder. A shadowy figure was running after them. Another slunk from between two parked cars. Then a third—

"Run, Jayne, run!"

Run, Jayne, run. Remy's words reverberated in her mind, sounding surreal. She thought of Dick and Jane and Spot, which made her think of childhood—and the potential threat to the baby.

"Damn it, Jayne!"

Both her need to protect the baby and Remy's rough cussing lit a fire under her feet. It was as if she were an Olympic runner and Remy's voice the pistol that sounded before a career-making race. The heels of her pumps beat an uneven tattoo across the pavement. Why hadn't she worn her glasses? The cars and curbs were nothing more than blurs of color muted by darkness. *But no one's really chasing us. They can't be.*

She and Remy had made it to another street; she didn't know which one. Everything seemed intensified—the sound of distant car horns, the affirming grasp of Remy's work-roughened fingers, the sting of her pearl necklace beating against her blouse as she ran. She gasped for breath as Remy rounded a corner. When he pulled her into an alleyway, she raggedly whispered, "Why am I letting you do this to me?"

But she knew why. She'd let this man do anything.

He gently pushed her between two garbage cans. "Get down."

As she dutifully hunkered down, a run raced up her panty hose. *Second pair in two days.* She winced, crinkling her nose against the offensive environs. "If anyone was chasing us, I really think they're gone," she said nervously.

Remy didn't respond. He didn't seem winded, either. That unnerved her nearly as much as the empty soup can that rolled right next to her high heel. She shifted her weight on her haunches. Squinting, she followed Remy's watchful gaze, expecting to find the street empty.

It wasn't. A block away, three menacing-looking shadows were approaching. They were mere blurs, hugging parked cars and melting into the darkness. Jayne fumbled in her pocket for her glasses, but her trembling fingers wound up twined around the heart-shaped beads. She found herself wishing she was a Catholic—and that the beads were a rosary. Were the men muggers? Had they mistaken her and Remy for cash-carrying tourists?

She clutched the Mardi Gras beads tightly. Her free hand shot to her abdomen, as if to protect the life within. Her mind racing, she squinted into the winter night—until she thought she saw a garage-style door. The large building looked like a warehouse, and there was a foot of space between the door and the pavement. She tugged Remy's sleeve. "Remy?" she mouthed.

His eyebrows arched.

Jayne jerked her head toward the door. Remy nodded, and they began to edge down the alley. When they reached the door, he whispered, "Roll underneath, *chère.*"

Here goes the suit. She lay on her back, then scooted. If she'd been a month more pregnant, she wouldn't have fit. Once inside, she scurried to her feet. Something warm touched her ankle, and she spun around. "Wha—"

"It's just me, sweetheart."

Remy rose behind her, taking her hand. Together, they tiptoed through the darkness, paper crinkling beneath their feet. *Newspapers?*

She yelped when fingers trailed across her cheeks. *They're feathers.* "Where are we?" she croaked.

"Please, Jayne."

She wished Remy would quit saying that. Without her glasses, and with the added impediment of the interior darkness, it was impossible to read his face. She told herself to don her glasses, but her fingers had frozen around that darn strand of plastic hearts.

Remy squeezed her other hand tightly.

She bit back a scream.

A giant monster was smiling at them!

Jayne turned to flee and ran smack-dab into Remy. For a moment, her nose remained pressed against his chest, and she wished she could remain there forever. But she forced herself to turn around and squint.

A mammoth alligator stared back at her. The giant jaws hung open, and the thick lips were curled into a grin. Huge pointy teeth seemed ready to gnash intruders. Jayne's body quaked with a head-to-toe shudder.

"One of the parade krewes," Remy whispered, moving toward the alligator.

Just as Jayne realized she'd been staring at a Mardi Gras float, Remy stepped inside the gator's mouth, pulling her behind him. She couldn't see, but felt the built-in stairs at the back of the gator's throat. They creaked as she and Remy ascended. Behind the alligator's eyes was a wide plank, and Jayne seated herself next to Remy on it. Outside, pounding footsteps drew closer and closer—then to an abrupt halt.

"Go ahead," a man said from the other side of the door.

"No, I'll stand watch out here."

The second voice was nasal. Jayne tried to ignore her fear—how her pulse was ticking dangerously fast, how her heart was pounding so hard that the men might hear it. She forced herself to squint in concentration. She knew that nasal voice. Where had she heard it before?

"You go first, Speedo," said a third man with a New York accent.

Remy's arm circled Jayne's shoulders, and he hugged her against his chest. It was crazy, but it was starting to seem as if men really *were* chasing her.

In the course of her career, she'd defended many accused criminals. Since justice always won out, some had gone to jail, too. Did she recognize the nasal voice because she'd defended the man? Maybe he'd decided in prison that Jayne hadn't given him the best possible defense and, now released, had come after her for revenge.

She heard one of the men roll under the door. A second later, metal grated and the door rolled upward on its chains. A light snapped on. Jayne blinked, her eyes a mere fraction away from the chicken wire that covered the alligator's eyes. Illumination from the room angled into the float, and Remy forced her downward, so that she was lying across his lap. With her cheek pressed against the hard muscles of his thigh, she could still see through one of the gator's eyes.

Two fuzzy figures were angrily pacing around the room. One man was squat and heavy, with black hair. He wore a black leather jacket and a black beret. At the top of the other man's skinny, trench-coat-clad body was a mop of blurry bright red hair. Jayne realized that the tan blob at which she was squinting was her own raincoat. It was draped over the rail-thin redhead's arm.

Giant wings, probably part of a Mardi Gras costume, rested against the door and accounted for the feathers that had swept across her face. The squat man charged past the wings, upsetting an open box of plastic bead necklaces that sat on a worktable. The newspapers beneath his feet were littered with toy alligators that had probably been thrown from the float during a parade.

"Find them yet, Speedo?" called Nasal Voice from outside.

"Give us a minute, would ya?" returned the rail-thin redhead.

Silver washtubs of the sort used to hold beer kegs were stacked against the walls. Speedo moved them, one by one, as if she and Remy might be hiding behind them.

"Smiley, are they in there or not?" called Nasal.

Where had she heard that voice? Jayne wondered again. As the squat man named Smiley headed for the float, Jayne's hand slid over her abdomen. Why hadn't she told Remy about the baby? He had every right to know. If she'd done the honest thing and confronted him, none of this would be happening.

Below, Smiley walked inside the gator's jaws. Silently Remy shimmied down next to Jayne, his steadying arms wrapping around her waist. She'd never imagined that anyone could be so still. Remy wasn't so much as breathing.

What if they were caught? Could she negotiate a deal? She'd give these men anything—as long as she and Remy and their unborn baby were safe. She just wished Remy knew the truth—and how high the stakes were. She turned her head, as if she could tell him. He turned just as she did, and their mouths almost brushed. Then Smiley changed directions and stomped out of the float.

At Jayne's audible sigh, Speedo said, "Did you hear something?"

"I think so," Smiley said.

Jayne wanted to scream, to simply announce herself and end this nightmare. In the shadowy interior of the gator, Remy's eyes glinted like silver bullets—the kind that could make mincemeat of bad guys and even vanquish werewolves. Then his lips gently covered Jayne's. Her fear vanished, but the soft pressure of Remy's mouth made her pulse accelerate and her heart pound again. Still, she wanted to tell him that no kiss—not even his—could take her mind from what was happening.

Except that it did. At the sweet, languorous touch of his tongue, heat infused her limbs. Speedo and Smiley and Nasal Voice disappeared. In fact, they'd never even existed.

Jayne was no longer hiding inside a musty Mardi Gras alligator float. She was in heaven....

Outside, footsteps thundered past the warehouse door. If more men were coming to attack them, Jayne didn't care. Remy was just the man to protect her.

Send a whole army, Jayne thought illogically as she snaked her arms around Remy's neck. Send the bad-guy army and the Marines. Even the thug equivalent for the navy SEALs could come—if only it meant Remy would keep kissing her.

"It's them!" Nasal Voice yelled. "Running down the alley!"

As Speedo and Smiley clambered noisily for the street, Jayne arched toward Remy. The men were gone, she and Remy were safe, and he was kissing her. Everything seemed right with the world. The engagement ring on her finger seemed as insubstantial as a pop lid. For a moment, she allowed herself to forget that Remy hadn't been informed of his impending daddyhood.

"Sorry..." Remy said, abruptly severing their kiss. "But I was afraid you'd start screaming."

"I DO NOT SCREAM." Pain pinched the bridge of Jayne's nose, and she massaged the spot, warding off a full-blown headache. She just wished Remy hadn't kissed her. Or that he'd meant something by it. But he'd only wanted to silence her. Once again, she'd mistaken his motives. *Just thank your lucky stars you didn't tell him everything in that moment of weakness, Jayne.*

"I saved your life, *chère,*" Remy pointed out as he urged her out of the warehouse. "So would you mind telling me what you're so riled up about? And keep close to the buildings, would you?"

Riled up? she thought. *Who uses expressions like that nowadays?* "We're no longer attempting to evade our mysterious attackers," she said dryly.

"*Your* attackers."

"Right." The way Remy steered her toward the buildings again, she had to fight not to remind him she wasn't a motor vehicle that he could simply hop in and drive. They turned down Orleans Street, then headed toward Jackson Square.

Suddenly, she stopped. Her hand shot to her throat, checking to make sure her pearls were in place. Staring down at her legs, she twisted right and left, turning her ankles to better view the damage. She had three irreparable runs. A great smear trekked diagonally across her lap. Heaven only knew how she looked from behind. She was freezing, too. Not that she'd let Remy see her shiver. She realized he looked furious. "What?"

"Are you going to stand there all day, Jayne?"

"It's night." She clamped her chattering teeth together and started walking. At least the drizzle had stopped. If her hair got any wetter, the curls would show. Remy's jacket was dusty, and there was a damp rain spot on his jeans. But then, dishevelment suited him.

Face it, Jayne, you're just angry because you're feeling defensive. You're lying to the man, so you want to act like he's the one doing something wrong. "Thank you for saving my life so gallantly," she finally ventured.

His mouth quirked. "If I'd known what the job entailed, I might have declined."

Still feeling his lips on hers, she couldn't help but smile tentatively. "But a man of Parker's stature is so difficult to turn down?"

"So you *do* believe Parker sent me?"

"No, and I don't think those men were chasing me specifically."

"They said, 'We know you have Jayne Wright.'" Remy started walking faster. "I didn't hear any mention of Remy Lafitte."

"The voice was muffled," she returned, feeling determined to remain reasonable. "That man could have said Jase Rice. Or Wainright. Or something that rhymes, such as 'in plain sight.' Maybe those men saw us get out of the cab in the French Quarter, thought we were tourists or easy marks, and..."

She let her voice trail off, hoping she was right, and desperately wishing she could check her reflection in the sideview mirror of a parked car. She smoothed the smeared front of her wrinkled skirt and sniffed.

Remy's eyes were focused straight ahead. "Don't you go acting like I hired those men to chase you, Jayne."

Watching his lips move, she thought that while Remy's kisses might be as sweet as a bee's honey, each carried the stinging reminder that he didn't want her. "No one is chasing me." *Including you.* Jayne tossed her head pridefully. "You know, I'm a big girl. I don't mind seeing myself home."

"What is it with you people?"

Her hand shot defensively to her pearls. "What people?"

"Rich people."

"Movie stars are rich, not attorneys." Jayne sent him a sideways glance. "What did I do wrong, anyway?" As soon as the words were out, she cringed. Her money made Remy uncomfortable, and she knew it. Besides, she was withholding some rather pertinent information. All day she'd dropped liberal hints. It was cowardly. But she felt so confused—wanting to keep quiet and save her pride, wanting him to guess, wanting to tell him.

He finally shrugged. "Well, you charged into my office a little over four months ago and..." His voice trailed off. "And then you and Parker have a fight, and he..."

"Parker and I didn't have a fight." Jayne disengaged a bobby pin and stabbed it back into her bun.

"If that subpoena's fake, then it's Parker's doing. And if it is, why did Parker send me to retrieve his renegade fiancée? And why, when I say guys are shooting at us, do you act like you don't believe me?"

At the mention of weapons, Jayne's well-manicured fingers shook. Somehow she pulled another pin from her mussed hair.

"You're driving me out of my mind, *chère.*" Remy quickly crossed the space between them, placed his strong hands on her shoulders and stared deeply into her eyes.

"What?" she managed to croak.

"This." He started tugging pins from her hair and tossing them to the pavement.

With the removal of each pin, his fingers seemed to linger just a fraction longer, caressing her hair. Fortunately, he left her ponytail intact, so she was saved from having a frizzy mop down to her shoulders. After a moment, he merely gazed into her eyes, as if he'd forgotten what he was doing. Not that he had. He wasn't attracted to her, and she vowed never to forget it again. He'd made love to her without feeling anything, just as he'd kissed her to silence her.

"There," he said gruffly.

When he shoved his hand into her blazer pocket unexpectedly, she tried to look offended. "What do you think you're doing?"

Remy withdrew her glasses, untangling them from the heart-shaped beads. He looped the beads around her neck, then slid the glasses onto her nose.

"Oh," she said.

"In my humble opinion, your hair looks better down." Remy raised his hand, as if to fend off the protests he expected would follow. "Now, I'm sure Parker likes it the other way..."

She tried to recall whether or not Parker had ever commented on her hair—and couldn't. Trying not to sound defensive, she said, "He most certainly does."

"Well, you're not with Parker at the moment," Remy said, his voice rusty. "And would you please keep your glasses on? I know you think they're unattractive, but I'm tired of having you squint at me."

"I'm sorry."

"Ah, *chère,*" he said with a sigh, "you don't have to apologize for squinting."

Somehow, he was making her feel like an idiot. "Sometimes I wear contacts, but they can make my headaches worse."

Remy merely shrugged out of his suede coat, then slung it around her shoulders. "Here."

He started walking again, and she watched the muscles of his back ripple beneath his tight white T-shirt. Now that he was in focus, Jayne let her gaze drift from his broad shoulders all the way down to his perfect tush. When he rounded a corner without a backward glance, she hurried after him. "I thought we were going to Parker's."

"I've got to stop at the Cha-cha Club."

Was this his way of saying he wanted to buy her a drink? "I don't really care for a cocktail," she murmured. "But I'm sure hungry," she added quickly. "Dinner would be great. I do realize you *wisely* told me to eat on the plane, but—"

"My car's parked at the Cha-cha Club, and I need to use the phone."

"Why don't you use one of those?" She pointed at a bank of phones on the corner.

"In private."

She'd probably made him late for a hot date. The realization was more painful than she could comfortably admit. "Maybe I should go home before you attend to your *private* calls."

He shot her a quelling glance. Those beautiful silver eyes, which she could see with absolute clarity now, said she had no right to be jealous. "I'm calling Parker."

For the thousandth time, Jayne fought the urge to calmly inform him that they'd made a baby together. And then she thought of her family and Parker and the wedding plans. She glanced down at her engagement ring. "Parker's probably still at the office." He was such a good, hardworking man. "It's only eight blocks away from the Cha-cha Club, just on the other side of Canal," she forced herself to say. "So why are we *calling* him?"

All at once, Remy turned and stared at her, his light eyes burning like twin spotlights. Twenty-three years fell away, and Jayne was the lead cherub in her fourth-grade Valentine's Day play. The spotlights, which were her cue to sing, had just snapped on. She'd frozen then—just as she did now.

Remy leaned and reached right inside the breast pocket of the jacket around her shoulders. He was merely getting his cigarettes, but at the fleeting pressure of his fingers, the tips of her breasts constricted. In the following flare of his lighter, she saw dawning awareness cross his features. She gulped and forced herself not to glance down at her belly.

"What are you and Parker up to?" he demanded.

"What?" she asked shakily. "We're not '*up to*' anything. We're getting married." After a few false starts, she finally cleared her throat. Then she tried to smile. "I went to law school, and I know for a fact that betrothal's not a crime."

Remy scrutinized her from head to toe. "Who are Speedo and Smiley?"

Her jaw dropped in horror. "Remy, I don't know those men who were in the warehouse."

"I don't buy it," Remy said. "Ever since last night, you've been staring at me in the weirdest way."

Jayne's knees nearly buckled, but she locked them tight. "What way?"

"Like you're guilty of something. I want to know what you're involved in that nearly got me killed tonight. Who were those men, and what did they want?"

Jayne swallowed hard. How could Remy believe she was involved in something underhanded? *Well, aren't you, Jayne?* Heat seeped into her cheeks, and her eyes darted toward the curb. "I don't know those men," she finally said, wishing her voice wasn't quavering.

"If you didn't, you'd be more shaken up." Suddenly, what might have been a smile curled the corners of his mouth. "Even you aren't so repressed that you could ignore a gunshot."

"If you're trying to goad me into some sort of confession by calling me repressed, it won't work. I didn't ignore any gunshot." She'd heard something, but believing that a man had shot at her was simply beyond her powers of imagination.

"So you admit to hearing it?"

She didn't want to commit one way or the other. If Remy was telling the truth and Parker had given him a falsified subpoena, was it also conceivable that there was something more to this latest incident than met the eye?

Remy exhaled a stream of smoke. "C'mon."

Jayne fell into step beside him. As she tugged his warm suede coat more tightly around her shoulders, a manly scent wafted from the collar. Then his tobacco smoke trailed across her face.

"You really shouldn't smoke," she whispered. "It's bad for you."

When they reached a trash can, he stopped, lifted his foot and ground the cigarette out on his heel. "Let me guess," he drawled as he dropped the butt in the can. "You don't like litter, either."

"I'm an advocate of recycling." When her gaze met his, she wished she'd kept her mouth shut. "Sorry," she murmured.

"You should be." He broke their gaze and started walking again. He was taller, with longer legs, and she had to walk fast to keep pace. They'd gone another silent block when Remy gruffly said, "You warm enough, *chère?*"

She glanced quickly in his direction, wondering if that was his way of apologizing for the tension between them. He was staring straight ahead. "I'm fine," she said gently. "Are you, Remy?"

His eyes crinkled in a wry wince. "I think I'll make it, Jayne."

How COULD a woman who looked so bad look so good? Remy wondered as he stared through the door of the Chacha Club's back office and dialed Bradford and Wright. Jayne was wedged between two burly tequila drinkers at the bar, and she kept glaring at Remy's friend, Eva, who was bartending. Remy didn't know which he felt more—flattered by Jayne's obvious jealousy or just plain worried. He'd started to assure Jayne that Eva was only a friend, but he'd felt awkward doing so, since Jayne was getting married in less than a week.

"Lynn?" Remy said into the receiver. "Could you put Parker on the line?"

Lynn put Remy on hold. In the bar, the Cajun Music Masters were onstage, and the drums were so loud that Remy could barely hear. He'd meant to shut the office door, but he'd decided against leaving Jayne to fend for herself. One of the burly men reached past her for the salt and lemons.

Maybe they should swing by her place, so that she could freshen up before she saw Parker. Remy simply couldn't figure out her hair. If he hadn't known it was straight, he would have thought it was trying to curl. His favorite jacket was draped over her shoulders and she was clutching her pearls and the heart-shaped beads. Her glasses had slid down to the tip of her nose.

"Remy?"

Parker's voice grated on every last one of Remy's nerves. *So what if I'm attracted to the man's fiancée?* "Hey, Parker."

"Where's Jayne?"

"With me."

"Why haven't you brought her here?"

For a lot of reasons. If Jayne said she had no traffic violations, that meant Parker had given him a false subpoena for some reason. But why? Given Jayne's guilty glances, maybe she knew more than she was telling. Remy sighed, deciding to go for broke. "I'll bring Jayne in when you tell me why two men took a shot at us when we got back to town."

Parker's gasp didn't sound genuine. "Excuse me?"

"Somebody started gunning for us near Orleans Street."

Parker sighed in relief. "Surely those shots were firecrackers, or cap guns. It could have been anything, if you're in the French Quarter. Still, I want you to be extra careful with Jayne when you bring her back."

Remy's eyes narrowed. It was hard to tell whether Parker knew what was going on or not. "Why's that?"

"She's pregnant," Parker said.

Remy gasped. "Mind repeating that?"

"She's going to have a baby."

Remy's eyes shot to Jayne. So, that was what she was hiding. How could he have missed it—the glowing skin, her fuller figure, the way her palm kept resting on her belly?

His breath caught. Lord, why hadn't she told him? The poor woman must have been terrified when he pushed her between those parked cars. That she'd kept mum hurt. After the night they'd shared, didn't she even trust him as a friend?

Now everything was falling into place. This explained her hasty marriage to Parker. The man had probably falsified the subpoena, thinking it would be easier to hire Remy that way. If Remy's own fiancée had vanished with his unborn child, Remy would have hired a professional tracker to get her back, too. Maybe that supposed shot had been a firecracker, after all. And maybe the guy in the street had said Jase Rice or Wainright. "So, Jayne's having a baby?" Remy finally said.

"Just bring her back!" Parker exclaimed.

Remy chuckled softly. Impending fatherhood was clearly making the man nervous. In a soft drawl, he said, "Are you all right, Parker?"

"No! Ever since Jayne went and got herself into trouble, things around here have been highly unusual. Boyd Laney can't possibly handle her caseload, the election is just around the corner, I had to fire Celeste, my wedding's in less than a week, and—"

Remy didn't hear a word after "got herself in trouble." He'd lived in the South all his life, and he knew good and well what that euphemism meant. His heart stopped, dropped to his feet, then came back up, pounding. "It's not your baby?" he asked.

"No! I don't know whose it is!"

No? Remy thought in shock. But Jayne Wright wasn't the type to fool around. At least not much. "How pregnant?"

"Four months or so," Parker said in exasperation.

No wonder Jayne had looked at him as if she were guilty. Because she was. She was pregnant with his child, and had absolutely no intention of telling him.

"Remy, are you bringing Jayne back here or not?"

Remy said, "No."

And then, very gently, he hung up the phone.

PARKER LISTENED to the dial tone until the intermittent buzz sounded, telling him the phone was off the hook. What had gotten into Remy Lafitte? It was absolutely essential that Parker get Jayne back tonight.

He grabbed his Rolodex and spun the dial. "*A, B, C...*" he muttered, wishing he knew who had fathered Jayne's baby. He'd waited patiently, expecting Jayne to tell him. He should have demanded to know. Because the mystery daddy was the one man, other than Remy Lafitte, whom Jayne might turn to. "*W...*" he whispered.

When he got Buddy Wyatt on the line, he said, "I need you to track Jayne and Remy Lafitte. They're in the French Quarter right now." During a thoroughly unnerving pause, Parker could almost see Buddy hike his jeans and pat his expansive belly.

"Now, Parker," Buddy said in a lazy drawl, "those two are oil and water. I wouldn't worry about them being together. Not unless you're afraid they'll kill each other."

Parker's voice rose with hysteria. "Buddy, I need help!"

"You think they *really* ran off together?" Buddy blew out a long whistle. "You need not explain. I like Remy, but women sure fall for him like a house of cards. I could have sworn Jayne had more common sense, though. I'll round her up faster'n you can say spit."

"Thank you," Parker managed. He dropped the phone receiver into its cradle, whirled around in his swivel chair and stared through the glass walls of his office. In the distance, Canal Street was still slick with rain. Puddles shimmered beneath headlights, reflecting colors.

Parker peered toward the Quarter, as if Jayne and Remy might suddenly run within the scope of his vision. But there was only open space. The endless city stretched before him—the Crescent City...the City That Care Forgot...the Big Easy.... It had all been within his grasp.

Lights still shone below as if beckoning him. But a sudden rush of vertigo made him gasp, and Parker Bradford flung out his arm, knowing he was just about to fall.

Because Jayne Wright was in real danger.

And it was all his fault.

Chapter Five

Jayne wrenched around in the seat of Remy's freshly waxed fire-engine-red vintage Cadillac convertible. Her eyes swept over the interior—seemingly noting that the car was well maintained and probably Remy's pride and joy, which it was—and then she stared back in the direction of the sign that said Leaving Orleans Parish. "What do you think you're doing?" she wailed.

Taking my baby with me, Remy thought illogically. Aloud, he said, "Please, Jayne. I'm trying to think." He clenched his jaw and gripped the steering wheel harder. What *was* he doing? All he knew was that the woman next to him in the seat was carrying his unborn child. And with all his heart, and with his every last breath, he wanted to protect her—or kill her.

His insides felt all knotted up, like one of those long rubbery balloons that street mimes in the French Quarter twisted into animals for little kids. A heart-crushing desire to love, honor and cherish was all jumbled up with overwhelming fury. Remy just wished some magician would appear, glance over his internal knots, then say a quick "Abracadabra" and set him free.

He wanted his baby. That much he knew. He just couldn't believe that four and a half whole months had passed. Day in, day out. The sun rising and setting. The moon revolving around the earth. And every second of every day, the hands of the clocks in Orleans Parish had been turning. But Jayne Wright hadn't so much as given him the time of day.

Oh, sure, she'd stare into his eyes with a look as deep as the Mississippi River. She'd kiss him, too—clinging to his neck, arching in need, whispering ragged incantations against his lips—but she wasn't about to give him the privileged information that he was about to be a daddy. Lord, what kind of a woman was she?

The guilt-stricken expression he'd been trying to interpret for the past twenty-four hours now made sense—and made his blood boil. Those shockingly clear blue gray eyes of hers had stared directly into his own, and her cheeks had turned as fiery red as a sailor's sunset—but she still hadn't uttered her oh-so-secret confession.

He'd been so worried that Parker had drawn sweet, upstanding Jayne into some dishonest business. But all the while, it had been Jayne who was the liar. Jayne had been playing him for a fool.

An image of her parents' dining table flashed through his mind. Remy tried to ignore it, concentrating his attention through the windshield on the straight white strip of road and the arrowed sign that whizzed past, pointing toward Lake Salvador. He scanned the increasingly empty landscape and saw that it was turning ever more watery, dotted with houses on stilts and raised bridges and old wooden docks.

But all Remy really saw was the cherrywood that had shone through the Wrights' fancy tablecloth. A delicate silver spoon had tilted—angled just so—from a jar of sugar cubes. Everything on that table had been so heartbreakingly perfect. Every object as dainty as Jayne's slender hands—one finger of which sported an engagement ring.

Did she really believe Parker deserved to father Remy's child just because he was rich? Or did she love the man? Perhaps she was marrying to appease her family.

I'll show her how the other half lives. For the first time, Remy realized he was taking her down deep into the bayous. Somehow he felt like one of those poor, outcast phantoms from old movies who dragged beautiful singing maidens through tunnels beneath cities or darkened caves beneath the sea. Yeah, it was damn tempting to simply lock Jayne up on Bayou Mystique—at least until his baby was born.

"Remy!" she yelled over the wind and the car motor.

His mind still reeling, he calculated the dates, thinking he had every right to keep Jayne home until summer, when the baby came.

"Remy!"

His mind jerked from the road, and he stared at her.

"You can't kidnap me!" she shouted, as if she were reading his mind.

"I just did," he said. But that was a joke. After all, it was *she* who, in some strange sense, had kidnapped *him*— or at least his baby.

He realized she looked terrified. And cold. He glanced at the speedometer and gasped. He was going far too fast. *Cool your jets, Remy.* He eased up on the gas pedal and searched for a place to pull over; but they were now in the middle of a bridge that spanned a slender, watery finger of Lake Salvador.

Jayne and I are crossing a bridge, all right, he thought. Four and a half months ago was on one side, their unknown future was on the other.

This was all Parker's fault. After Jayne's fool fiancé so unwittingly delivered the news about Jayne, Remy had acted on pure instinct. With one surge of adrenaline, he'd hauled Jayne out of the Cha-cha Club, installed her in his car, wordlessly buckled her seat belt for her, and then driven her right out of town. He hadn't stopped to put up the car's roof, even though the temperature was in the fifties.

Once they crossed the bridge, Remy pulled over. He intended to continue ignoring Jayne—at least for the moment. He had absolutely no idea how a man was supposed to react to a woman when he heard something like this so suddenly. *Usually the mother-to-be prepares the guy. She makes a nice dinner, gets some flowers, wears a special dress. She says, "Honey, you better sit down, because I have something to tell you...."*

Placing his hands at the top of the steering wheel, Remy interlaced his fingers and rested his forehead on his knuckles. At the periphery of his vision, he could see the full moon reflecting off the lake waters. Jayne was staring at him. Had he gone into actual, physical shock?

Jayne probably thought he'd gone crazy.

Hell, maybe he had.

And maybe he had a right to.

He was going to be a father. All his life, he'd ruminated on how Georges LeJeure had deserted him. As a kid, he'd lain awake in the hot, sticky summers, staring through his open window, past the tightly meshed screen and the rope swing in the big old cypress tree. He'd stared into the curling night mists, listening to the high-pitched whines of skitters and crickets and to the deep bass croaks of bullfrogs and gators. And all night long, while he listened to the song of the swamp playing through that open window, he'd planned his fatherhood.

Usually he'd imagined a son whom he taught how to trap crawfish and crack open oysters and run trotlines through the bayou waters. And everything Remy imagined doing with that son had been one hundred and eighty degrees different from the way Georges LeJeure would have done it.

Countless times Remy had imagined a woman telling him she was pregnant, just the way his own mother, Jenny Lafitte, must have said it to Georges LeJeure. Each time Remy had pulled the nameless, faceless mystery mother into his arms. He'd sworn he'd stay with her forever—cross his heart and hope to die—vowing never to run away as his father had. But Remy had never once imagined that the woman would be named Jayne Wright.

Oh, he imagined so many things, but never this. Never that the mother of his own child would try to rob the cradle. And by default, yet. By not even telling him about the pregnancy. Wasn't fathering this baby his God-given right? No woman was going to deny him his opportunity to be a real father. When he heard the news from the very man who was apparently going to give his child a name, Remy had very nearly lost his mind.

"Remy?"

Her voice fluttered, the way the collars of her blouses and the hems of her skirts might on a breezy day. In fact, her wavering voice seemed to sing like a soft wind whistling through whisper-thin reeds in the bayous.

Remy gulped. He was getting awful damn poetic about Jayne. But then, maybe he was powerless not to wax romantic over the woman who was going to bear his child.

"Remy? What's wrong with you? Aren't you going to say something?"

He wouldn't know where to begin. Surely, by now, Jayne guessed that Parker had told him.

But maybe not. Jayne was smart—probably even brilliant when it came to the law—but she didn't seem overly gifted with people sense. She unbuckled her seat belt and scooted closer. Her left hand grazed his shoulder, coming just near enough that Remy could feel the back of her engagement band through his T-shirt. It was almost as if she were afraid to touch him too hard.

"Are you all right?" she whispered.

He raised his head a fraction and stared over the steering wheel through the windshield. What in the world should he do? What should he say? When he looked at her, his heart twisted with a bittersweet feeling.

A car approached. As it turned off the bridge, its rounding headlights swept over Jayne—illuminating her face, making shadows dance on her cheeks. In that instant, her skin was iridescent, shimmering, glowing. Then darkness fell again. The curling gold tendrils of her hair seemed to turn black, becoming sultry silhouettes framing her oval face, her oversize glasses.

Remy's eyes drifted to her belly, and he sucked in a breath. She should be starting to show now, but he couldn't tell because she was wearing his jacket. He found himself wishing she belonged to him. He wanted to touch her belly, run his palms over it, mold his fingers to its contours. There was no help for it. The second he realized she was pregnant with his child, the attraction he kept trying to deny had become a compulsion.

"Sorry—" His voice creaked in a way it hadn't since adolescence, and he cleared his throat. "I... started feeling sick there for a minute," he lied. "Must have been the food on the plane."

Jayne's mouth quirked. "Do you always drive too fast when you're sick?"

"I just didn't see a place to pull over."

Jayne peered at him with concern. "Better now?"

He nodded. The interior of the car was so quiet that the urgent tattoo of his heart sounded deafening. Somewhere far off a fish splashed in the lake. Closer, Remy could actually hear the wind lift the loose wisps of Jayne's hair. She slipped her hand from his shoulder and placed it primly in her lap.

"Cold?" he asked.

"Freezing."

He nodded again. He got out, circled the car and replaced the convertible's top. Then he got back inside and slammed the door. Turning on the heater, he put the car into drive and pulled onto the road again.

Warily she said, "What did Parker say that was so bad?"

Fear coiled in Remy's gut—and he hoped her pregnancy was all she was hiding. Why had she fled from Parker's house the previous night? Once again he wondered if his kiss had prompted her to leave—but this time he hoped it had. "Did you *expect* Parker to say something bad?"

"No, but you hung up, practically carried me to this car and then drove off like a maniac."

Remy couldn't help but chuckle. "And you still trust me?"

A small smile tugged at the corners of her lips. "Sure," she said. "But don't ask me why."

Since she hadn't scooted to the other side of the seat, Remy started to put his arm around her, then reminded himself that they were in an awfully sticky situation. Thinking of the baby, he said, "If you're going to sit here, *chère,* do me a favor and use that middle seat belt."

As deceitful as Jayne had been, they were going to have to work this thing out together, he thought, watching her buckle up. It would be tough, but some long, hard talks would render a workable solution. Fortunately, Remy was fairly sure she wasn't mixed up in anything shady. Maybe Parker wasn't, either.

Thinking that was sure better than the alternative—that Remy's unborn child and Jayne were in jeopardy. Gingerly he lifted one hand from the wheel, cupped Jayne's chin and turned her face. His eyes darted from the road just long enough to gaze into hers. "Do you believe Parker gave me the subpoena and hired me?"

"Yes." Jayne lifted a hand and pinched the bridge of her nose.

He frowned. Was she getting one of those headaches she'd mentioned?

"If I believe you, Remy," she said, "you have to believe me, too."

That she was asking him to trust her was a bit unsettling under the circumstances, but he nodded. Then his mouth turned dry. "Trust you about what?"

"I don't have to be in court tomorrow. Those are trumped-up charges, Remy."

He exhaled slowly. He'd felt so sure she was going to tell him they'd made a baby together. "You really have no traffic violations or unpaid fines?"

Jayne shook her head, plainly worried. "No."

When her hand dropped to her belly, Remy's heart softened. Lord, she looked so alone, as if she needed to protect her child from an unseen menace all by herself. He reminded himself that it was her own darn fault she was alone, but it was no use. His anger had ebbed away. He wondered if Parker had been any help to her at all—and somehow doubted it.

His chest constricted. Jayne hadn't even told Parker that the baby was Remy's. Parker was as blue-blooded as

Jayne; maybe she thought Parker wouldn't marry her if he knew. That would mean their relationship wasn't all that loving. Still, Remy wasn't sure he blamed her for hiding his identity. Her own father had thought Remy had come to rob them.

Arresting her on false charges was just as bad. Ditto for kidnapping. And then there was the illegitimate child. Remy winced and reached for a cigarette. Then he thought of secondhand smoke and Jayne's condition. He tossed the pack onto the dashboard. "Look…"

"Parker said something on the phone that convinced you he's involved in something bad, didn't he, Remy?" Jayne asked.

Was that why she'd allowed him to drive toward some mysterious destination without any explanation? Did she want to find out what Remy knew about Parker, so that she could protect the man? Remy shrugged, thinking that Parker *had* sounded nervous on the phone. "I'm sure I heard a gunshot in the Quarter. Even if I'm wrong, there were definitely people chasing us."

Jayne's eyebrows furrowed. In the darkness, her skin looked as pale as the china that had graced her mother's dining table. Remy didn't want to frighten her, especially since he wasn't sure whether she was in danger or not, but he felt desperate for a good excuse to take her away for a few days. *Maybe even until after next Tuesday, her wedding day.*

"Jayne, I'd like to get you out of town, just long enough to be sure…"

She thrust her chin upward and blew out a long sigh. "You can't expect me to believe that my own fiancé's gunning for me."

"I never said anything like that." Remy tried not to notice that his gut wrenched with jealousy at the way she leaped to Parker's defense. He *did* have doubts about Parker's basic moral fiber—not that he'd say it. "Your fiancé handed me what's apparently a fake subpoena, and he paid me double the going rate to find you. I just want to stay out here...overnight. I'll call Buddy. He hears just about everything."

"Buddy Wyatt?"

Remy nodded. "I'm friends with a detective at the NOPD, too. Dan Stanley."

Jayne sent Remy a grateful glance. Uneasily he thought back to the scene in the Quarter. It made no sense. He said thoughtfully, "Wasn't Boyd Laney accused of embezzlement a few years back?"

"Yes, but there was absolutely no proof."

Jayne and Parker were friends with Hal Knowles, too, Remy thought. And Knowles had beadier eyes than a snake. "Would anyone have a reason to hurt you?"

She shrugged. "Maybe a defendant who felt I'd mishandled his case."

Remy shook his head and grunted softly in disagreement. "I can't imagine you not doing your job to the letter."

"Thank you," Jayne said quietly, sounding surprised.

He nodded. Still, someone had been chasing her. Or maybe the thugs had been after him. In his line of work, he made his share of enemies. Suddenly his stomach clenched and he actually did feel queasy. He'd have protected Jayne under any circumstances, but now, with the baby...

"Look, I'm sure those guys just picked us out as random targets," he said, hoping with every last drop of his lifeblood it was true.

"I hope so, too," she returned. "Mind if I ask where exactly we're going?"

"To my father's place." Remy wanted to kick himself for putting it like that.

"Your dad's?" Jayne said with a soft chuckle. "I'd like to meet him."

"I would have, too," Remy shot back, more roughly than he'd intended. When Jayne squinted at him, he gruffly explained, "I never knew him." Even as he smiled in apology for his tone, he searched her face, almost hoping the words made her feel guilty. She turned as red as a crawfish.

"What happened to your dad?" she asked raspily.

Remy sighed. Why had he mentioned Georges Le-Jeure? "When my mother got pregnant, he left town and joined the Marines. I always heard he drank too much. Six or seven years after he left, his father died and left my mother the old LeJeure place on Bayou Mystique. She raised me there. She's got a house on Bayou Lafourche now. We can pick up my boat there. There's a shell road to Bayou Mystique but taking the boat's faster."

"You never knew your father at all?"

The sympathetic surprise in her voice conjured up images of that huge family gathered around her parents' dining table. Remy shrugged, as if it didn't matter too much. "Never even met him." Against his will, he found himself adding, "I guess I really hated it, not knowing my own father."

"And he..."

"Got killed. Drunk-driving accident, when I was in my late teens. He'd made a career out of the Marines, and it happened in Amsterdam, where he'd been stationed. No one else was in the car. He hit a phone pole...." Remy shifted his weight uncomfortably in the seat. When had he gone from wanting her to feel guilty to simply wanting her to know? With these few facts, he was telling her everything, too. All the words anyone had ever bothered to offer him about his father.

The silence in the car turned thick. Remy felt submerged. He felt as if he were swimming and a bayou water snake had looped itself around his chest and squeezed, pulling him into ever-deeper waters.

The lights of the city were long gone. Mile by mile, they'd been drawn toward the darkness of the swamps. Everywhere he looked were the ancient old trees he loved, with their clawlike roots that sprawled over the ground's surface and cracked the pavement. They'd driven far enough out that nature was starting to encroach upon the road.

Softly Jayne said, "Remy, I'm really sorry about your dad."

"Me, too." He sighed at the understatement. "When you don't have a father, you don't have any roots. You don't know who you are or where you're from. Because of that, sometimes you don't know where you're going." *Like right now, tonight. When I'm headed into the bayous, with you—the captive mother of my child.*

In the silence, the wheels spun. The car bumped over a root that had grown onto the road, and Remy found himself thinking that his own roots were just that shallow. He said, "The worst thing is that I spent my whole life hating that man, and he didn't even care that I existed."

That said, everything fell utterly still—except the air. It seemed alive, charged with secrets.

It was so quiet that Remy could hear the sound of Jayne's lips parting. And he *knew* she was going to tell him then.

But she didn't.

He realized how much he wanted her confession and apology. How desperately he needed the truth. But he was just as sure he wouldn't confront her.

And he didn't know why.

"THIS HERBAL concoction's perfectly safe." Remy ambled around the kitchen and placed a mug of milky-looking liquid on a rustic wooden table. "Kids and pregnant women use it all the time," he added, as if it was an afterthought.

At the words, Jayne nearly choked. Had Remy guessed she couldn't take aspirin—and why? Her headache was so bad she wasn't even sure she cared if he knew about the pregnancy. In the past hour, everything had become a blur.

The trip to Jenny Lafitte's had melted into a lamplit pirogue ride through twisted trees. That brought them to this crazy quilt of a house. Nestled cozily in a cypress stand, the stilted place was a patchwork of added spaces, screened porches and alcoves. Apparently Remy had an apartment in the Quarter that he also called home.

Jayne barely recalled the mumbled apology she'd offered her parents when she called, or the noncommittal ringing of Parker's phone. She'd showered immediately, hoping stinging-hot water would relax the tender, tense muscles of her shoulders. Then she'd donned a long-sleeved blue cotton dress and boots that were among the items she'd borrowed from Jenny Lafitte. But everything had taken a back seat to her headache.

When Remy's eyes urged her to drink, their dreamy depths nearly convinced her she was about to imbibe a love potion, rather than a headache cure. She slowly brought Remy's homemade elixir to her lips and sipped. It tasted surprisingly good—for a drink made of sap and roots. As soon as she was done, Remy's hand rested beneath her elbow, and he led her to a couch in the next room.

"I don't even know when it started," she whispered.

But that was a lie. The headache had begun twenty-four hours ago, when she'd seen Remy again. Orchestrated by guilt, it had started with a quick rat-a-tat of pain here, a vibrating strain of pain there—until it had become a throbbing, symphonic crescendo. No doubt she deserved it, as a punishment for being so deceitful.

As Remy laid a warm compress over her eyebrows, his throaty voice whispered near her ear. "*Chère,* this ol' headache of yours'll be gone by the time I fix your grub."

She wanted to smile. Remy's mother had given him a cooler full of food, as if he were about to leave home, never to return again. Just as Jayne opened her eyes to teensy slits, Remy dimmed the light. She winced against the pain of her headache and whispered hoarsely, "What did you say your grandfather was?"

"Just a healer . . . an herbalist."

Remy had used a French word, too, but she couldn't remember it now. She managed to lift a hand and lightly touch his. "See," she said as her eyes drifted shut again. "You do have roots."

He chuckled. "You're already making jokes."

Jayne thought of the various plant roots in his kitchen and smiled. "I meant you've followed in your grandfather's footsteps," she whispered after a moment.

Having her headache ebb away was as unexpected as the fact that it was Remy who was curing her. Maybe the drink hadn't actually helped. Maybe the real cure was the realization that Remy cared. She could feel it in how he nestled a soft velvet pillow behind her head, in how his chuckle was calculated to soothe.

Even though she wanted to look at Remy's house again, she kept her eyes shut. The place was airy. She'd noticed that much. It stood high on stilts near the water, a screened-in porch facing the front. At the end of a long hallway, she'd glimpsed the floor-to-ceiling windows in Remy's bedroom.

In the kitchen, bunches of herbs hung from the ceiling rafters, gnarled roots sat in old mayonnaise jars, and plank shelves held Ziploc bags that contained leaves and seeds. Messages had been tacked on the front door, saying that one trusted neighbor or another had borrowed a country cure in Remy's absence. One note said Marie's baby was due soon.

"You wouldn't happen to have anything for allergies, would you?" Jayne thought of all the minor ailments for which she could no longer take medicine. With the spring season just around the corner, she'd been dreading her hay fever.

"Sure. We inherited herbs and bottles of medicines for just about everything with the house," Remy said, his drawl calming her like a lullaby. "As soon as we moved in, people started showing up, expecting my mother and me to know how to help them. Little by little, we figured out which herbs went with which illnesses. When we ran out, I started gathering them."

"I should thank my lucky stars," Jayne whispered.

"You just rest," Remy said. "I'll heat you up some gumbo."

Jayne listened to his retreating steps. They were so even, so steady. He walked like a tracker. But for all his perceptiveness, she was sure he hadn't guessed she was pregnant. He was a man of action, and he'd have confronted her if he knew.

But she was going to tell him.

In fact, she shuddered to think of what might have happened if she hadn't seen him again. She'd been so wrong to withhold the information about the baby from Remy. It was unethical. Probably even a sin. And, as a lawyer, she could cite cases that had set precedents for the illegalities.

But it was more than that. No matter what his response—and she feared the worst—she *wanted* him to know. That was why she was lying here in the dark with her head and heart pounding.

The secret had been on her lips all night, along with the taste of his kiss. When he told her about his father's desertion, everything else had seemed light-years away—her wedding, the election, Parker.

Jayne let herself drift to the sound of rattling pots and pans in the kitchen. How would she tell him? Maybe by candlelight, while they were dancing to soft music. He'd move behind her, his arms circling her waist, his hands on her belly. With her enclosed in his embrace, so safe and warm, maybe he wouldn't get upset. Maybe he'd say he thought he could fall in love with her. . . .

Lord, hadn't she learned her lesson yet? It was absolute madness to fantasize like this.

"Chère."

The word came out of the darkness.

"Darling," she almost whispered in return.

"Jayne?"

She realized it was no dream. The object of her fantasies, the man who had haunted her nights for the past year, was right beside her, his warm breath touching her cheeks, his lips hovering just above hers. She opened her eyes, her own breath catching.

Remy smiled at her.

She realized that in these past twenty-four hours he'd started to become a real person. Before now, he hadn't seemed like flesh and blood—not really. The first moment she saw him, such an unbelievable attraction had gripped her that she was barely able to speak when he was around. And then, one lonely night, she'd mustered her courage and headed to his office near the wharves.

He was watching her carefully, as if he knew exactly what she was thinking. "Hungry yet?"

"I could eat a horse."

"If I'd known that, I would've cooked you one."

The flirtation made sadness touch her soul. The baby wasn't the only issue here. As clearly as if it had happened this morning, she could see Parker kneeling in front of her and proposing. Parker loved her, Remy didn't. And Parker's career would be ruined if she called off the wedding. The polls indicated that the voters wanted a married man.

"Penny for your thoughts."

When she stretched, Remy caught her hands and pulled her to her feet. "No thoughts," she lied.

"C'mon." Without releasing her hand, Remy paused and depressed a button on the stereo. The reel-to-reel tape deck began to turn. The tail end of some wild zydeco segued into "Moon River."

"You're full of surprises," Jayne managed once they reached the screened-in front porch.

A round wooden table had been set with straw place mats and two tall, flickering candles. Heavenly-smelling steam rolled upward from a crock of seafood gumbo at the table's center. Two bowls were already filled, and myriad other dishes had been placed within easy reach. Remy's hand rested on her waist, and then he formally seated her. Jayne tried to fight it, but the man could be positively irresistible.

"Care for a Turbo Dog, or a Dixie?"

"Water or milk would be just great." As soon as the words were out, Jayne frowned. Both had been placed next to her plate already.

Remy grinned, opened a longneck Dixie beer and said, "Dig in."

The seafood gumbo was hearty, the best she'd ever eaten. Between bites she told Remy how much she liked his house and how much she'd enjoyed meeting his mother. She downed her share of raw oysters, then tried a thick slice of homemade bread.

"Trying to make me feel guilty for the way I hauled you out of your parents'?" he finally asked.

She looked up—and found herself staring into those gorgeous eyes of his. Shrugging, she said, "They were having roast beef and stewed tomatoes. I'll take your mother's gumbo any day."

"You sure look like you've got a taste for it, *chère.*"

And for you. She blushed. *Why is it you can't love the man you're marrying?* Lou Reed began singing "Sweet Jane," making her realize that Remy's music collection was as eclectic as hers.

Through the porch screens, she could see the bayou waters shimmering below. Tall, thin reeds stood straight in the shallows, like soldiers standing guard. Between the water and the house was a narrow strip of land, and two trees flanked the porch. Fishing nets, which Remy had said he was repairing, were strung from tree to tree. Jayne had nearly entangled herself in them on her way to the house.

The environs were as mysterious as Remy. The moonlight was by turns hauntingly eerie, then strangely inviting. The dark air was hazy with mist and, farther out, the waters seemed deep with the unknown. Hadn't she always suspected there was more to Remy than met the eye? Wasn't that why she'd reacted to him with such need, such desire? If only she knew how he was going to react to her pregnancy.

"Having untoward thoughts?" Remy asked.

"Now, stop that," she teased.

His grin was infectious. "What?"

"Reading my mind," she couldn't help but say.

As he picked up his fork, it glinted in the candlelight. He swirled sauce into an oyster shell and, in a very practiced and sexy way, lifted the shell and let the raw oyster slide down his throat. He washed it down with a gulp of beer. Then he did a double take and frowned at the bottle.

Jayne squinted at him. "Sudden rush of temperance, Remy?"

He shrugged. "Maybe."

She laughed, thinking that would be the day. The tape on the stereo broke into a bit of patter, and the announcer introduced "Tell It Like It Is." Seconds into the soulful melody, Jayne felt as if Aaron Neville himself were commanding her to tell Remy the truth. She sang the first few bars.

"You've got a good voice, *chère.*"

Jayne smiled. "I've always liked singing."

"Ah..." Remy chuckled. "Didn't I see you late one night with the BonTemps Band? Or were you with some other group?"

"My church choir," Jayne admitted in a stage whisper.

"In one of those—" Remy wiggled his eyebrows playfully "—long black robes?"

Leave it to Remy to make a choir vestment sound like a negligee. "Ours were maroon."

"Well, I like you in that dress," he said.

She glanced down at the blue cotton dress—and remembered that, instead of her pearls, she'd worn the plastic hearts Remy had looped around her neck.

What were she and Remy really doing here? she wondered shakily. Why, when Remy was previously so desperate to get rid of her, had he brought her out here, only to start flirting with her?

She decided she didn't want to know. Not really. She only knew she felt compelled to be near this man. They were so alone out here. There was candlelight and soft music. *Tell him, Jayne.* "You cooked," she found herself saying. "Why don't you let me do the dishes?" The words sounded so domestic that she gulped.

"Ah, *chère*—" Remy rose and circled the table "—we've got better things to do than a bunch of dishes."

"Like what?" she managed to croak.

"A little two-step?" he suggested.

She should have known Remy would be a good dancer, she thought a moment later. Each of his lithe movements recalled the way he'd held her four and a half months ago—as if they were meant to be. They anticipated each other, swaying together as if in response to the same breeze. Heaven help her, but it made her ache for him. Just breathing in his scent, she could forget that anything else existed. "About what happened in the Quarter..." she began, hoping to remind them both of why they were here.

"Forget the Quarter."

"I'm getting married," she whispered.

"That's usually my line," Remy returned. And then his lips settled on hers and he lifted her right off her feet and into his arms.

Chapter Six

"Remy, we can't," Jayne said, in breathless surprise. "We just—"

Wordlessly, his mouth covered hers again, the touch of his lips alone saying *Yes, we can, chère.*

He paused, just long enough to blow out the candles. He hadn't even known he was going to kiss her, much less lift her into a cradling embrace; like so many things between him and Jayne, it had just happened.

When he first saw her, the attraction had been electrifying—startling him, leaving him shaken. He'd denied it. Later, when she all but propositioned him, her sheer unpredictability had excited him even more. Then he'd discovered that her prim starchiness concealed a softness so heavenly that it didn't belong on earth. And her pregnancy had been as unexpected as the way he was holding her now—as if he'd never let her go.

"I don't know what I want..." she began raspingly.

He didn't, either. At first he'd wanted to protect her, then he'd wanted to seduce the truth from her. Now his kisses were capturing both her protests and her confessions. That soft voice of hers kept singing to him, but it wasn't really a song—just the sudden catch of her breath as they'd danced, the gasp of delight as he'd lifted her from the floor, the raggedness of her words. *We can't.*

"We sure can," he murmured against her lips as he carried her through the living room and toward the hallway.

They were both keeping secrets, yes. But maybe the only real truth was in the perfect fit of her small body against his large frame. Not because of sex, but because he and Jayne shared the kind of fundamental man-woman chemistry from which everything else could just naturally follow.

If only they could hold on to that—and to each other—wouldn't the rest fall into place? Kissing her, delving his tongue deeply between her lips, he wanted to believe that. And he wanted to make love to her again. This time knowing she carried his child.

"Please . . ."

Her whispered word wasn't an invitation or a refusal. It carried no telling inflection, but hung in midair, as if confused as to its final destination. Remy's mouth caught the word, turning that *please* into pure pleasure. As his lips covered hers again, he hugged her to his chest, curling his one arm all the way beneath her bent knees, wrapping the other around her shoulders.

She clung to his neck. With every step, he realized she'd made him feel a tenderness he hadn't suspected he possessed. Somewhere between the porch and his bedroom, his kisses became ever slower and more languid. He swept his tongue across her lips, grazing, barely touching.

She moaned, as if to say that she was powerless to stop what was happening. "Whatever it is we do to one another—"

"Is undeniable, Jayne." Remy's words sounded thick to his own ears. "Even if we are fire and water."

"Which are you, exactly?" she murmured on a sigh.

"Fire," he drawled without hesitation, tilting his head and flickering his warm tongue between her lips, letting the flamelike touches stoke the warm heat that he knew curled in her veins—and his.

Moonlight streamed through the narrow floor-to-ceiling windows of his bedroom. As if only now aware of where they were, Jayne said huskily, "Please, Remy, this is an attraction we have to fight."

The lack of conviction in her voice was the sweetest thing he'd ever heard; the way she stretched in his arms, the sweetest movement he'd ever felt. He just wished that for every kiss they'd shared, a lie hadn't passed between them....

"Ah, but, *chère*—" he stopped at the bed and whispered between kisses "—why fight a battle we can only lose?"

More insistently, she whispered, "We can't..."

"But we are."

Beyond his window, tinged by the mists of the bayou's waters, the moonlight had turned the color of Jayne's blue dress. His childhood swing, which hung from an old cypress tree, was a dark silhouette swaying with the night breeze. Tree branches broke across the moon's face in black slivers.

In that light, Remy surveyed Jayne's face. As he laid her on the bed, the skirt of her dress draped over his white coverlet like an opening fan. Covering her body with his own, he let her feel his full weight, his arousal. His feelings were as tangled as their tussling tongues had been a moment before. Could they work things out? Could they capture the wild energy that pulsed between them—tame it and domesticate it, for the baby's sake? Remy pushed thoughts of Parker far from his mind.

"All during dinner, I was imagining making love to you," he said. Staring down at her, he felt oddly raw, as if all his pretenses had been swept away by the last brush of her lips.

Jayne's hands unclasped at his neck, and her palms cupped his nape beneath his hair. He expected her to say that he shouldn't be thinking of that. Instead, she whispered, "Really?"

He nodded, nuzzling against her freshly washed, faintly damp hair, which he now knew wasn't straight at all, but full of sensual waves. During dinner, he'd noticed the beginnings of her thickening belly for the first time. Now, with that softness cushioning him, he pressed his hips to hers. On a soft moan, he drawled, "Jayne, you smell so sweet that it makes me think of raw sugarcane in the rain."

"But, Parker..." she whispered back, her hands molding over his shoulders.

Gently Remy whispered, "Guess what?"

She smiled into his eyes. "What?"

"I don't give a damn about Parker."

It wasn't exactly true. He didn't believe in kissing engaged women, either. But then, Jayne was carrying his baby. "Do you love him?"

She turned her head to the side, and her damp honey curls left wet spots on Remy's pillow. "Parker loves me," she whispered urgently.

But that wasn't what Remy had asked.

"Parker's always stood by me, and we've planned a whole life together. A good life."

It was all she was going to say. But Remy knew she'd never allow this intimacy if she was really in love with Parker. He nestled a palm against her waist. "Why is it that I feel so inclined to try to steal you away from your fiancé?" he asked her.

"Remy, I . . ."

He drew in a sharp, silent breath, then he fell utterly still and waited. *Tell me.*

After a long moment, she whispered, "You don't really want to steal me away from Parker. Not really."

But he did. Every touch and kiss and word was calculated to do exactly that. Just what he'd do with Jayne afterward, Remy wasn't quite sure. Suddenly Jayne arched against him in one fluid motion that stole away his breath—until he realized that she was actually wrenching away.

"No, Remy!" she gasped.

Before he even knew what was happening, she'd squirmed out from beneath him and scooted away, tugging down her dress. He quickly rolled onto his back and caught her wrist. "Ah, *chère* . . ."

She jerked away her hand as if she'd been burned. "No!"

Even though she was doing her level best to hide it, her loose, disheveled hair and heaving chest announced her excitement. The worst thing was that she looked so pretty, sitting on his bed in that blue dress, that his heart ached right to the point of breaking. "Jayne..." he began gently.

"A woman has a right to say no anytime she so chooses," she said calmly.

"Of course she does." But he'd been thinking of how fresh Jayne's hair smelled, how blue the moon looked. How could she be so sanctimonious, when it was she who was lying to him? Realizing he'd sounded testy, he said, "Look, that's not what I—"

"What *do* you mean?"

He stared at her.

"Please, do not become angry with me just because I have changed my mind and would prefer not to, er..."

Remy's jaw set. She was smoothing her dress as if she'd wholly forgotten how close she'd just come to having it removed, and that formal tone was calculated to force a distance between them. This time it wasn't going to work. "I'm not angry."

"You sound angry."

"If you'd rather talk than make love—" his eyes pierced the darkness, seeking hers "—it's fine with me."

She smiled, trying to get them on the track that led in the direction opposite from the bedroom. "Is there anything in particular you want to talk about?"

He said, "The baby."

JAYNE FLED THE BED. She was all the way across the room before she realized she'd moved. Or that her hands—which had been outstretched, with the fingers splayed like extended claws—now clutched the bodice of her dress in fistfuls, as if that might stop her heart from beating so hard.

"You knew?" When she reached one of the floor-to-ceiling windows, she whirled around—her back against the panes, her mind racing. "When...and from whom?"

Silence.

He hadn't even moved. He remained a prone silhouette in the bluish moonlight. Powerfully masculine, utterly still. His hands were clasped behind his neck, his taut white T-shirt receding into the white of the coverlet, while his tanned biceps and forearms were dark against the stiff white pillowcase.

"Aren't you even going to do me the courtesy of answering me, Remy?"

"The way you did me the courtesy of *telling* me, Jayne?" he drawled, with deceptive softness.

She couldn't breathe—not with her chest squeezing, the air thinning, her heart pounding. Her hand slid across the window glass, but the light switch was obviously elsewhere. Nervously she twirled her engagement ring on her finger. Why had she run in this direction? In panic, she wondered why she'd come here at all.

She didn't even trust herself to cross the room and find the light—because in the dark she might well stumble into his arms again. Or into his bed. Not that he'd catch her. Even in the darkness, she could feel the eyes of judgment pinning her right where she stood. Remy's eyes.

She wished with all her heart that he'd just say something.

Ever so slowly, he sat up. The uncanny silence of his movements was as unnerving as the other silences he'd apparently been maintaining. She wished he was anywhere other than on that well-made bed, too. A starched sheet peeked from a turned-back triangle of the coverlet, looking as clean and inviting as he was strong and warm. Jayne licked at her well-kissed lips. Thoughts were running through her mind so fast that she couldn't barely catch a one.

All night long, she'd wondered how to tell him. In the car. While they'd eaten. When he'd carried her across the threshold into this very room.

But he'd known.

All along, he'd known.

That was why Remy had told her about his father. He'd said pregnant women could drink the herb tea, too. And he'd given her milk and water at dinner, knowing she wouldn't take a beer. Jayne's cheeks stung with such heat that Remy might have slapped her.

The whole evening raced back to her—the candlelit dinner, the dance, the way he'd lifted her into his arms. The man had done it again—called her *chère* and danced her through the moonlight. And she'd thought...

Lord, I wanted to pretend he's falling in love with me.

She cleared her throat. "I do believe that you so kindly informed me about your father..." Her words were twisting uncontrollably, turning stilted, but she forged on. "...to try to make me feel guilty."

"You'd fault me for that?"

"Were you trying to seduce me into telling you?"

He didn't say anything, which she took to be his admission that it was the truth. She suddenly remembered how she'd danced alone to old 45s when she was a kid, singing softly and snapping her fingers, dreaming of true love. She blinked, vowing that hell would freeze over before she ever let a tear fall in front of Remy Lafitte. Ever since she'd first seen him, she'd ached for him, as if he were the man she'd dreamed about all those years ago. And now they'd made a baby together. But he'd just been leading her on tonight... again.

"You *knew,* and you were trying to make love to me," she said accusingly.

A chuckle of warning sounded from the bed. "You weren't putting up too much protest, Jayne."

"I did indeed—" Her words fell in a halting, forced staccato. Just one look at Remy, and she wanted to fall apart, to stamp her feet and cry like a baby—if for no other reason than that he might offer her his strength. Oh, he brought out the very worst in her. And she had to rein it all in, pull herself under control. For the baby's sake. "I'm on the opposite side of the room, Remy."

"*Now* you are."

The lithe way he rose from the bed seemed to say that they wouldn't remain so far apart for long.

"Stay over there," she said.

"Why?"

"Because..." Because the relationship between them was so complex. Because their one night together had bound them forever. *And because I want you, Remy, but you don't care.* As he approached, Jayne edged sideways, sinking back against the wood of the window molding.

"Because?" he repeated.

"Because we need to talk."

"Afraid we can't talk if I'm standing next to you, *chère?*"

Yes. "Please—" With his every nearing step, Jayne's knees got weaker, her voice shakier. Her fingers shot to her neck, felt the absence of her pearls and twined nervously around the red heart-shaped beads. "Please, can't we sit down and discuss this reasonably? You know, like two adults?"

But the man kept coming.

And coming.

Right about the time she started feeling faint, he stopped in front of her. Then he placed his hand on the wall beside her, angling his body right against hers, as if to keep her from fleeing. Not that she would. She'd had it with running from Remy. No, this time she'd take her stand.

Jayne just wished she could do so from a little farther away. Feeling the heat rise from his skin and hearing his breaths, she wished she had an alter ego, too—one who was better equipped to deal with a bad-boy bounty hunter who also happened to be the father of one's baby. But, of course, she didn't.

When Remy leaned away, her whole side felt bereft. But Remy was touching the air, and then the air was touching her—and although that might not amount to much in the books of most people, it was more than enough to send Jayne's senses into overdrive. Finally she whispered miserably, "How could you try to make love to me when you knew?"

In the moonlight, Remy's expression softened. "It wasn't all that difficult, Jayne," he whispered back.

Her flushed warm skin turned hot. Remy was no longer touching her—a half foot separated their bodies—but she could still feel his broad chest and lean torso and hard-muscled middle pressing down the length of her side.

"I'm pregnant." She said it as if he didn't know... as if that fact had nothing to do with why he'd backed her against the wall...as if she were merely protesting how his proximity unsettled her.

He lifted a lock of her loose hair and let it fall. "You're pregnant, and I wanted to be with you tonight."

Her heart fluttered. She damned her breath for catching. Remy *would* think it was just that easy. But why was he being nice? She'd imagined him cursing and slamming doors. Didn't he realize that making love was truly out of the question now? "Remy..." She fought the huskiness in her voice, tried to deepen her shallow breaths. "There's more to being with someone than sharing physical attraction."

"Parker tell you that?" Remy drawled.

Parker. At the name, Jayne became conscious of where she was—alone with Remy, in the middle of nowhere. But no, they were *somewhere.* Inside Remy's house on stilts in the bayou. They were in a bedroom where they'd nearly made love again, to the lullaby of crickets and the blue light of the moon.

And they were talking about *their* baby.

Oh, they were somewhere, all right. And Parker Bradford, the man Jayne had sworn to marry, simply did not belong. After a long moment, she said, "Maybe."

"And physical attraction is all we've ever shared—" Remy leaned a fraction closer, his words sounding hard-edged "—or *could* ever share."

She knew he didn't want more from her. She felt her heart breaking, and knew her words would waver when she spoke. "That's right."

They were so close to the window that moonlight was pouring over her shoulder and illuminating Remy. His face was as still as the rest of him. Hard to read. When his lips did part, the movement was a catalyst. Like a stone cast into still waters, it created a ripple of effects over his face. The lines beside his expressive mouth deepened, the corners of his silver eyes crinkled, the hollows of his cheeks danced with shadows.

"Were you ever going to tell me?"

It wasn't a question. In fact, his voice insinuated she was the worst kind of liar.

"I was."

He came so close that his cheek grazed hers. "We'll never know for sure now, will we?"

Her temper flared, and she slipped away—ducking beneath his arm. Striding toward the opposite side of the bedroom, she told herself she really wasn't running from him, but simply searching for the light. His reaction was too difficult to gauge without it.

"Four and a half months is a long time to keep me in the dark, Jayne."

There it was again. That sound of accusation. "Believe whatever you like, Remy." Jayne pivoted at the doorway and reached for the light switch—but the man's fingers curled over hers. She gasped. "I didn't hear you behind me!"

"Most people don't." His low drawl came from deep inside his chest; his breath was so close she could feel it. "I track the dishonest for a living—or have you forgotten?"

"I was going to tell you!" she nearly wailed. "Why won't you believe me?"

"Why should I?"

He had a point, but as a lawyer, Jayne knew better than to admit it. Barely perceptibly, his fingers tightened over hers. She said, "Are you calling me a liar?"

He leaned closer. "Yes."

"Well, what about you?"

He dropped her hand. "Meaning?"

"You…" *Never called me, Remy. You made love to me when it meant nothing to you.* Telling herself she only meant to keep him at bay, Jayne splayed her fingers on his chest. Feeling his muscles ripple in response, she knew it had been a mistake to touch him. "You didn't have to scare me tonight in order to discuss the baby," she said angrily.

Remy arched his eyebrows. "I scared you?"

"You made sly insinuations about my fiancé. In the car, you grilled me about who might be chasing me as if I'm involved in some sort of criminal activity. And you said you heard a gunshot."

Remy merely grunted. "You think I made that up?"

She nodded, feeling on surer ground. Argumentation was the one thing in the world at which she truly excelled. Whether she actually believed the line of reasoning was immaterial. "I very strongly feel you said those things as an excuse to get me out here. Alone."

"To talk about the baby?"

"No." Jayne sighed, feeling as if she were on trial. "To torture me."

"Don't skirt the issues, Jayne."

"Which are?" she shot back.

"Number one is that Parker Bradford's not going to touch hide nor hair of my child," Remy said.

Instinctively Jayne grabbed for the wall. Her pulse accelerated, throbbing at her wrists, her throat. A headache pain zinged into her left eye, and she realized her glasses had slid downward on her nose. Surely she'd misunderstood. Pushing her glasses into place, she said, "Excuse me?"

"You heard me."

Jayne could only stare. Long fingers of sadness for what could never be slid around her heart. They squeezed hard, as if they never meant to let go.

Remy continued, "Tonight, all I want you to understand is that this baby is mine. No one else's. Mine."

At the words, irrational fury coursed through her veins. "Yours," she said venomously. "Where have *you* been?"

"You didn't give me the chance to be anywhere," Remy shot back tersely. Then he leaned so close that only her splayed hand separated them. When he spoke again, his voice was hoarse and ragged. "Why, Jayne? Did you really think Parker would make a better father for *my* baby?"

He'd tried to mask it, but she'd heard the pain. What on earth had she been thinking? What had she done? "No, Remy. No..." When she heard that warning chuckle again, Jayne withdrew her hand.

"Of course you did, Jayne. Parker'll send our child to the right schools in the right clothes in the right beige BMW. He or she'll come home to a nanny in a nursery in that mansion of his in the Garden District."

It was true.

But it wasn't why she hadn't told Remy.

All at once, with a quick sweep of his arm, Remy flicked the switch, bathing the room in light. His eyes didn't so much as narrow against the sudden brightness. "And to hell with my rights, Jayne?"

She squinted against the light and stamped her foot. "I was going to tell you, Remy."

He merely stared at her. "Want to know why you didn't?"

Not particularly. Especially since she knew why, even if she wasn't about to say it. "Why?"

"Because you want me. And every time you see me, you wonder if I'd cut my hair for your class reunion. Or you see your political ambitions go out the window. You imagine a future that could never work."

"That's enough."

"Not by a long shot," he returned. "I work hard and make a good living. But you have absolutely no idea who I am. In spite of your attraction to me, and in spite of the fact that you're pregnant with my child—" his eyes trailed over her, scalding everywhere they touched "—you haven't even bothered to so much as start to find out."

Jayne couldn't do anything but stare. Did people really talk this boldly—and then face each other in the morning? She flushed, thinking of the night she'd spent with Remy. *People do all sorts of things and then face each other.* "You're wrong about me," she managed to say.

"Prove me wrong," he shot back.

Oh, how she wanted to.

But it would mean admitting the truth. That she'd stared through her office window countless times—only to realize she was dreaming about Remy. Or she'd glance down at doodles on her legal pads and see that she'd been scribbling his name. She caught herself staring at phones—desk phones, wall phones, phones in booths—as if willing them all to ring. And on restless nights she'd wandered the streets, aimlessly searching, only to find herself on his doorstep.

Then, once, she'd knocked on his door. She'd thrown herself at him, begged him to make love to her. And he had, touching her body and soul. But he'd never called. And if he'd wanted to, he would have. Because Remy Lafitte was the kind of man who did what he damn well pleased.

And so she couldn't tell him.

Because she couldn't bear for Remy to know how much she'd feared his rejection—of both her and the baby.

"So, prove me wrong, Jayne."

She'd meant to stand her ground. Instead she turned and fled.

REMY TOLD HIMSELF not to follow her.

He flicked off the light, feeling more comfortable in the dark, then crossed the room and leaned casually against the window molding. Apart from the music, the house was utterly silent. He was so conscious of how alone he and Jayne were that he imagined an invisible string connecting them . . . as if all they needed to open the lines of communication were two Dixie cups. For a very long time, he stared into the face of the blue moon, wondering what she was thinking.

As one song segued into another, a wry smile flickered over his lips. Of all things, "Blue Moon" was playing.

"I saw you standing alone . . ." Remy whispered.

Jayne was alone in the dark living room, and Remy could sense her movements as surely as if she were standing next to him. She was lying on her back, staring at the ceiling. The skirt of her dress was draped over the side of the couch, grazing the braided rug on the hardwood floor.

He hadn't become a tracker for nothing.

He just wished he knew what was going on inside her head and heart—what she was thinking, feeling.

He hummed along with the song, vaguely wondering what had possessed him to choose a tape that was so full of songs about love and loneliness. Maybe he'd thought it would make Jayne tell him the truth. And maybe, he thought dryly, given the barely suppressed heat of their exchange, it would have been better to set the tone with some hard-edged rock and roll. Or heavy metal.

"Oh, hell," he muttered.

And then he did what he'd told himself not to—and followed Jayne.

Sure enough, she was lying on the couch. He patted her thigh softly. To his amazement, she actually scooted over so that he could sit next to her.

"Jayne?"

She squinted at him warily. "Yes?"

Had she been crying? It was hard to tell. Hers was a determined expression—chin thrust forward, eyes fixed on a point somewhere above his, lips pursed. He realized he didn't have a clue about what he wanted to say. When he first learned about the pregnancy, working things out with Jayne had seemed an easy enough proposition. Now he wasn't sure.

"I'm not going to apologize for the things I said, *chère*."

Her chuckle sounded nearly as wry as one of his. "You came all the way in here to tell me that?"

Her tone communicated something like "Don't go too far out of your way for my sake, Buster."

So much for the animal chemistry that was supposed to make everything else fall into place. Remy sighed. "No, I wanted to tell you..."

What? Remy didn't quite know how to put it, but while he was staring at the moon, he'd realized why he'd always been so attracted to Jayne Wright.

As a bounty hunter, he came into contact with more than the average number of unsavory characters. He'd been blessed with a sixth sense about people, too, and that came in handy in his line of work. Even the most apparently upstanding people were sometimes not exactly as they seemed. But the second Remy saw Jayne, he'd known she was the genuine article—honest, ethical, the salt of the earth.

Sounding nervous, she said, "Go ahead and tell me whatever it is, Remy."

"You're one of the best lawyers in Orleans Parish."

She shifted her weight on the couch, making just a tad more room. "Thanks," she said, sounding surprised.

"The first time I ever saw you, you were down at the lockup."

"You remember seeing me for the first time?"

At the catch in her voice, his spirits lifted. He nodded. "You looked so..." He paused, trying to think of the right word. "So *trim*, in your gray suit and pearls, and you were surrounded by..."

"Criminals?" she supplied.

"All manner of lowlife." Seeing her there, his first impulse had been to pick her up by the gray lapels and haul her outside. He chuckled softly. "You kind of stood out in the environment."

A smile twitched at her lips. "I should hope so."

He shifted his weight again, feeling uncomfortable. This talking business could be unnerving. "Damn it,

Jayne,'' he suddenly said, "the main reason I'm mad is that I wanted you, *expected* you, to be honest." He licked his lips, craving a cigarette. Somehow, what he meant to say wasn't coming out right. "I mean, it might not be fair, but I realize I kind of hold you up as, er . . ." He was digging himself in deeper with every word.

"As what?" she asked insistently.

"Well, as a kind of standard."

There was a weighty pause. At that moment, the long reel-to-reel tape reached its end. When it clicked off, the silence was excruciating.

She didn't say anything, so Remy continued, "When I called Parker, he said you were pregnant. I just guessed the baby was mine. . . ." His voice trailed off. He wasn't sure what kind of response he wanted or expected from her. Was she still upset because he knew?

"Remy?" Jayne whispered.

Her voice sounded small, somehow. "Hmm?"

Instead of answering, she reached out and gently took his hand in hers. As she placed his palm on her belly, he could feel her fingers trembling. It was as if she sensed how much he wanted to touch her there. He felt as if he'd suddenly flown from sea level to the top of the highest mountain; the thinner air was making him breathless and the height was making his head spin. Was this Jayne's silent way of telling him that she recognized his rights?

They sat like that for a long time, his palm rounding to the contours of her belly. Beneath, he felt the soft cotton of her dress, the warmth of her skin, the rim of her panty line. He found himself praying he'd imagined that gunshot tonight. If one of them had to be in danger, why couldn't it be him? Tomorrow he'd return to New Orleans and find out what was happening.

"Remy?" she finally said, so softly that he barely heard.

"Yeah?"

"Everything you said is true," she whispered. "But it's not why I didn't tell you."

"It's all right." He no longer cared. The truth was out in the open. Jayne had said with a gesture that they'd work out something between them. Remy no longer wanted to lay blame.

"I...ran away from Parker's party because I knew I had to tell you, and I was afraid."

So, she *had* left because of him. The news made his heart soar. "Afraid?"

She shrugged helplessly. "I didn't know what you'd do. I thought..."

Remy squinted at her. He guessed Jayne didn't feel much more comfortable than he did. "Hmm?"

She sighed. "I thought you'd offer me money, at best. Maybe tell me to get lost. Tell me it wasn't your problem. Tell me the baby wasn't even yours."

With every word, Remy's jaw dropped another notch. And he could read between the lines. Jayne had had too much pride to face his possible rejection. He lifted his hand from her belly and cupped her chin. "But, *chère,*" he said softly, "whatever made you think I'm that kind of man?"

Chapter Seven

"Hey, are you Remy's new girlfriend?"

I sure am. Feeling positive she was dreaming, Jayne smiled drowsily, snuggled deeper into the sofa and nuzzled her nose into a fresh-smelling down-filled pillow.

"Hey, didn't you hear me?"

Jayne stretched lazily, then realized her legs were confined. *They were bound at the ankles!* She was trapped! Those horrible creeps from the French Quarter had found her. Would Remy hear and rescue her? Jayne's scream lodged in her throat, and she started kicking in earnest.

A high-pitched squeal sounded. "Watch it, lady! Hey, quit kicking me!"

"Who are you?" Jayne croaked in groggy panic. When she opened her eyes in the darkness, she realized her feet were merely tangled in a heavy knit afghan. She wasn't in mortal peril.

Oh, Jayne, you're just dreaming. Those thugs who'd chased her and Remy were long gone. That Remy had covered her with the afghan sent a smile across her lips. Who would have believed such a tough guy could be such an old softy? As she'd drifted to sleep, he'd remained beside her, his fingers threaded through hers and resting on her belly.

Nearby, a foot stamped on the hardwood floor. "Hey, wake up!"

That's a real voice.

Jayne shimmied to her elbows, suddenly wishing whoever it was would quit using the word *hey* so darn much. She fumbled for her glasses, swiftly slipped them on, then tugged a lamp cord—and gasped. Not an inch from her nose, a small, pixieish face peered back. The faint yellow lamplight illuminated the living room, but a quick glance through a window said it was still the middle of the night. Remy was probably fast asleep in his bedroom.

So who was the child glaring at Jayne?

In a demanding tone, the little girl said, "Well?"

She couldn't have been but nine years old, and her bright blue eyes were every bit as piercing as her needle-thin voice. She was all restless nerves and crackling energy, with a frame that was fittingly wiry.

"Hey, are you his new girlfriend, or what?" she repeated.

Deciding that the child in front of her was simply adorable, Jayne couldn't help but ask, "Just who was Remy's *old* girlfriend?" When no answer was forthcoming, Jayne became half convinced this was a very real dream. She chuckled sleepily and said, "Who are *you?*"

"Belle—" At the intense squeak in her own voice, the little girl's blue eyes popped open wider. Looking startled, she hopped from one knobby-kneed leg to the other and back again. Then, in one extremely long, uninterrupted squeal, she said, "My name's Belle Burdette and I live near the shell road that comes in from Bayou Lafourche and my daddy, Claude, he sent me and he told me I had better hurry up or else!"

Belle Burdette? "Doesn't ring a bell," Jayne managed to say, feeling punchy from lack of sleep. The child spoke so quickly, she'd barely registered the whole of what she'd said. "I'm Jayne Wright."

"Okay, but do I have to call you Miz Wright?"

"Jayne's fine."

Blinking herself awake, Jayne glanced toward the hallway, wishing a sleepy, half-clad Remy would appear. When he didn't, she looked Belle over from head to toe, searching for additional clues as to the reason for her visit. All she discovered was that Belle had lovely auburn hair that hung in two tight braids to her waist and an impish face that was sprinkled with reddish freckles, most of which seemed concentrated near the tip of her upturned nose.

Jayne frowned. Belle was wearing what looked to be a Catholic-school uniform. A plaid skirt of navy, green and yellow was hemmed sharply at her knees, her crisp white blouse had been buttoned cockeyed, and her yellow knee socks, which had lost their elastic, were pooled around her ankles.

The child had been running! That was why her socks had fallen down. At the revelation, Jayne came fully awake. Her hand shot to her neck, nervously toying with the strand of heart-shaped beads. Apparently Belle had grabbed her school clothes, dressed in a flash, then run to Remy's, scampering as fast as her gangly legs could carry her. And in the middle of the night, Jayne thought, suddenly worried.

"What's the matter?" Jayne had fallen asleep in her dress, so she swung her feet over the side of the sofa and slipped them right into the leather boots Jenny Lafitte had loaned her. "What's happened?"

Belle said, "We gotta find Remy!"

"Remy!" Jayne called out. Lowering her voice and knotting her shoelaces with lightning speed, Jayne said,

"Don't worry, Belle. I'm sure Remy's just asleep. Could you please tell me what's happened?"

"But I went to Remy's room first!" Belle wailed.

Jayne placed the little girl's hand firmly in her own and stood. Apparently, out here, people made themselves right at home. Jayne was hardly accustomed to open-door policies, but she liked that people looked out for one another. She started searching the house for Remy, wishing Belle would divulge the nature of her troubles. If it was a medical situation, they'd have to hurry—Remy or no Remy.

Belle's fingers curled tightly around Jayne's hand. "My daddy woke me up when I was fast asleep," she offered in a shocked voice.

"That sounds a little scary," Jayne said gently. "But now we're on our way. Did your daddy say why he needs Remy?"

"Daddy says everything's okay. So far, anyway." The furrowed white line of Belle's eyebrows said she didn't believe it.

Remy wasn't in the bedroom. Or the bathroom. Or on the back porch. *Where's he gone?* Something about his quiet watchfulness always inspired a sense of safety. Whatever had happened, Jayne wanted him with her. *Just thank your lucky stars you were here, Jayne.*

"The ambulance can't come—" Belle's death grip loosened somewhat, as if the child were calming. "The only one's got all tied up on account of Mrs. Cleary, who had to have her fake angina again. And Daddy can't drive the truck, on account of his transmission."

Claude Burdette had called for an ambulance? So, it *was* a medical emergency. Jayne hastened her steps. Maybe Belle's mother was ill...or had had an accident.

Maybe another child was sick. Jayne shot a reassuring glance in Belle's direction.

"Hey—" An answering smile hovered on the little girl's lips. "It's gonna be okay, right, Jayne?"

Jayne told herself to be strong for Belle. "Absolutely."

Internally her temper flared. The scarcity of ambulances in all the parishes was causing local political debates. If she was running for office, instead of Parker, she'd do something to correct the situation. "If Remy's not in the kitchen, then we'll head back by ourselves, Belle."

"But you're not a doctor," Belle protested.

Neither was Remy, but Jayne decided this wasn't the best time to point that out. Besides, as surprising as it was, Remy did provide care for the community. "I know a little medicine," Jayne said firmly, just wishing she'd done more than take quickie day courses in basic first aid. She was trained only for heart attacks, high fevers, strokes, choking, snakebites....

The kitchen was empty.

"I just knew it!" Belle moaned.

The kitchen clock said 3:00 a.m., and the only evidence of Remy's presence was in the dish drainer, which held the clean dinner dishes. After Jayne fell asleep, he must have washed them. A fleeting image of one of Remy's naked shoulders sporting a clean dish towel entered her mind, but she suppressed it. This was no time to contemplate the unexpected features of Remy's personality.

"Hey, what's my mama gonna do if we can't find Remy?"

So it was Belle's mother who was ill. "Not to worry," Jayne assured. Quickly she headed to the front door, with Belle in tow, and grabbed a sweater from Remy's coatrack. "Here—" She gently wrestled Belle's arms into the sleeves and rolled back the cuffs.

"Hey, Remy's sweater fits me like a midi coat!" Belle remarked bravely.

Jayne smiled at the sight of the sweater's hem sweeping Belle's calves, then whisked the little girl through Remy's front door—and hit something hard. Remy's hand—at least Jayne *hoped* it was Remy's—closed around her upper arm.

"Trying to escape in the night, *chère?*" he asked with a throaty chuckle.

"I ran right into you," she said huskily. The way his fingers curled around her arm was meant to steady her, but the touch did everything but.

"No problem," he told her.

In spite of Remy's unsettling proximity, Jayne had never felt so relieved. He'd changed into a pale blue T-shirt and a navy cardigan. Because his raven hair was drawn back, his high forehead was accentuated. His sleep-swollen silver eyes were the steadiest she'd ever seen. "This is Belle Burdette, and she says her father sent—"

"I should have *known* our little Belle would be the culprit who'd aid you in your escape, Jayne."

Under any other circumstances, Remy's irresistible smile would have been infectious. "Remy," Jayne said gravely, "I believe there's a medical emergency."

Remy merely guffawed, then leaned down and scooped Belle into his arms.

"Remy, Daddy sent me," Belle said in a stern rebuke.

Another chuckle rumbled in Remy's chest. "Heard you coming from a mile away, too, crashing through the trees like a wild animal. So I got up, got dressed and went out to get some sassafras."

"For medicine…" Jayne murmured in relief. Remy was clearly acquainted with Mrs. Burdette's illness.

"Nope." Remy grinned at Jayne in the darkness, his teeth flashing white. "For sassafras tea, in case I want some." He glanced down at Belle. "So Mrs. Cleary had an attack of hypochondria tonight, eh?"

Belle nodded and put her arms around Remy's neck matter-of-factly, as if accustomed to his embrace.

He glanced at Jayne. "And you gave this little urchin my best sweater?"

Belle giggled shakily. "Hey, you're the big urchin, Remy."

"Don't you think we'd better go?" Jayne managed to say.

"Well, Florence Nightingale." Remy looked at her for a long moment. "Were you really going out alone on a mercy mission?"

The approval in his eyes made Jayne's heart swell.

I'm not that kind of person, Remy. The words came back to her, unbidden. *Prove it to me, Jayne.*

Maybe she just had.

The Wright residence was the sort of place where professionals came running on call. Remy seemed surprised that she'd wake in the night and head for an uncertain destination to aid a stranger in need. She never would have thought to do otherwise. But maybe this would help change Remy's opinion of her. His sudden laughter broke her reverie.

"Since you're up for this," he drawled, "I guess I can go on back to bed."

The next thing Jayne knew, a worn green army-issue pouch was thrust into her hands. Staring down, she was sure it contained country remedies. Remy swung Belle around in a sweeping circle, deposited her soundly on the front porch, and then brushed past Jayne and through the front door.

"What am I supposed to do with this?" Jayne asked in rising panic, staring from the pouch to Remy's retreating back.

Remy shrugged and shot her a grin over his shoulder. "Deliver Marie Burdette's baby."

"HEY, ARE YOU *sure* Mama's not going to die?"

"I promise, Belle," Jayne whispered gently. She was seated beside Belle on the steps outside the bedroom door. Inside, Remy was still with Marie and Claude Burdette. "We just won't let that happen."

Remy had merely been teasing when he said Jayne was going to have to play doctor. She'd headed outside with Belle—her mind racing over every fact she'd learned about babies in the past months—but Remy had appeared again, this time carrying a bona fide black leather medical bag.

"You're *sure* she's okay, Jayne?" Belle asked again.

Jayne gave her a quick hug. "There's no doubt in my mind," she said, thinking of the way Remy had piggybacked Belle most of the way home. After Belle wriggled down, she'd walked between Remy and Jayne, holding both their hands.

Jayne tried to remember whether she and Parker had ever been together with a child—and couldn't. Meeting voters and their babies after political speeches didn't count. Would a child respond to Parker the way Belle did to Remy?

Quit comparing Remy and Parker, Jayne.

But she couldn't help it. Tonight, it was she and Remy, not she and Parker, who were working as a team. He'd protected her in the French Quarter. And now, as much as Jayne wanted to help Remy with Marie, she was needed to occupy Belle. Marie's cries of pain had terrified her only daughter.

"Hey, what's an urchin, Jayne?"

Jayne drew her arm more tightly around Belle's shoulders, tilted her head and thought for a moment. Twining the fingers of her free hand through the beads she was wearing, she said, "An urchin is a mischievous youngster."

"What's mischievous?"

Jayne chuckled. "Inclined to get into trouble."

"Hey, I'm good."

"You sure are." Jayne glanced down fondly, wondering if her own child would be at all like Belle. Then she thought about the woman who was going through the birthing process that Jayne herself would experience in a few short months. She kept imagining the possibility of Remy delivering his own child . . . their child. Jayne whispered, "Remy just likes to tease. So, when he calls you an urchin, it means he likes you bunches."

"Oh," Belle said, sounding pleased. "He teases me lots."

He teases me, too. But, in Jayne's case, it was harder to tell why. It had been a long day, with little opportunity to process the many events. Intense feelings were sparking between her and Remy, but then, they always had.

Belle stretched her legs out straight. Swinging them back and forth, she murmured, "I wish the amb'lance would come."

"It will."

But instead of a siren, there was a bloodcurdling scream. A long series of rushed, high-pitched pants followed. Belle's gaze shot to Jayne's.

"She's fine," Jayne cooed, smoothing Belle's auburn hair and glancing around the dimly lit staircase. The exterior of the Burdette's house was in need of fresh paint, and the furniture in the interior was worn, but the place was cozy and warm. It was a good home for a child...for Belle. Remy had envisioned their baby living in Parker's Garden District mansion. But didn't he realize that Jayne knew a child could be happy anywhere—with enough love? Parker had sworn his love was so strong that it might make up for her lack, but Jayne wasn't so sure now.

"Hey, I'm *never* having a baby!" Belle suddenly declared. "Not ever!"

"You may change your mind." Because sometimes it was an unexpected surprise, a gift that changed your life overnight. The words Jayne had been thinking for the past hour slipped past her lips. "I'm going to have a baby, too, Belle."

Belle stared at Jayne's midsection, looking curiously doubtful.

Jayne chuckled softly. By now, Belle clearly knew some of the basic facts of life, but the details probably remained sketchy. "In a few more months you'll be able to tell better," Jayne explained.

Belle's nose crinkled. "If you go to the hospital, can they give you a painkiller?"

"It still hurts." Jayne hugged Belle again, and then rocked her. "Were you ever so happy that you cried?"

Belle promptly said, "Once when I was seven and Daddy brought me a brand-new bike by complete surprise."

"Well, that's what this is like," Jayne said.

Belle said, "Hey, that might be okay."

Nearby, something rustled.

Jayne glanced up. The bedroom door was open, and Remy was leaning against the jamb, backlit by a triangle of intensely bright light. He looked as if he'd been standing there for a few moments—head cocked, shoulders against the doorjamb, surgical mask slung around his neck. He'd been listening to Jayne talking to Belle. Now he nodded his head in the direction of the bedroom.

As if on cue, one long, loud wail sounded.

A baby's wail.

Jayne's lips parted in astonishment. Remy looked tired, but a slow smile curled his lips. He shook his head, saying, "Somehow I knew the quiet wasn't going to last."

"Mama!" Belle shot from the steps toward the bedroom. Remy caught her by the scruff of the neck, just long enough to slow her down. For an instant, her running feet merely churned in midair, cartoonlike. Then Remy set her down again, allowing her to proceed into the room at a walk, rather than a run.

Jayne stood and all but tiptoed toward Remy and the room. "The baby's okay?"

Remy ran a palm over the top of his head, slicking back his hair. He nodded. "Yeah."

"C'mon in," Marie called weakly.

"Hey, Jayne—" Belle yelled excitedly, her voice turning squeaky again. "It's a sister! I wasn't gonna say it in case it didn't turn out right, but hey, a sister is what I wanted!"

Jayne smiled, then realized Remy was staring at her. "Hmm?"

"I guess you want to see the new urchin, too, eh, *chère?*" Even though his voice was strained, he wasn't so tired he couldn't tease.

Jayne stepped reverently inside the room, just wishing she'd seen Remy deliver the baby. Marie was already dressed in a fresh gown, and she held up a fuzzy pink bundle. Claude grinned and fussed with the fluffy stack of pillows at the headboard. Out of the corner of her eye Jayne could see towels, used linens, gauze and surgical scissors.

"Be right back," Remy drawled softly, heading toward the bed. A moment later, he returned, saying, "Jayne Wright, meet Lisa Leigh Burdette. Go on and get acquainted."

Jayne's mouth went dry. She wasn't sure if it was because of the newborn—or Remy. She could only stare at the pair. Inside the blanket, Lisa Leigh was adorable—all naked and wrinkled and red. In perfect health, too, judging by the way she was wiggling.

"She's so beautiful," Jayne whispered, tears stinging her eyes.

So was Remy. Little Lisa Leigh was curled in the crook of his strong, corded forearm, her fuzzy pink blanket bunched against the pale blue of his shirt. Remy's cupped free hand supported her tiny head, molding to the contours, his long fingers sweeping across her forehead. No man had ever looked larger or more masculine, no baby so small or so safe. *The lion lies down with the lamb,* Jayne thought.

Far in the distance, a siren screamed in the night.

But the ambulance was too late. Because Remy had already come to the rescue.

"You know how you said I'd never gotten to know you?" Jayne murmured, so that only Remy could hear.

He nodded.

"It's true...but only because I've always felt so nervous around you."

At the words, Remy smiled, warmth touching his tired eyes. Then he leaned forward, his arm the perfect cradle.

As Jayne gingerly took the baby, she whispered, "Oh, Remy, you're a man of surprises."

Hearing Remy's soft chuckle, Lisa Leigh quit squirming and exhaled one soft, contented baby-sigh. Remy shot Jayne an arch glance and said, "You ain't seen nothin' yet, *chère*."

"SCARED?" Remy asked softly, teasingly.

Jayne smiled into his eyes. "How could I be scared, when I've got a professional tough guy watching my back?"

"Ah, is that all I am to you?" Remy pressed a palm over his heart, as if he were mortally wounded. With his other hand, he swung his black leather medical bag, lifting a banana leaf that had fallen across a narrow section of the footpath.

As Jayne ducked beneath the wide, flat frond, she shrugged, as if to say, "We'll see, Remy." But her smile said he meant much more to her. And he did. He always had.

The banana leaf rustled, falling behind her in the semidarkness. "Thanks," she said, trying and failing to fight the huskiness in her voice. When Remy moved next to her, she inadvertently bumped against him and his caressing hand slipped beneath her elbow.

He said, "Just protecting you as best I can."

Was he ever! She was all grown up, but Jayne found herself the recipient of a touch as gentle as that which Remy had bestowed on little Lisa Leigh. And earlier, when he carried her into his bedroom, Jayne had felt as fragile as a newborn. She could still imagine Remy's strong fingers molding to her nape, his corded forearms cradling her back and his muscular chest catching her, keeping her from falling.

Images of the day's crazy events were suddenly jumbled together with thoughts of Parker and the baby she'd made with Remy. Jayne had to fight not to turn to the man beside her and speak her deepest, secret wish. *Just keep me from falling, Remy. Keep me from making a mistake.*

Clearing her throat, she said, "Sure is strange out here, isn't it?" When Remy smiled back casually, she knew he meant to keep to their unspoken pact—the one that said they were too tired to discuss the future of their own unborn child.

"You can live here forever and never get used to it."

"I keep expecting to see a dinosaur."

Remy chuckled. "A gator, anyway."

Jayne's eyes shot heavenward. "Or some snake dangling down from one of these old trees."

"Now, *chère,*" Remy drawled. "Don't get overly dramatic."

She wasn't. The first fingers of light were touching the swamplands. A low-lying, seemingly phosphorescent sea green mist had settled along the footpath between Remy's and the Burdettes', and the sheer eeriness of the primordial landscape would have chilled Jayne to the very bone—if she'd had any guide other than Remy. But Remy was here, ready to catch her if she fell.

"The air smells salty," she commented in a sleepy whisper. It smelled of vegetation, too—moss and ferns and mushrooms. It was moist, and Jayne's cheeks were as dew-damp as the iridescent green leaves all around them. The more she stared ahead, the more the ghostly predawn haze seemed to take on a life of its own. Its long tongue licked around the swaying fronds of plants, while their slender arms reached heavenward and waved at the fading blue moon, as if saying goodbye. Gnarled hands of ancient tree roots stretched their claws across the surface of the dark soil.

"Watch out," Remy said softly. His gentle grip tightened on her elbow.

Are those men from the French Quarter chasing us again? Jayne wondered. But Remy merely steered her around a tree root.

Then a silence fell between them—one that was as comfortable as the navy cardigan he'd given her. Jayne hugged the sweater around her shoulders as tightly as if she were hugging Remy, and she tucked her cool hands into the folds of the wool. Was this man—this country healer and deliverer of babies—really the father of her child? Somehow, she didn't quite believe it. She was so awed by what had transpired tonight that her chest got tight every time she looked at him.

But Remy hadn't changed. She had. In the strange light of this new morning, she was looking at him for the first time. He'd been so right when he accused her of never having seen the real him. The initial effect he had on her had been so overpowering that she was incapable of simply getting to know him. Could something between them possibly work? If so, could she leave Parker, knowing it would ruin his career?

"Correct me if I'm wrong," she said on a sigh, "but has this been a very long day?"

A belly laugh rumbled on the quiet air. "Very."

Even though Jayne felt bone-tired, she chuckled. Had it really only been last afternoon that Remy dropped her gray pump on her parents' dining table?

After a few moments, Remy said, "Earth to Jayne."

"Earth," she repeated as Remy's house came into sight. "I feel like we traversed it today. We went from Virginia to New Orleans to here...."

"Nearly to heaven and back," Remy said softly.

Her breath caught. When she glanced into his eyes, there was no mistaking his meaning. Tonight, he'd carried her into his bedroom, and they'd nearly made love. Judging from the way Remy was looking at her now, he hadn't merely been trying to seduce the truth about the baby from her. She felt a quick, wrenching sense of need, a longing.

"Remy, I'm sorry I didn't—"

His index finger pressed against her lips.

Tell you everything.

"It's forgotten," he said huskily.

But she didn't want forgotten. She wanted forgiven. Remy trailed his finger from her lips, across her cheek, and tilted his head, angling it downward. Then he leaned back again, clearly having second thoughts about kissing her. There was so much between them—their baby bringing them together, her marriage keeping them apart. There was no room for thoughtlessness, no doorway or window through which foolishness could beat a hasty retreat. They couldn't afford any wrong moves.

He nodded in the direction of his house. "Let's get home."

Home. Her heart ached at the word. Staring at Remy's little house in the wilderness—that cozy, crazy-quilt house with the added porches and the sagging roof and the shingled siding—she couldn't help but see herself a week hence. Would she really be living in Parker's Garden District mansion? How would Remy fit into her life then? And the baby...

She sighed. Whatever the solution, she wouldn't discover it tonight.

"Watch out, Jayne."

The warning came too late. Jayne had run right into the fishing nets Remy was repairing. Instinctively she flailed her arms, but she only trapped herself further. Because the nets were of transparent threads, she hadn't seen them. "I wasn't paying attention to where I was going."

"When you don't watch out," Remy said gently, moving to the other side of the nets to free her, "you're likely to get all tangled up, *chère.*"

Remy's words seemed weightier than they actually were. Feeling sure he was thinking of the tangled web of their relationship, she said, "Isn't that the truth?" She felt just as trapped by her upcoming marriage to Parker as she was by the nets. "You think it's a mistake for me to marry Parker, don't you?"

"Let's just say I don't think you're well suited."

Well suited. The night they made love, that had been exactly why she said she and Remy couldn't be together. Did he remember? "Parker and I have a lot in common."

Remy merely shrugged. Then he finished helping free her, caught her hand and started toward the house.

"So, what kind of a man do you think I need?" she asked. As soon as the words were out, she realized she was fishing—and hard. Heaven help her, but she wanted Remy to say he was the kind of man she needed. The old Remy would have said it, too. Not that he'd have meant it.

The new Remy said, "Only you can decide that, Jayne."

She parted her lips, maybe to protest. What she wound up saying was "Sweeny."

Remy's mouth quirked. "If Sweeny's the man for you, I'd rather not know. You're marrying Parker next week, and—" he shot her a quick smile "—having my baby this coming summer. Jayne, another man in your life might be more than I can handle."

"The voice outside," she clarified. Why hadn't she realized it before? Her heart pounded with excitement. A century seemed to have passed since she'd been trapped inside the Mardi Gras float with Remy, but she was sure she was right. "The man outside the garage in the French Quarter tonight was Smoothtalk Sweeny!"

"You're sure?" They ascended the stairs to Remy's front porch and his arm draped protectively around her shoulders, as if Smoothtalk might be inside the house.

Jayne nodded. "I'm good with voices."

"You've got a hell of a good singing voice, anyway."

In spite of the revelation about Sweeny, Jayne found herself gazing deeply into Remy's eyes. As she hoarsely said, "Thanks," her sweater slipped from her shoulder. Remy gingerly slid it into place, even though they'd reached the porch and were seconds from entering the warm house. He held open the door for her.

"But Sweeny knows us." Jayne tamped down a flush as she entered the living room and turned on the lamp. After all, the night she propositioned Remy, she'd also hired him to find Smoothtalk Sweeny. "I can't believe he'd try to rob us."

"He's a criminal," Remy reminded. "You've defended him."

The charge had been mugging, too. Still, Smoothtalk Sweeny had actually apologized to his unharmed victim. Besides, Smoothtalk's mother doted on him, and he seemed more misguided than menacing. Jayne shrugged. "We could track him down. Maybe he'll shed some light on whether or not he and his cronies were specifically chasing us." She felt the warm traces of Remy's fingertips across the small of her back.

He smiled at her. "Bright and early tomorrow, which means as soon as I get an hour's worth of shut-eye, I'll head back to the city and find him."

Her eyes fixed pointedly on his. "You say that as if you're going alone."

"If those guys are really after you, Jayne, you'll be safer waiting at my mother's." Remy's eyes drifted over her figure and lingered on her belly, making it clear that he meant to protect both her and the baby.

Not that Jayne was about to stay on Bayou Lafourche. But she was too tired to argue, so she turned and sank onto the sofa.

"Jayne, darlin', why don't you do me a huge favor and take the bed?"

At the mention of his bed, her pulse quickened. Her mind raced back to how he'd kissed her earlier in the evening, the full weight of him covering her. The memory of his arousal, the hard heat of it scarcely masked by his clothes, made tremors move inside her, as if she had a bellyful of butterflies. And the night they'd made love... Even now, the mere thought of how they'd moved together made her feel breathless, senseless. Damp heat prickled her nape. Over Remy's shoulder, she tried not to notice the last vestiges of tonight's blue moon. "I was fine out here before," she said shakily.

Before he could argue, she continued, "Strange..."

Pulling an ottoman next to the sofa, Remy seated himself and tugged off her boots. He gently massaged her sock-clad feet, working the pads of his thumbs into her insteps. "Hmm?"

"The whole time we were in that float, I kept trying to place Smoothtalk Sweeny's voice." But Remy's proximity had distracted her, just as his foot massage was distracting her now. She willed herself to remember Parker and, with a fleeting, apologetic smile, withdrew her feet and curled them beneath herself.

Suddenly she clamped a hand over her mouth, catching a yawn. "It's just strange that when his name was the farthest thing from my mind, it popped out." She shook her head sleepily. "Does that ever happen to you? I mean, you're searching for something and you're not even sure exactly what it is...and then, right out of the blue, it just comes to you? Know what I mean?"

"I sure do, Jayne."

He said it as if he'd been searching for *her.*

She glanced up, into those gorgeous silver eyes. They were rimmed with eyelashes that were as black as his hair, and in the dim light the pupils made her think of shimmering silver seas on steamy tropical nights. The look in those eyes seemed fathoms deep. As her heart pounded against her ribs, stealing her breath, Jayne begged herself to hang on to reason. They were worlds apart. She was marrying Parker in less than a week. And it was naive, crazy even, to think that a baby could bring them together.

Except it didn't seem so crazy when Remy's lips brushed hers, then settled on her mouth with a silken, persistent pressure. No, it didn't seem crazy at all.

"Night," he said huskily.

"Sleep tight," she whispered, her insides shaking.

He chuckled as he stood. "Don't let Remy bite."

With a final grin, he shoved his hands deep into the front pockets of his jeans. As he turned on the heels of his dusty alligator boots, then strode toward his bedroom, it took every last one of Jayne's prim, proper Wright-family genes not to follow him.

Chapter Eight

"Those books are here somewhere." As the man inhaled a quick, invigorating sniff of the sharp winter air, he stepped onto the porch, threaded his fingers through his silver hair and scanned the terrain. The upper windows of the white-brick town houses were dark. Early-spring buds peeped over the tops of window boxes, and freshly painted white bricks had been planted in a circle around the willow in the yard.

One by one, he tugged on snug black gloves, liking the efficient sound the Lycra made when it snapped against his wrists. He glanced over each of his shoulders—the left then the right—but he saw only the calm early-morning New Orleans street and, directly behind him, the unbroken bright blue surface of Lake Pontchartrain.

So far, so good. From the inner pocket of his gray sport coat, he withdrew a slim case containing his lock picks. Reaching into a mail basket next to the door, he plucked out a red envelope, which he found contained a heart-shaped, doily-edged Valentine signed "Love, Mother and the Judge." Pretending to read the card, he wedged his body between the screen and storm doors, then proceeded to wiggle a pick into the first of three locks.

Jayne's lakefront town house would be open to him in mere moments. Because she had information that could send him to prison, he hardly felt guilty about breaking and entering. If she'd taken the books with her when she fled town, Remy Lafitte would have delivered them to the police already. But Remy hadn't, which meant the books were probably inside.

The man just wished Smoothtalk, Speedo and Smiley could have done this job. But his hired thugs were chasing the real prize—Jayne. They'd found her, too, in Lafourche Parish. By now the motley crew, whom he'd privately nicknamed the Three Stooges, were probably bringing Jayne back to New Orleans.

Unless Remy'd stopped them. The bounty hunter could be one tough customer. Nevertheless, it would be three against one. He sighed, hoping the Stooges remembered Jayne wasn't to be harmed—at least not yet. According to Smoothtalk, Speedo had become overzealous last night in the French Quarter and fired a shot.

Well, the books had to be found—and at all costs. Once they were in his possession, Jayne would be inconsequential. Without the evidence, it would be a simple matter of her word against his. Of course, if the authorities *did* get the books, it would take time to decode them. There was also the distinct possibility that his partner in crime would break down, confess and try to plea-bargain.

When the cylinders turned over, he smiled. "A Medeco," he said of the next lock, his gloved hands sliding downward. Medecos were the toughest locks to beat, terribly sturdy. On the road, a blue Porsche whizzed past without the driver giving him so much as a second glance.

Suddenly he frowned. What if Jayne and Remy passed the Three Stooges on the road? There was a chance Jayne could return home while he was searching her town house. If Remy was with her, things could turn nasty.

He cursed under his breath. Jayne was smart. She should have known better than to team up with Remy. After all, that was what made it obvious she knew something. Oh, the night before last, when she ran away from Parker's party, he'd suspected she had the books. Especially since the safe in the study had been left open.

But now there was no doubt. Jayne had discovered the books and told Remy everything. Why else would the two have fled the Cha-cha Club together—and in such a hurry? Jayne and Remy weren't even friends. According to Speedo, two burly tequila drinkers with loose tongues swore Remy had hopped into his red convertible with Jayne and squealed away from the curb. Clearly, Remy was hell-bent on protecting the woman. It was just a shame he wasn't the type who could be bought off.

Jayne's second dead bolt clicked. "Good," he whispered, his gloved fingers skittering down to the third lock, which looked flimsy.

Yes, Jayne had made a royal mess of things. If she'd left town due to a case of prenuptial jitters, as Parker had suggested, then Remy would never have taken her to the bayous. No, Jayne had obviously hired Remy to protect her—and to escort her and the incriminating books safely to the police.

He blew out a short, pursed-lipped sigh. His own situation had very definitely intensified. He just hoped Jayne had hidden the evidence in her town house.

The final lock clicked, and he silently pushed open Jayne's door. Momentarily forgetting he'd come to ransack the place, he thoughtfully swiped the soles of his expensive Italian loafers across her welcome mat. Then he replaced the lock picks in his sport coat pocket and stepped across the threshold. He called out, "Anybody home?"

Tilting his head, he listened. Nothing. With a self-satisfied sigh, he closed the door and wondered where he should begin. He bypassed the living room and headed down a long hallway, methodically flinging open the doors on either side. As he passed the kitchen, his stomach rumbled. Maybe he'd fix himself a snack. Surely his hostess would have *beignets* and coffee. In Jayne's bedroom, he saw that her wedding gown was laid out on the bed. At the far end of the hallway, he came to a dead halt.

"Inviting," he whispered as he stepped inside the small yellow room. Bags from various toy stores were spread across a Persian rug that covered the hardwood floor. In one corner was an assembled crib; in another, a rocking chair with a seatful of navy-and-white plastic bags from the Baby Gap store. As he walked through the room, his body stirred the air, making a ceiling mobile spin; small cats and mice made of stuffed gingham chased each other around in circles.

"A nursery," he whispered in surprise. But who on earth had gotten Jayne pregnant? Somehow he doubted it was Parker. Shaking his head as if to clear it of confusion, he reminded himself that Remy Lafitte was his problem—not whoever had made a baby with Jayne.

Again he looked around the nursery, and smiled. This would be the least likely place one might look for incriminating evidence. With a start, he headed toward the crib.

He had to find his missing books.

Then he had to make sure Jayne and Remy couldn't testify against him.

With that in mind, one of his black-gloved hands reached right inside the crib, forcefully grasped the mattress and flung it across the room.

"JAYNE?"

To whom did that intrusive voice belong? Jayne wondered hazily. Did Lisa Leigh need attention? Maybe a bottle, or a diaper change? Jayne nestled into Remy's sofa, imagining him cuddling the newborn.

Then everything turned pink and white. Jayne was lounging on a bed stacked with pillows, wearing a pearl-colored satin gown. A bare-chested Remy was reclining on his elbow next to her, with the sheet covering him to his waist. They were both gazing at the fuzzy bundle of pink blanket in her arms.

"Lisa Leigh?" Jayne thought she whispered.

Remy merely shook his head and smoothed his palm over the blanket. Against the pink fuzz, his hand looked huge and dark, and in response to his calming touch, the fuzz stopped wiggling. Remy tugged the blanket's satin edge so that Jayne could better see the baby.

But the bundle of joy wasn't Lisa Leigh. The face was too square, and a black tuft of hair grew from the top of the baby's head. It was their baby—hers and Remy's—dressed in the sweet white lace christening gown that all the Wright girls had worn. It was the morning of the christening, they had to hurry and wake up and—

"Darn it, darlin'."

At Remy's exasperated whisper, Jayne felt the cool sidepieces of her glasses slide over her cheeks until the curled ends hooked around her ears.

"Jayne, can't you hear me?"

Not again, Jayne thought foggily. Those strong hands that had looked so masculine against the baby's blanket were actually shaking her shoulders. "Does no one here awaken in a normal fashion?" she croaked.

"How's that?"

"You know, with that marvelous electronic device that citizens of the civilized world call an alarm clock," she murmured, drifting back to sleep.

"If we had more time," Remy throatily returned, "I'd awaken you with an alarming kiss, *chère*."

"More time?" Groggily she decided that if Remy wanted to kiss her, she'd darn well *make* more time. She parted her lips in an alluring manner, her mind drifting...

Until Remy yanked her into his arms. The abrupt movement sent the afghan flying and her glasses sliding downward. Just as her sock-clad feet hit the floor, her eyes flew open—and she realized her specs were teetering right on the tip of her nose.

Heavens, was Remy in focus! He was fully dressed, in well-worn jeans and a faded pink T-shirt, which meant she'd been dreaming about being in bed with him and the baby.

Pushing her glasses into place, she could only stare at him—deliverer of infants, seducer of women, tracker of men. He looked so well rested. It was as if magic elves had come in the night. They'd ironed away the frown lines on Remy's forehead, smoothed the laugh lines beside his lips and straightened the creases at the corners of his eyes. They'd taken soft rags and polished—until the pupils of his eyes gleamed a solid silver. Before sunup, they'd slung their pickaxes over their shoulders, pocketed their rags and headed home—leaving Remy looking fabulous.

The best thing was that the man's lively eyes were all asparkle, and his luscious lips stretched into a devilish smile meant just for Jayne. He drawled, "Don't side-track me."

She grinned, then realized he had a firm grip on her elbow. As he started guiding her down the hallway, she tugged at the hemline of her blue dress, which had served as sleepwear. "It must be nearly noon," she said, wondering where he was headed.

"Somebody's comin' down the bayou, *chère.*"

"Who?"

"When I find out, I'll let you know." As they crossed the threshold of his bedroom, Remy smiled reassuringly, as if to tell her she needn't concern herself with the visitors. "Jayne, you sure sleep like a log."

Jayne's eyes landed on his lusciously mussed, unmade bed. Seeing the imprint of Remy's body on the exposed sheet, she drew in a wavering breath. Maybe the visitors needed herbal cures. Were she and Remy going to pretend not to be home? Was he thinking of something romantic?

When Remy opened the closet door and pointed inside, Jayne surveyed the shirts and sweaters that hung so sloppily on their wire hangers. She started to reach inside and straighten them, but the thought of wearing another of Remy's cardigans stopped her. Her insides melted. A new day stretched before them ... and she wouldn't think of Parker at all. She'd wrap herself in Remy's sweater, Remy's scent.

He grunted softly in exasperation. "Jayne."

She eyed the sweaters. "Green," she returned on a sigh.

When he didn't respond, her eyes darted to his. He was squinting at her.

He said, "Excuse me?"

She tapped the bridge of her nose with her index finger, ensuring that her glasses were in place and that she'd indeed seen and chosen the correct sweater. "Is something wrong with the green one?"

"Jayne, would you please just get in the closet?"

She gulped. "Hmm?"

He gently pushed her inside. Right before she was left in utter darkness, he added, "Do me a favor and don't come out."

The sound of the door clicking shut sure woke her up. The air smelled faintly of cedar and mothballs. Wool sweaters brushed her nose, making it itch. Was Remy tricking her—trying to see how gullible she was, how much she'd let him get away with? Heaven knew, men could be like that.

But no, he'd said people were coming. Pure cold curled in her belly, and a shiver zipped down her spine. Remy was hiding her.

Once again he had placed himself in the role of her protector. This time she'd been fast asleep—defenseless, a target. But what if Remy needed *her* help? After all, she had a responsibility to make sure her baby wasn't fatherless.

Jayne cracked open the closet door. Seeing nothing, she crept into the bedroom. No movement was discernible through the windows. *Good.* She crouched down—heading through the hallway, ducking into the kitchen, seeking a weapon. Her eyes scanned the drawers—but a knife seemed too dangerous, the broom too wimpy. She snatched a cast-iron fryer from the stove. She proceeded onward, weapon raised and ready for combat.

When she reached the front door, Jayne carefully peeked through the porch screens. "Remy?" she called out hesitantly.

The fishing nets had been torn from the trees. They were strewn across the ground, and a number of men—

she couldn't tell exactly how many—were rolling over and over each other, hopelessly tangled.

She quit breathing. Becoming perfectly still, she listened to her heart pounding in her ears. All her senses were heightened, put on red alert. She didn't question what was in her heart—she merely heeded the fierce call of it. No one was going to hurt Remy. If he was going to protect her, she could protect him, too.

Jayne whooped like a crane. Then she flew down the steps of the stilted house in her stocking feet. With one tight fist, she kept her glasses pressed to her nose. With the other, she clutched the skillet, raising it high above her head. Heart pounding, she skidded to a halt. She peered into the nets, into the mess of flailing arms and legs, until she caught rolling snatches of worn denim and faded pink. She skidded to a halt, yelling, "Get 'em, Remy!"

Just as she was about to brain the first intruder, the man rolled onto his back and gasped. "Jayne?"

Buddy Wyatt looked mortified. Everything in his voice said he expected better behavior from her, and she was so surprised that she nearly lost her grip on the skillet. "Buddy?" she said, in shock. "Buddy Wyatt?"

Remy fought his way out of the nets and rose to his feet, saying, "Don't you two guys move."

Remy was better than intact. As gorgeous as ever, he was squinting against the strong sun, the way a cowboy might. Jayne felt vaguely disappointed, since she hadn't rescued him from grave peril. She set down her frying pan and turned her attention back to Buddy. Within seconds, she disentangled the cumbersome man.

With a loud grunt, Buddy pulled himself from his haunches to a standing position, saying, "Thanks a bunch, Jayne."

"Get offa me, Smiley!"

Sure enough, the two men remaining in the nets were the culprits who'd chased her and Remy through the French Quarter. The transparent nylon netting had wound around their faces so many times that the men were virtually cocooned in a thick, milky webbing.

"I've been watching the place for the last hour." Buddy dusted his hands against his jeans. "Knew something was about to happen. Felt my nose wiggle."

Jayne supposed that was bounty hunter talk for having a hunch. She stared into the nets again. In spite of Remy's warning, Smiley and Speedo were squirming to get free. Each movement only served to further ensnare them.

"The guys from the French Quarter," Remy said simply.

For an instant, panic kept Jayne from breathing. The men had obviously followed her and Remy here from New Orleans. No doubt one of them had called out Jayne's name last night, too. They were chasing her. But why? And what did Smoothtalk Sweeny have to do with it? Her eyes trailed over the rail-thin redhead named Speedo. With a start, she realized he was wearing an ankle holster. Fortunately, he couldn't reach the gun.

"Well, they're sure wrapped up." Buddy nodded at the nets, as if not particularly interested in how or why the thugs had shown up here. "Parker sent me." Buddy shot Remy a chastising glance. "The man wants his fiancé back."

Jayne flushed when Buddy's eyes landed on her next.

"Jayne, you at least owe Parker an explanation," Buddy continued. "If you two head back to the city, I'll drop these guys with the Lafourche PD. We can hold them on a concealed-weapons charge."

But what explanation could Jayne give Parker? She didn't know what she thought, what she felt. All she knew was that from the moment she'd seen Remy again, she couldn't bear the thought of her marriage. She *was* getting married, though. There was too much at stake—and she was too good a girl to do otherwise.

"So where's Smoothtalk Sweeny?" Remy was saying.

Jayne focused her attention on the thugs again. Speedo and Smiley continued to bat at the nylon ineffectually. Sprawled and wiggling inside the nets, they looked like insects caught in a giant spider's lair.

"Smoothtalk called in sick this morning," Smiley grumbled.

"Don't tell them anything," Speedo told him threateningly.

So, the voice outside the warehouse had definitely belonged to Sweeny, just as Jayne had thought. But why had the three men been chasing her and Remy?

"Who sent you?" Remy asked.

The men merely stared at Remy through the diamond-shaped gaps in the nets. It was clear from the looks on their faces that they weren't going to talk.

"Hey," Buddy said, "didn't I see you two on Parker's veranda night before last? You were talking to...you know, that tall, silver-haired fellow."

"Boyd Laney?" Jayne croaked.

Buddy shrugged. "I don't know the guy."

"Hal Knowles?" Remy asked.

Jayne wanted to protest, but she was too shocked to speak. What was Remy talking about? "They couldn't work for Hal," she managed to say.

Remy's eyes seemed to dare her. "Why not, *chère?*"

"Because..."

Because Hal Knowles is an ex-Tulane quarterback from old New Orleans money, that's why, she thought. His house had graced the pages of *Southern World* magazine, and he owned no fewer than four sugarcane refineries in the area. He gainfully employed countless people, including many in Lafourche Parish, and he actively campaigned for charities.

Besides, Boyd Laney had been the only other tall, silver-haired man at Parker's party. And Boyd had been accused of crimes in the past.

Remy arched his dark eyebrows. "Because?"

Jayne's most lawyerly, poker-faced expression masked the fact that her insides shook like jelly. "Just because," she said. Because it seemed clear now that someone was out to harm her.

And because Hal Knowles and her fiancé were as thick as thieves.

"WHY WOULD SOMEONE be chasing you? Can you think of *anything,* Jayne?"

Defensive silence.

Remy tossed the *Times-Picayune* between them on the car seat, wishing he'd never mentioned Hal Knowles. Then he pulled out of the gas station, wondering how Jayne had wound up in the car at all. He'd laid down the law. He'd said hell would freeze over before she accompanied him to New Orleans to track down Smoothtalk Sweeny.

But Jayne had pulled an F. Lee Bailey act and talked rings around him. Or, maybe he'd let her. Last night, in his bedroom, he'd kissed her long and hard. He'd held her hand and touched her belly and seen her eyes fill with wonder when she looked at Lisa Leigh. Then he'd bumped shoulders with her on the footpath home and kissed her good-night. He wanted to protect her, all right. And he just plain wanted her with him.

Besides, she'd be safer with him. Not that she couldn't take care of herself, judging by the way she'd brandished that frying pan. He shot her a quick glance. Another of his mother's dresses, this one green cotton, draped over her graceful figure. She'd removed the strand of plastic hearts, probably because she was mad about the Knowles business. Her pearls lay against her throat again—as iridescent as her skin in the afternoon light. Her hands were folded in her lap.

As they passed the sign announcing the Orleans Parish limits, Remy found himself wishing Jayne wasn't so determined to protect Parker. "Please, just tell me whatever you know," he finally said.

"I don't know anything," she returned, her voice sounding strained. "Why are you so mad at me?"

He wasn't. But he stared through the windshield again, thinking he had a right to be furious. Would he always wonder if she'd meant to tell him about the baby? "When Speedo and Smiley turned up," he found himself saying, "I had asked you to stay inside the house."

"Don't you mean inside the closet?" she asked dryly.

Remy was sure she was feigning annoyance so that he wouldn't ask her about Parker's activities. As softly as he could, he said, "I was only trying to protect you, Jayne."

"The same way you were trying to protect me when you demanded that I remain at your mother's for an unspecified duration?"

Remy swore under his breath. If Jayne wasn't the mother of his child, if the stakes weren't so high, he just might lose his temper.

"Sorry, Remy," she continued. "But you have to understand that I've got a career in town, clients and bills to pay."

He turned his eyes from the road and stared at her. "I want to make sure you're safe. Is that so horrible, *chère?*"

When her expression softened, he told himself to scowl. If he wasn't very careful, she'd dog every step of his investigation. And if there was any more trouble, he meant to make sure she was out of the line of fire.

He ought to move her into his place. At least until he got some answers. That way he could also make sure she ate right, saw a doctor and took vitamins. He started to tell Jayne his game plan, then thought better of it. "Jayne, what exactly is the relationship between Parker and Hal Knowles?"

Her sigh sounded resigned. "Parker works as a legal consultant for Hal's refineries." She shot Remy a quick smile. "Business law's really Parker's area, you know."

Jayne sounded more like Parker's press secretary than his fiancée. "I wasn't aware of that."

"Suspecting Hal of hiring thugs to chase me is absolutely ludicrous, Remy."

"Why?"

The way Jayne rolled her eyes didn't jibe with her prim posture, somehow. "Hal Knowles is an extremely well-known member of the New Orleans community, and you know it."

"A man of distinction," Remy drawled.

"Yes." Jayne whirled toward Remy in the seat. "He's upstanding, respectable."

"Rich folks can be just as crooked as poor ones," Remy reminded her softly.

"Of course they can," Jayne shot back, temper coloring her cheeks. "I'm not naive."

He disagreed. Jayne knew things from books, not the school of hard knocks. And right now, if life's tougher blows came pounding on her door, Remy meant to answer for her. At least until something more concrete about the baby's future was decided.

"So," he murmured, "Parker's a consultant to Knowles. Everybody knows Boyd Laney was accused of embezzlement a few years ago, but it never stuck. And Sweeny's an ex-client." At his words, worry lines creased Jayne's forehead, replacing her angry expression. Remy reached across the seat and rubbed them away with a brush of his thumb.

"I guess we have to assume someone hired Speedo, Smiley and Smoothtalk to chase us last night in the French Quarter," Jayne said glumly, stating the obvious.

Remy nodded, wishing he and Buddy had been able to coerce the two men into talking. Well, he'd call Dan Stanley at the NOPD. Maybe Dan would have better luck. "Can you think of anything unusual that's happened—or that's going to happen?"

Jayne shrugged. "My wedding?"

Remy clenched his jaw. *Of course she's still getting married.* Had he really thought that last night's kisses would stop her? Or that his knowing about the baby would change anything? He sighed, telling himself to concentrate on her safety—and that of their unborn child. Later he'd worry about the tangled web of their relationships—her, Parker, him, the baby. Hell, none of it would matter if something happened to Jayne. He gripped the steering wheel tighter. "What about the election?"

Jayne shook her head. "Everything's going wonderfully. The polls show that Parker'll definitely win. At least if..."

"If?"

"If I marry him."

Remy gaped at her. "What?"

She cleared her throat. "The voters won't elect Parker—or any other candidate—unless he has a stable family life. The new member of the House of Representatives will be happily married...."

With a baby on the way? Remy wondered. Was Jayne marrying Parker because she loved him or because of the election? Did she feel she owed Parker something—and, if so, why? Feeling frustrated, Remy reached for the dashboard, then realized he'd left his cigarettes on Bayou Mystique. With the baby coming, he'd just have to ignore the cravings.

He sighed. Things were more complex than he'd imagined. The upcoming election, the one Parker needed Jayne to win, might lead to an important long-term Washington career for the man. "Somehow, I never took you for a political wife." As soon as the words were out, Remy wished he hadn't sounded so confrontational.

"What's that supposed to mean?"

"You're your own woman, Jayne," Remy found himself saying. "Not the woman behind the man."

At the backhanded compliment, a smile flickered over her lips. "Hillary Clinton didn't do badly for herself," she returned.

Remy's mind raced. Something was out of the ordinary. Something in the past few days. "Did you really leave Parker's party because you were afraid to tell me about the baby?" he asked.

Her piqued sigh said she couldn't believe his lack of trust. "There's absolutely no reason to think Hal or Boyd is involved in some shady business. These are the facts...." She ticked them off on her well-manicured fingers. "Buddy Wyatt saw Speedo and Smiley talk to a silver-haired man at Parker's party. I heard Smoothtalk

Sweeny outside the warehouse where Speedo and Smiley were looking for us. You *think* you heard—"

"Definitely heard."

"*Think* you heard one of those men yell my name when we were in the French Quarter last night."

When Jayne put it that way, it didn't sound like much. Of course, she'd failed to mention that Speedo and Smiley had followed her for two days running. And why hadn't Parker answered his phone since last night? *Maybe he's driving around, looking for Jayne.* "I still don't understand why Parker handed me a false subpoena and paid me a king's ransom to find you."

Jayne's shoulders slumped, her perfect posture crumbling. Her hand skated across the seat and settled on the newspaper. "I honestly don't know. Maybe Parker thought I was backing out of the wedding. If he was too embarrassed to admit that, he might have forged the subpoena, so that he'd have an excuse to hire you."

Her fingers started toying with an upper edge of the newspaper. "Why are you so desperate to make yourself Parker's judge and jury, Remy?" she continued. "I mean, a man's innocent in this country until proven guilty."

Remy held his breath, then slowly exhaled. Didn't Jayne know why? His own son or daughter was about to wind up calling Parker Bradford Daddy. Remy would be driving up to that damn mansion in the Garden District to see his own baby. But maybe Jayne was right. Maybe he was looking for connections where there were none. If he could remove Parker from the equation, it would leave only the baby, himself and Jayne.

Not that he loved her. Whatever his feelings, they were impossibly tangled with those about the baby now. Parker had always made his nose wiggle—but did that mean Parker was unethical, or that Remy was jealous?

"Sorry I'm being so hard on Parker," he finally said, thinking he had to keep a clear head, for Jayne's sake and the baby's. He handed her the *Times-Picayune.* "Here," he said gently. "I know you're friends with Boyd Laney and Hal Knowles, but I want to check them out. Maybe the paper will say which Mardi Gras balls they're attending."

Jayne's breath caught. "The Venus ball. It's day after tomorrow—Sunday night—and Parker and I were going, dressed as a masked bride and groom."

Were going. Did that mean she wouldn't be going to the ball with Parker now? In spite of how Jayne defended Parker, was she secretly harboring suspicions? Or had last night's kisses convinced her to take a few days away from her fiancé?

The thought of Jayne and Parker in wedding garments at the *bal masqué* was more than Remy could bear. After a moment, he squinted at Jayne, wishing she didn't sound so devastated about missing the party. She was blushing.

"I didn't go to many dances when I was a teenager, okay?"

So that was it. Gently Remy said, "If you don't go with Parker, I'll take you."

She smiled tentatively. "I guess you'll get me that rose corsage I always wanted, too?"

Remy smiled back. "Time will tell." How dangerous could the Venus ball be, if Jayne was well disguised? He frowned, half listening to Jayne crinkling the newspaper's pages. "It *is* a costume ball, right, Jayne?" When she didn't respond, he said, *"Chère?"*

Glancing from the windshield to Jayne's face, he realized that her glowing skin had turned ashen. He looked at the *Times-Picayune,* and his lips parted in astonishment.

Even from where he was, he could read the Living section's headline:

Surprise Bride!
Parker Bradford's Surprise Bride Is... Guess Who?

"'Last night...'" Jayne admirably masked any shock she felt and began reading the article. "'We spied our favorite political couple, rubbing elbows at yet another *bal masqué*. While the king and queen were crowned, veiled bride Jayne Wright and soon-to-be-hubby Parker Bradford practiced for their upcoming nuptials.'"

In the accompanying photograph Parker was dressed in a wedding tux, with a pleated shirt and wide cummerbund. He waved jauntily at the unseen cameraman, his Lone Ranger-style mask in hand. On his arm was a heavily veiled woman in a bridal gown.

"Is that the gown you were going to wear Sunday night?" Remy forced himself to ask.

"I—I'm not sure. I was supposed to pick up the dress at a costume store." Jayne licked her lips. "I, er...guess someone saw Parker and just assumed this woman was me."

"Or else Parker's got someone else playing proxy bride."

Chapter Nine

Jayne trained her gaze away from the surprise bride's photograph and stared through the windshield at Lake Pontchartrain. Because the sky was reflected in the lake's surface, the world looked topsy-turvy. Seemingly submerged clouds rippled with the breeze, as if wavering deep down in the water. Taking in the miragelike illusion, Jayne assured herself that Remy's barely veiled insinuations about Parker were groundless. Because Remy didn't want Parker in the baby's life, he couldn't help but want to turn her against Parker.

As if to break the tension, Remy chuckled softly. "Hey, Jayne, look."

She found herself smiling. Near the lake, a dogwood tree had been strung with thousands of strands of Mardi Gras beads. For weeks now, as people left parades, they'd been draping the inexpensive plastic necklaces over the boughs. From a distance, the brightly colored beads made it look as if the dogwood were decorated with Christmas lights.

"Mardi Gras," she murmured.

Remy nodded. "Carnival...when nothing's as it seems."

The pointed way his eyes landed on the picture of Parker and the surprise bride made Jayne wish she'd turned to another page. She stared at the rippling reflections on the lake's surface again, wondering if the surprise bride was really a rival for Parker's affections. Could the veiled woman be someone Jayne knew? And what if the sting Jayne felt wasn't jealousy over Parker at all—but merely wounded pride and ego masquerading as that emotion? "Well, it's good to be home," she said with a traveler's sigh, as if the experiences of the past two days didn't bother her.

Remy turned into the driveway and parked in the carport behind her Volvo. For the first time Jayne wondered where they were supposed to go from here. She shot him a sideways glance. "It seems like..." *Like you intend to come inside.*

"Yeah?" Remy turned off the engine.

"Like we've been together awhile," Jayne finished. With Smoothtalk on the loose and Speedo and Smiley only temporarily out of commission, Jayne wasn't exactly thrilled about relinquishing her unofficial bodyguard. Not that that was the only reason she wanted Remy to stay. She imagined going into her living room alone, surreptitiously lifting an edge of a lace curtain and watching the father of her baby drive away.

Remy sure has eyes, she thought as he lifted them from the society column. Set in his tanned, chiseled face, those slants of pure silver fixed on her. When the sun kissed the windshield, his eyes reflected the beams. Gray white light, like melting metal, shimmered just beneath the silver surface of the irises, reminding her of how the lake looked at night, under the stars. How many romantic, moonlit midnights had she spent staring at that lake... alone?

After a moment, he said, "I want you to stay with me, Jayne. At least until we figure out what's going on."

Nothing's going on, she wanted to protest. But men were chasing her. And after seeing the newspaper, she wasn't so sure about Parker's integrity. Not that she'd admit it to Remy. "I really ought to stay here," she said, nervously twisting her engagement ring on her finger. One more night with Remy and there was no doubt in her mind what would happen. Just by kissing him, she'd already risked far too many sure things—her marriage, a family environment for the baby, her law partnership and Parker's political future.

Remy merely nodded in response, got out and circled the car. Funny, Jayne thought, digging in a pocket for her keys. The idea that Parker might have been out with another woman wasn't nearly as unnerving as Remy's awareness of it. *You care far too much what Remy thinks of you, Jayne,* she decided, knowing she'd sooner tell a thousand lies than have him see her exposed, knowing she'd been played for a fool.

But Parker wasn't with another woman, Jayne.

She gulped. Wasn't *she* with another man? Her door swung open, and she mustered a smile as she got out. "Thanks."

Remy slammed her door shut. "I sure am thirsty."

Her tentative smile became more genuine. "I may have a Dixie longneck." Walking toward her front porch, she felt obliged to add, "Parker likes them."

"If it's Parker's," Remy shot back, "I'm having none of it." Then he chuckled, grabbed her waist and drew her right next to him for a quick squeeze. "Unless, of course, it's you."

She tried not to react, to tell herself that she was with Remy because she might be in danger, but a giggle escaped. "I already feel guilty enough, Remy."

"You should, *chère.*" As they climbed the porch steps, he playfully rubbed one index finger across the other as if to say, "Shame."

"If I hear that racket again," a woman shouted, "I'll call the police!"

Jayne whirled around, seeing nothing. When Remy pointed, she followed the line of his finger upward. A twenty-something woman was leaning out of the open upstairs window of the adjacent town house. Her blond tresses were wrapped in pink rollers and her face was flushed with anger.

"Excuse me?" Jayne called in a worried tone.

"I said if you don't keep it down, I'll report you!" The woman's head popped back inside, and the window shut with a resounding thud.

"My new neighbor," Jayne murmured.

"Well, when you have these wild parties, Jayne, you really should invite me," Remy teased. "I look great wearing nothing but a lamp shade. Are you *sure* that subpoena wasn't real?"

Jayne shot Remy a wicked smile. In a drawl meant to mimic his, she said, "I *am* known as something of a troublemaker."

Remy laughed. "Well, given your neighbor's attitude, I sure wouldn't bake her any apple pies."

Turning serious, Jayne shook her head. "This is usually such a quiet street. I wonder what—" Just as she slid between the screen and the door and inserted the key in the top lock, Remy's hands circled her waist. "Remy," she said in censure.

"Jayne."

There was a certain tone they took when they said each other's names. Familiar and habitual, it usually made her smile. But this time Remy's tone was sharp. He slipped in front of her, an arm outstretched as if to shield her from an enemy.

"Get back in the car," he said.

Only her eyes moved. She watched Remy flatten his palm against her door. When he shoved, the keys dangling from the lock jingled. As the door swung inward, Jayne gasped. She groped for Remy and caught fistfuls of the back of his shirt. "I've been robbed!"

Remy glanced over his shoulder, his eyes acknowledging the truth of it. "They either got in with a lock pick or a key."

"Parker's the only one with a key." As soon as the words were out, she wanted to retract them. "Maybe he came over to look for me," she quickly added, "and then forgot to lock the door."

Remy smoothed Jayne's forehead, brushing away a stray tendril of her hair. As if the intruder might still be inside, Remy whispered, "If you won't go to the car, then promise you'll stay on the porch."

Jayne nodded. "Okay."

Remy headed inside, moving slowly and cautiously down the long first-floor hallway. In spite of her promise and the possible danger, Jayne couldn't help but follow.

As she crossed the threshold, her body temperature dropped, her veins running with pure ice. Thin needles of cold pain wiggled at her temples. "Oh, no," she murmured. *No wonder there was noise.* Her living room had been utterly destroyed. Yellow foam gaped from long diagonal slits in the sofa cushions. Books and CDs had been torn from shelves, strewn across the floor.

Feeling as if her heart had just been ripped out, Jayne whispered, "Not my 45s." She took two zombified steps across the carpet—unable to believe that those well-loved records from her girlhood had been reduced to jagged slivers of broken black vinyl on the floor. She'd spent hours dreaming of love, dancing alone to those 45s. Now she could almost hear Bette Midler's cover of "Do You Wanna Dance?" And Paul Anka softly, soulfully singing, "She's Having My Baby."

"Jayne."

Her unseeing eyes lurched toward Remy's voice. After a moment, she realized she was staring at his broad chest and lifted her gaze. "This makes me feel so…dirty," she said weakly. "Violated."

Swiftly Remy crossed the space between them and wrapped her in his embrace. She hugged him back, squeezing her eyes shut, wishing it was all her imagination, or a bad dream, but knowing it wasn't. "Nothing like this has ever happened to me," she said in a strangled whisper.

Remy's lips brushed across the top of her head. "Whoever it was is long gone," he said gently.

She swallowed hard, then looked into his eyes. "How do you know?"

"He fixed himself—"

"It was a man?"

Still holding her, Remy nodded toward a footprint on the carpet. "About a size twelve," he said. "He fixed himself a *beignet*. Since it's rock-hard, I guess the guy's been gone six or seven hours."

Jayne took a shaky breath. Stepping away from Remy, she placed her hand on his forearm for support. "C'mon," she said, "I want to…"

She didn't finish, but slowly walked down the hallway with him at her side. At her bedroom doorway, she stopped and shuddered. Her dresser drawers had been systematically removed and the contents dumped on the floor. Suits had been ripped from their hangers and tossed in a heap. Some remained in the open closet, along with the red gown she'd bought the day after she made love to Remy. Her wedding dress was oddly undisturbed on the bed, and as she stared at it, she could feel Remy's eyes on her face.

"You don't have to look at this." Remy put his arm around her shoulders. "I can phone the police. If you want to wait in the kitchen, I'll start folding some of this."

Jayne turned to face him. "You'd do that?"

He cupped her chin, running his thumb tenderly over her jaw. "Do what?"

She felt on the verge of tears. "Fold my things for me."

"Of course I would."

Jayne bit her lower lip. "Really?"

Remy leaned against the doorjamb, drawing her against him. He murmured, "Where'd you get such a lousy impression of me?"

She swallowed hard. How could she have been so very wrong about him? "I guess I'm not always the best judge of character." Their eyes met and held. He looked as if he had something to say but kept thinking better of it. "What, Remy?"

"You'll have to check, but I don't think the guy took anything. The TV, VCR and CD player are all still in the living room."

When Remy ran his hand over her back, smoothing her dress, she could feel the warmth from his palm through her clothes. Glancing into her bedroom, she said hoarsely,

"You're right. It doesn't look like he even opened my jewelry box."

"And you're sure you don't know what he was looking for?" Remy probed gently.

Jayne shook her head. Then she wrenched herself from his arms with a strangled cry. A surge of adrenaline propelled her down the hallway. She heard Remy's footsteps—six of them—pound right on the heels of hers. Grabbing the frame of the door to the nursery, she swung inside the room.

Even the steadying pressure of Remy's hands on her shoulders couldn't stop the tremor that shook her body. She felt stung. Betrayed. The little crib that she'd so lovingly picked out, so painstakingly put together had been destroyed. The intruder had pawed through the bags of new baby clothing. When she saw that a gingham mouse had been torn from the ceiling mobile, she could no longer hold back her tears. One fell, splashing down her cheek. Whirling toward Remy, she swiped it away.

"He could have my things," she managed to say. "He could destroy whatever he wanted." Her furniture, her pictures, her books, her music. "But the baby..." she continued, her tone suddenly venomous. "How could he do this to the baby's things? What kind of monster would do this?"

Remy pulled her into his arms again. "I promise I'll find him, Jayne."

"I know you will." And he would. No man was going to mess with Remy's baby and get away with it. Right now, in his embrace, Jayne could feel her own vengeful anger emanating from his strong body, making the muscles of his flat, hard abdomen clench.

She sank against him, wanting to give comfort as much as to take it, knowing she shouldn't and feeling unable to stop herself. She just wished everything was different. But even if she changed her mind, even if her marriage was only a sham and she later left Parker, she couldn't call off the wedding now and ruin Parker's career.

She couldn't let Remy fool her, either. Surely he was processing the news about the baby, confusing it with what he wanted from her.

But it was Remy who was here, not Parker. And she needed comfort. When she drew away and gazed up at him, he looked back at her the way he often did, with his head tilted and his eyes watchful, as if he were waiting for her to say some magic word.

Who's been here, and why? his eyes seemed to ask.

"I have no idea," she said simply. When she blinked, two more tears slid from beneath the frames of her glasses and rolled down her cheeks.

"Ah, *chère*—" Remy pressed her face against the soft cotton of his shirt. "Just let go."

A second later, racking sobs shook Jayne's shoulders. She cried so long she forgot why she was crying. Someone had violated her home, but the feeling of betrayal ran deeper. Women like Jayne weren't supposed to suffer intruders. But they weren't supposed to marry men they didn't love, either.

"I could just...just tear that man apart," she finally said.

"Good girl," Remy whispered softly.

She managed a sniff and leaned back in his arms. "Anger makes me feel less helpless, anyway."

"I'll call Dan Stanley again." Remy swept his lips lightly over her forehead. "Then I'll help you pack an overnight bag. Even if you don't want to stay with me, I can't let you stay here."

A smile tugged at the corners of Jayne's mouth. Where Parker was deferential, Remy was an Old Guard man's man. "I need to try to call Parker again," she forced herself to say.

At the name, Remy's concerned features reassembled themselves into a perfect mask. His lips lapsed into complete repose—neither a frown, nor a smile—and his eyes turned unreadable. His face was so expressionless that he might have been sleeping dreamlessly.

Jayne cleared her throat guiltily. She could remember the sincerity of Parker's proposal as surely as she recalled the newspaper photo in the car. "Parker loves me," she said. When he proposed, he'd knelt and tears had come into his eyes. "I know him...I've known him for years."

There was a long silence.

They should have been cleaning the house, calling the police and Parker, packing her bags. But they hadn't moved. The whole length of Remy's hard body was pressed against hers. After long moments, her eyes narrowed. "Remy, I'm sure Parker has nothing to do with this."

Remy's lips parted as if he might protest. Then, very softly, he whispered, "Well, I guess Parker's not here to defend himself."

He kissed her on the lips then, his mouth firm and soft, hard and gentle. For the first time since entering the house, Jayne felt truly safe. Each familiar brush of Remy's lips swept away her fear, and each silken sweep of his tongue said Parker Bradford had never mattered.

Slow heat curled between them—rising upward, warming and melting her. As Jayne kissed him back, her eyes opened to slits, drinking in his handsome face. Parker and her wedding—like the disarray all around her—were nothing more than a soft haze just beyond the reach of her vision. "Remy..."

His palms molded over her hips, feeling hot. "Hmm?"

"Remy..." This time Jayne spoke his name on a sigh. She moved her head from side to side, telling herself her lips were trying to evade his kisses, knowing that with each turn of her head, his mouth only found hers again.

"Let me take care of you tonight," he whispered raggedly.

"I—" Her breath caught—audibly, sharply. "I can stay here. I really can." *I must.*

"I'll pack you a bag," Remy said simply.

Any further protest died on her lips. Because he was already gone.

STILL FEELING GROGGY from her nap, Jayne tilted her head and listened. *No, Remy's not back yet.* He'd given her prenatal vitamins, made some herbal tea to stave off her impending headache, then left her to nap while he returned to her town house to meet Dan Stanley. Now she lifted the receiver of the bedside telephone and punched in the direct number for Parker's office. *Just because he wears a size-twelve shoe, that doesn't mean anything, Jayne.*

"C'mon, Parker." Jayne listened to the ringing phone, wishing Remy hadn't so pointedly told her Parker would never find her here. She also wished Remy's hideaway in the French Quarter didn't point up the complementary differences in their personalities. Where she preferred wide-open spaces, Remy favored nooks and crannies. Her town house was like a peaceful desert landscape, but Remy lived in the middle of a multicolored collage.

She liked his sitting room best. It was an odd room— octagonal and painted clay red. Black shelves, messily jammed with books and CDs, lined the walls. Two ceiling fans whirled overhead, circulating cool air from the partially open floor-to-ceiling windows. A Maxwell House coffee can full of harmonicas, tin whistles and kazoos was perched on top of the glossy baby grand piano that dominated the room's center.

"Hey, Scamper." Jayne chuckled, glancing down at the scrappy kitty who lived in the courtyard and who Remy fed when he was home. With his orange and black splotches, the skittish Scamper looked as if he were costumed for Halloween. Suddenly, he arched his back, his hairs bristling as if he were terrified; then he pranced through another door, into Remy's bathroom.

"Why isn't Parker answering?" Jayne sighed and replaced the receiver.

Her eyes darted toward the bedroom door. Had she heard something? No, she was just edgy because of the break-in. She blew out a shaky breath, hoping her intruder had used lock picks. After all, Parker kept an extra set of keys in case Jayne was ever locked out.

Glancing down at the long cream-and-black kimono-style robe she was wearing, she wondered what had possessed her to let Remy pack her bag. Grabbing a presumptuously large suitcase, he'd filled it with every unworn birthday gift she'd ever received from her matchmaking sisters. That meant a virtual Victoria's Secret catalog of silk teddies and lacy peignoirs.

Maybe she should have been angry. But instead, she was taking a certain pleasure in being seated on Remy's rumpled bedcovers in the sexy robe. Everywhere—on the sheets, on the pillowcases—she recognized the masculine scent of his skin. Remy could have led her here blindfolded, and she still would have known she was in his bed.

She stared through the closed French doors toward a balcony that was crowded with wrought-iron chairs, hanging spider plants and philodendrons. Then she picked up the phone again and called Parker's house. Unexpectedly, someone picked up on the second ring. Jayne gasped. "Parker?"

There was a long pause. Then the receiver at Parker's end thudded on a hard surface. Was it the kitchen countertop, or the bedside table in Parker's room?

"I think it's Jayne," a muffled female voice said.

Jayne was so shocked that the phone receiver slipped. Quickly catching it, she sandwiched it between her ear and shoulder. She crossed her arms over her kimono, feeling livid.

"Jayne?" Parker said breathlessly. "Is that you? Where have you been?"

Jayne's jaw set defensively. The sheer relief in Parker's tone seemed somehow...overblown. "You're not my keeper. Maybe the better question is, who's with you? Or are you entertaining your surprise bride?"

"Excuse me? Jayne, I've been worried sick."

Jayne shut her eyes, straining to hear the woman in Parker's house. "So, you haven't seen a paper?"

"No! I've been driving all over town searching for you."

Maybe so. But he was lying about not having seen the paper. Parker, ever the diligent up-and-coming politician read newspapers and magazines with a near-religious fervor—regardless of what was happening in his personal life. "Do you know anything about why I was shot at last night in the Quarter?"

"Why did you leave town?" Parker returned.

At the tone, Jayne's heart started thudding. Parker Bradford could have written the rule book for good manners, and his were slipping. Something was wrong. Dead wrong. She twined her fingers around the phone cord. "Why are you growling at me?" *And not answering my questions.* He'd evaded them all, so far. About the woman and the gunshot. "Did you ransack my house today?" she demanded.

He gasped. "What?"

"Who's the woman, Parker?"

"It's Celeste," he said. "Because you're not here, she's helping me put together our quarterly reports."

Plausible, Jayne thought. The quarterly reports that detailed the law firm's banking transactions were due to be compiled. She and Celeste usually took care of them. "Could you please put her on the phone?"

"She just left!" Parker answered, his voice booming.

Right. Something was fishy here. Jayne hadn't heard any goodbyes. No doors shutting. As Jayne's assistant, Celeste would have been more polite on the phone. "You will not take that tone with me, Parker," Jayne said flatly.

"Jayne—" Parker sounded furious. "You're going to marry me. You have exactly twenty-four hours to come here, or I'm calling in every favor I've got to find you. A certain someone is very angry about your disappearance." Parker's tone lowered. "And both he and I want those books."

"A certain someone? What books?"

There was a long silence.

"You know what books," Parker said. And then he slammed down the phone.

Jayne felt utterly stunned. Before today, Parker had been the most attentive man she'd ever known. Not passionate, but always ready with a kind word. But he hadn't even probed her about the break-in. The mention of a gunshot hadn't fazed him. The woman's voice in the background had been muffled, but Jayne felt sure it wasn't Celeste.

"The books?" she whispered. What were they? And had the intruder at her town house been searching for them?

When a loud crash suddenly sounded in the next room, Jayne was positive Speedo, Smiley and Smoothtalk were headed straight toward her.

Even though she knew he was gone, she shrieked "Remy!" And then she bolted for the door.

"SCAMPER," Remy muttered, opening his eyes just as the kitty streaked beneath the piano. Glancing around, Remy realized he was lying on his back, still wearing his glasses, with the crib's assembly directions on his chest and his toolbox beside him. He'd returned home while Jayne was napping, and he must have fallen asleep. He glanced toward the doorway—only to find himself staring at the vision of Jayne in her kimono.

"Scamper!" she exclaimed, pressing a hand to her heart.

Remy nodded. Scamper had knocked the Maxwell House can from the piano and the blues harps, tin whistles and kazoos were strewn across the floor. The cat now darted from beneath the piano and attacked Remy's shoulder.

"I didn't know you were home yet," Jayne said shakily. "He scared me to death."

Remy bit back a smile, remembering how she'd flown from his house earlier in the day, wielding a frying pan. "Thanks for coming to my rescue again."

"Anytime."

He wished. *Anytime as in Tuesday, when you're marrying Parker?* Feeling distracted, Remy scratched behind

Scamper's ears. At the gesture of affection, the skittish kitty sprang into the air, then scuttled sideways from the room, looking one way, then another, as if danger lurked at every turn. Maybe it did, Remy thought, glancing at Jayne.

She was gazing down at him—so intently that she hadn't yet noticed what he'd been doing. The long cream-and-black kimono suited her coloring. The hem swept her bare feet, the toenails of which were painted bright pink.

"You wear glasses," she said.

He slipped off the round silver wire-rims. "Only to read." He sure didn't need them to see how sexy Jayne was in the kimono. Just looking at her made his mouth go dry. He'd imagined her in every scrap of silk and lace he'd packed. In the red dress, too. He'd found it in her closet with the price tag still affixed to it, hanging between two gray suits. Unfortunately, it was probably too dangerously revealing for her to wear to the Venus ball.

Things are dangerous, all right. Falling in love had a way of making them dangerous. He should know. He'd fallen in love countless times—it had just never stuck. Was what he'd started to feel for Jayne the real thing?

Jayne smiled sleepily. "No wonder you're always telling me to put on my glasses."

Was he? "Headache gone?"

She nodded. "Never got worse than a pang."

"Take your vitamins?"

She started to speak, and then she breathlessly called his name.

She'd noticed. Without moving from where he was lying on his back in the floor, he arched an eyebrow. *"Chère?"*

Her gaze swept his sitting room. He'd brought in and refolded the baby's clothes and assembled a new mobile.

On the way back to the French Quarter, he'd stopped and bought a new crib that was identical to the broken one they'd left at Jayne's.

"I couldn't stand the thought of leaving the baby's things there," he finally said. The words didn't quite communicate the strength of what he felt. He'd thought he could kill whoever had ransacked the baby's things. Clearly Jayne had spent weeks putting together the adorable room.

But why had the nursery been at her town house? That reinforced Remy's gut-level suspicion that Parker wasn't all that involved with the baby...and maybe not even with Jayne. If he was, wouldn't Jayne have decorated a room in the Garden District mansion?

Who cares? Remy thought. Maybe all that mattered was how Jayne was staring at him now—as if he were the greatest guy in the world. His heart swelling, Remy realized he'd forgiven her earlier deception. Surely she'd been telling him the truth. She would have told him about the baby if he'd given her more of a chance.

Now they were getting to know each other, trusting each other, talking. In every exchange it was implied that they'd work things out—with or without Parker. It was crazy, but Remy kept wishing Parker would answer his phone and just break it off with Jayne.

She walked toward him, her silk kimono breezing open, exposing a sliver of her creamy leg. "You're so sweet."

Remy grinned and stretched an arm over the floor, grabbing one of the harmonicas. In his most gravelly voice, he sang, "Ain't nothin' plain about my little Jayne."

Color touched Jayne's cheeks as he punctuated the lyrics with a few bluesy bars.

"Nothing plain about Jayne except she's plain drivin' me insane," Remy sang.

She grinned, and her shoulders started to shake with merriment. After the terrifying events of the day, it was good to hear her laugh, and even better to be the one making her laugh.

"Must be that kimono Jayne's wearing." Remy guffawed and lost a note. "Because it sure is awful daring."

The song was so silly that Jayne, usually so prim, actually hooted. She seated herself next to Remy on the floor. Lifting another harmonica, she played a bar. "Remy better not give me any flak," she belted out. "Because Remy ain't doing nothing but lying on his back."

She continued with lyrics that brought tears of laughter to his eyes. He rolled up onto his elbow to get a better look at her. She was goofing around now, but she sure could sing. Not to mention play a blues harp.

"Learn that in your church choir?" he asked with a chuckle when she put down the harp.

"No," she said playfully. "During all those wild parties I've been having over at my place."

Lord, he wanted her, he thought. And yet there was something more now. It wasn't just the baby, or that they shared a love of music. It was how Jayne persevered that moved him. Her town house had been ruined today, the nursery destroyed, but she was forging ahead, joking and singing.

"Well, Jayne," he said, "I hate to tell you this but the directions for assembling this crib put me right to sleep."

Jayne plucked the booklet from his chest. "Here, I put the other one together by myself. The directions were fine—it was the screwdriving that gave me palpitations."

So Parker hadn't helped her with the crib. Remy fished in his toolbox and came up brandishing a screwdriver. She began to glance between the booklet and the new, unassembled crib. For a few peaceful moments, she silently pointed while he did the manual piecing together. "There's a beautiful antique cradle in Mom's attic," he found himself saying. "I bet I could refinish it." He knew darn well he could—but surely Jayne would reject the offer.

Instead, she murmured, "You could?"

His chest constricted. When their eyes met, hers promised they'd work out a reasonable arrangement. He wanted to confront her now, to demand to know concrete details. Because, by the second, Remy felt the stakes getting higher.

But it was nicer this way. Playing blues harps, assembling a crib, enjoying this moment together. It was how life was meant to be.

"What did Dan Stanley have to say?" she asked at one point.

"Not much. The man who broke into your place was definitely looking for something." Remy drove a screw into the wood of the crib, then tested one of the bars for sturdiness. "If we get ahold of Parker or Boyd, maybe one of them can shed some light on all this. Speedo and Smiley still won't talk, and Dan can't find Smoothtalk Sweeny. But Dan said whatever's missing could be connected to the law firm."

"Connected to the firm?" Jayne echoed.

Remy shrugged. "Who knows? Maybe some crazy ex-client wants to find his case files."

After a long moment Jayne said, "Do you have one of these little gizmos?"

Something in her tone made Remy glance up. She was pointing at a picture of a bracket in the direction booklet, but her face was turning crimson. He'd seen that look before...when she hadn't told him about their baby.

Damn, he wanted to trust her so much, but could he? Well, maybe she wasn't withholding information from him again. Maybe she felt guilty because she wanted to be here, instead of with Parker. Or was that just wishful thinking?

Remy's eyes roved over her hair. It was still in a bun—but this one was sleep-tousled, disheveled, and sexy as hell. A far cry from her old drum-tight French twists. He caught a stray tendril and twined it loosely around his finger. "Can't you postpone your wedding?" he found himself saying.

"Why?" she nearly whispered.

He shrugged. "Just to see what happens." *Between you and me. To see if we can't start up something—like a family.*

"It's a lot to ask."

A lot to ask without promises. He could hear the words as surely as if she'd spoken them aloud. He supposed it was. "But we deserve the chance to get to know each other better."

"It could cost a more solid home life for...for our child. It could cost my business and Parker's political future."

"But you should take the chance," Remy said huskily.

Jayne set down the booklet and gazed into his eyes. "How can you be so sure?"

He leaned toward her, the kiss he gave her nothing more than the firm, steady pressure of his lips against hers. When he drew away, he whispered, "Because a sure thing isn't always the right thing, Jayne."

Chapter Ten

"You can't hurt her." Parker Bradford was collapsing under the strain—his posture stiff, his voice cracking.

"Can't I?" Readjusting his round wire-rimmed glasses and snow-white beard, the man peered around the ballroom of the Windsor Court Hotel where the krewe of Venus's fortieth masked ball was under way. Which of the lovely costumed ladies, if any, was Jayne Wright?

"If Jayne has the books, she'll return them. For God's sake," Parker pleaded, "leave her alone. She's pregnant. Don't you possess a shred of decency?"

"Not really," the man admitted on a sigh. He'd dressed as Santa Claus even though the theme of the ball was Legendary Lovers, mostly because he'd found a suit at Bradford and Wright that was left over from the Christmas party. "You had your chance to find her, Parker," he said softly.

"Hurt her and I'll talk."

As Parker turned on his heel and strode through the crowd, the man murmured, "No, you won't."

Parker was too ambitious. By confessing, he'd be sacrificing his career to protect Jayne. Besides, the books were still missing—which meant Parker had no evidence.

Shaking his head in disgust, he wished the ledgers had been inside Jayne's town house. Speedo and Smiley were still incarcerated in Lafourche Parish. Smoothtalk was a permanent fixture in the French Quarter—just like the mounties and ironwork balconies—but now the man had simply vanished.

The stress was getting to be a bit much. Soon he'd look as pale as Parker. He kept awaiting the knock on his villa door that would announce that his reputation was ruined, his future finished. Surely he'd be arrested.

But why hadn't Jayne and Remy gone to the police? According to one source, Remy had been spotted in New Orleans this weekend—and the bounty hunter had spent time sniffing around Jayne's town house. What were he and Jayne waiting for? And where were they hiding? Maybe they weren't honest, after all. Had they guessed how desperate he was—and how much he'd pay for those books? Maybe they realized how far he'd go to retrieve them....

He squinted into the crowd, his lips parting in recognition. Where had he seen that shirtless Cupid with the gold-painted body? As the Cupid disappeared into the crowd—squeezing between Cleopatra and Marc Antony—Martha and George Washington appeared at the ballroom's entrance. Were they Jayne and Remy in disguise?

No, the woman was too tall. He suddenly peered at a milkmaid. She was clad in a peasant blouse and a checkered jumper, and was carrying a copper pail. A Jill looking for her Jack.

Was *she* Jayne Wright?

"WHO ARE YOU?" Remy whispered playfully, staring at his closed bedroom door and awaiting the metamorphosis. Scents of fragrant soap seeped from beneath the door, and he found himself imagining Jayne—wet, naked, and stepping from her hour-long bath.

He had no idea which of the rented costumes she'd choose, if any. Would she become the Egyptian princess... the belly dancer... the clown? *Or Parker Bradford's wife?* Remy pushed aside the thoughts about Parker. Maybe Jayne would wear that sexy red gown with a mask.

Remy glanced down. Not even his own mother would have spotted him in a crowd. Ruffled lace cuffs fell from beneath the sleeves of his double-breasted gold brocade jacket. Tight white breeches encased his legs to the knees, where they met his black lace-up boots.

Glancing into a mirror in the hallway, he straightened the black velvet ribbon that held the ponytail of his white wig. Next to his mouth, on his powdered skin, he'd drawn a dark mole that wiggled when he grinned. He didn't look half-bad for a seventeenth-century dandy, he decided. He pinched the tip of his long, pointy Cyrano de Bergerac nose—it was strung on either side with elastic—and moved it so that it hung around his neck. *"Chère?"* he yelled.

"Five more minutes!" Jayne called in a teasing singsong.

Remy smiled, loving the excitement of her tone. To hear her voice catch just one more time with that breathless anticipation, he knew he'd willingly wait all night. He loved knowing she was in some state of dishabille, too. Inside his bedroom and dressing just for him. He shifted a corsage box from one hand to the other, then headed down the hallway—only to have Scamper lunge at him from the kitchen.

Remy chuckled and drawled, "Don't hurt me."

At that, the wiry, alarmed-looking Scamper pounced again, batting Remy's toes. Then the kitty guiltily streaked down the hallway. At the bedroom door, Scamper whirled around and hunkered on his haunches, as if he were a guard kitty hired to protect Jayne from Remy.

"You like her, eh?" Remy murmured. *So do I.* He winked at Scamper, then continued down the hallway. He more than liked Jayne. He wanted her so much that the past two nights had been pure torture. He'd slept on the sofa, but he'd imagined her naked in his bed, warm between the sheets, aroused beneath his touch.

Not that he'd tried to make love to her. He'd stolen his share of kisses, though. And he could feel Jayne's desire—all bristling static beneath her clothes, all honeyed softness on the surface of her skin. But she kept holding back.

Maybe she stopped herself because of Parker. Or because loving Remy would mean something different now. Either way, it left him edgy, left him aching to be inside her. The moment when he'd make love to her again was always just out of reach. Everything in her eyes said: What about Parker? What about the baby? What about us?

The possibility of an "us" was making things downright unbearable. As if by unspoken agreement, they'd barely referred to the incidents that had brought them together. They'd spent yesterday relaxing and watching TV. Today they'd dressed in nominal disguises—a hat for him, loose hair for her—and rented costumes for tonight, then gone shopping for themselves and the baby. Remy supposed Jayne was giving him the chance he'd asked for.

He didn't want to blow it. But, Lord, did he ache to touch her! This morning had been gloriously sunny, the temperature soaring to a heavenly sixty degrees. When they breakfasted on the balcony, she'd been wearing that cream-and-black kimono—the one that made him feel less like a new daddy and more like a man.

During the meal, through the open French doors, Remy had had a view of the unmade bed in which she'd slept. His bed. At one point, he'd accidentally dropped his napkin. Bending beneath the covered patio table to retrieve it, he'd found himself staring at Jayne's bare feet. She'd been leaning her weight on her pink-painted toes, and one ankle was twined around a chair leg.

It had happened in a flash. His eyes had traveled upward from her feet. Realizing her bare legs were slightly parted at the knees, he'd felt a tug of arousal so strong that it took every last fiber of his moral being not to slide his hand between her legs.

When had he become such a gentleman? he wondered now. The robe had been so inviting. Held together by nothing more than a slippery sash, it would have opened so easily. When she felt his eyes and gently, surreptitiously pressed her parted knees together, he'd been sure he'd never been so turned on in his life.

He'd snatched his napkin and sat up straight, fully aware of how nervously she licked her pink-glossed lips, how hard she swallowed. She'd stared into her empty plate as if the crumbs there were as complex as rocket science.

In the sitting room, Remy set the corsage box on the piano, next to the Maxwell House can. Seating himself, he played a rapid set of scales, wishing his fingers were touching Jayne's ivory skin instead of the ivory keys. He began improvising a jazzy melody to occupy his mind.

But it kept returning to Jayne, maybe because music was really about relationships. Each piece was about how individual notes played with others. With scales, they followed in sequences. With chords, they melted together, becoming one. Notes, like people, could befriend—only to turn tail and run. Jayne's improvised song slowly took on a life of its own, leaving him to wonder where it was leading. What kind of love song was he playing with Jayne Wright?

He shut his eyes, concentrating and playing harder, until his shoulders rolled with the music. Time passed—he wasn't sure how much—and then he glanced upward, sensing something. On the keys, his fingers stilled.

"Don't stop," Jayne whispered huskily.

She was reclining on top of his piano, leaning on an elbow, her chin supported by a red-gloved hand. Just looking at those delicately shaped fingers, he had to fight not to peel off a glove and remove the engagement ring beneath.

How had she gotten onto the piano without him noticing? The woman seemed to short-circuit his brain waves, canceling out his tracking abilities. Still, he was sure he'd have no difficulty finding her and defending her if she were in danger.

But she *was* in danger. And not just from Speedo and Smiley. From him. After all, his senses weren't out of commission. His eyes never leaving hers, his fingers started trailing over the keys again. He thought of the many missing people he'd tracked down over the years. How he'd run through muddy swamps and modern skyscrapers. All that time, maybe he'd just been chasing Jayne.

Instead of a rental costume, she'd worn the red sheath. The gown was too classy to be truly vampy, but the long side slit left her leg exposed from ankle to thigh. Swaths of transparent fabric crisscrossed her shoulders, creating a red heart-shaped neckline that seemed redder still against her pale skin. The gloves extended from her fingertips to her upper arms. Remy had never seen them, or the red shoes she was wearing, and he found himself hoping she'd packed them in secret, planning to dress this way for him tonight.

He continued playing, letting the slow notes rise in ever-higher strains. He rode the natural wave of the song's building crescendo, stretching for the climax. Without apology, his eyes lingered on a strappy high-heeled sandal. Most of her slender foot was exposed—the squarish toes, now painted red, the stocking-clad arch. A delicate latch, nothing more than a strand of rhinestones, draped lazily over her ankle.

Remy's eyes traversed the length of Jayne's leg, moving as slowly as the notes he played—until they rested on her milky thigh. Then the voluptuous curve of her belly. Then her breasts. He took in her shoulders through the transparent veils of red. And every time his eyes touched a new space of bare skin, his fingers quickened on the keys.

She'd forgone her pearls. Only the strand of red Mardi Gras hearts circled her slender neck. Rhinestone drop earrings dangled from her earlobes, and her loosely coiled hair was piled high. Her perfume was bold and musky. Jayne Wright wasn't hiding tonight.

And yet she was.

Red and white feathers fanned from the sequined sides of the red mask that covered her eyes and nose. Apparently she'd worn her contacts.

"Who are you, mysterious lady?" he asked huskily. "Besides the mother of your child?"

One of those red feathers could have pushed him right off the piano bench. *Yes. And who are you to me?*

Jayne's red-glossed lips stretched into a sexy smile, as if she were reading his mind. "Roxanne to your Cyrano?" she suggested.

Cyrano. He imagined himself hiding in the darkness beneath Roxanne's bedroom window, singing her love songs. "Roxanne was in love with another man, at any rate," Remy said dryly.

"Let's not fight."

Was it Remy's imagination, or had her voice become deeper? It sounded so lilting and musical. As sensually haunting as whatever he was playing. His fingers glided faster over the keys, and the music rose in tempo. "*Chère,* you know what you're doing to me, don't you?"

"*Chère?*" She smiled like the Cheshire cat. "Are you sure you even know who I am?"

He raised his eyebrows. Carnival was a time for fantasies—for playing dress-up and pretending. But he'd have known her anywhere. "Jayne," he said simply.

She chuckled softly. "How do you know?"

"By my internal radar, that would pick you out of any crowd," Remy said. He leaned into the keyboard, pressing one of the foot pedals. "I think you excite me more than any other woman I've ever known."

"Think?"

Remy's mouth went dry. "I know you do, Jayne."

From somewhere within that mask, past the dark eyeholes, he sensed, rather than saw, her looking at him. It was hard to tell what she was thinking. Her lips were parted, and she looked a little breathless.

He wasn't sorry he'd told her how he felt. Not that it would stop her from marrying Parker. But by the minute Remy was feeling less inclined to let her go easily. How could he, when she was sleeping in his bed, lounging on top of his piano, wearing scraps of gowns calculated to entice him? The notes came faster, with more intensity. Then Remy's fingers stilled.

"Oh, Remy," she said in a near whisper, "please don't stop."

"I don't intend to." His dark eyes pierced her mask as he moved his fingers from the keyboard to her ankles. As he rose from the bench, his hands glided over the silk of her stockings. They slid right beneath the slit of her dress, tucking themselves into the folds of her skin. Just as she gasped, his lips claimed hers.

This time Remy gave no quarter. He didn't want to hear her protests—much less heed them. As his tongue plunged between her lips, she slid downward into his embrace. Her delectable behind landed on the keys, and the song, so hauntingly romantic before, ended abruptly in a succession of discordant crashes.

Listening to the sheer cacophony of those nonsensical notes, Remy gently parted her quivering knees and wedged his torso between them. When she moaned against his lips, the spark of his arousal ignited fully. Tongues of fire heated his blood and ate his oxygen, leaving him breathless.

"Remy..."

"You're the mother of my child, Jayne," he murmured against her lips. "Let me make love to you."

"I just can't, Remy."

Her soft panting, and the warmth of the ragged sigh on which she'd said his name, sent white heat streaming through his veins again. But, feeling how aroused he was, she'd come to her senses. As she gently attempted to disentangle herself from the embrace, he grunted softly. The pleasure he felt was every bit as intense as his frustrated need. Keeping her trapped between his body and the keyboard, he reached past her for the corsage box.

Opening the box, he held it between them. Inside, a single red rose was nestled on a bed of new leaves and baby's breath.

"You remembered," Jayne whispered.

Fixing his eyes on hers, Remy set the box aside. Then he slid an index finger deep between the neckline of her gown and her bare skin. At the touch, she groped behind herself—and her hand landed on the keyboard. The crashing sound involved a B flat, but was otherwise unrecognizable.

Smiling, glancing quickly toward the piano keys, Remy said, "Sounds like you're a little rusty, Jayne."

"It's been awhile since I've practiced," she returned raspily as he finished pinning the rose onto her dress.

How long? he wondered as his finger slipped from beneath the fabric of her dress again. Four and a half months? "Well, I did just make a play for you." He tilted his head and watched her lick her lips. When she glanced down, he followed her gaze, and he realized that the tips of her breasts had pebbled against her dress.

"Thank you for the rose..." Her throaty voice trailed off. "I missed my senior prom. And I guess I always wanted to dress like this and..."

Remy smiled. "Have a great-looking guy give you a rose corsage?"

Jayne nodded. As if sensing he was about to kiss her again, she said. "Don't forget, we've got bad guys to catch tonight, Remy."

"Darlin', I think you've already caught one."

She chuckled. "You're not one of the bad guys."

His eyes roved over her face, then flicked downward over her dress. "I wouldn't be too sure about that, Jayne."

"EXCUSE ME!" In the ballroom of the Windsor Court Hotel, Jayne found herself nose-to-nose with a man in a Santa Claus suit who seemed determined to knock her down. Cupping her hand around her corsage, she tried to protect it from the crowds squeezing past. If she'd known a simple trip to the ladies' room could be so perilous, she probably wouldn't have gone, she decided. "I said, excuse me!"

Giving up, Jayne tried to fishtail backward through the sea of dancers, but without success. She took a deep breath and drew an imaginary line between herself and Remy, who was at the punch table. Then she aggressively elbowed past Santa. The man whirled around and lunged toward her in a blur of red and white, seemingly intent on snatching her bodily. Just before he did, a sheikh slipped his arms around Jayne's waist—and spun her away from Santa.

"Mind if I kidnap you?"

"It's a little late to ask," Jayne managed to say.

"Just for one dance," the sheikh assured her in a muffled voice.

Jayne bit back a gasp. She recognized something—the man's tone, or his build, or the way he moved. As they danced, his long white robes swirled around her feet. Jayne peered at his face, but a white headpiece swept across his mouth and nose, entirely covered his head, then hung to his shoulders. His eyes were obscured by sunglasses, and the visible sliver of his face was painted silver.

Just thank your lucky stars you didn't say much, Jayne.
After all, someone might recognize her voice. And there
was the distinct possibility that whoever had ransacked
her town house was here tonight.

In the distance, Santa was dancing with an angel, Jayne
noticed with relief. The man had probably imbibed too
much of the free-flowing carnival spirits and then decided to woo a stranger. Jayne just hoped this sheikh was
equally harmless. She squinted at the man, who was
turning her under the soft lights.

He stared back with such intensity that she gulped.
What if it's Parker? Shameful heat burned her cheeks.
She'd let Remy kiss her again—longer and harder than she
should have. They'd arrived at the ball so late that they'd
barely caught the tail end of the pageant. The attendants
to the royal court—maids and dukes, pages and her-
alds—had been presented already. But she'd seen the entrance of the king and queen of Venus, the long trains of
their fur-trimmed red velvet robes sweeping the stage.

Jayne wanted to believe in the majestic magic of it all.
It was a night of fantasy. Of kings and queens and royal
courts.

And royal mistakes, she thought.

Still, she couldn't help but pretend that she and Remy,
not she and Parker, were to be married. Just for tonight,
anything seemed possible. All evening, standing beside the
man, she'd felt as if her dreams were coming true.

Until now.

Reality was intervening—and she could have sworn she
knew her dance partner. If she found definitive proof that
it was Parker, she would simply have to tell him who she
was. And yet she doubted she would. Their phone call had
been too upsetting.

Besides, tonight was her night—and Remy's. At the periphery of the dance floor, Remy was watching her carefully, holding their drinks, ready to intercede at the slightest indication. As if sensing another presence, the sheikh danced her into the thick of the crowd.

"Parker?" Jayne finally guessed.

"Parker's beside the food table. He's wearing a mask and black cape."

The voice! Recognizing it, she wrenched away. But it was too late. The sheikh had her in a death grip. Her eyes darted toward the food table—and she was rendered speechless. If that was Parker, then who was the woman on his arm who was dressed like a cat? Was it the same woman who'd dressed as the surprise bride? Jayne caught a final snatch of the woman's skin-tight leotard, twitching whiskers and long black tail just before another couple swirled by, blocking her vision of the mystery woman.

"Would you listen? I'm trying to do you a favor."

Jayne shook her head to clear it of confusion. "Smoothtalk Sweeny?" she managed to say.

"Keep your voice down, girl." Smoothtalk loosened his grip on her arm and leaned back. He didn't relinquish her, but lifted an edge of his sheikh's headpiece.

Jayne peeked beneath. Sure enough, a pile of dreadlocks was stuffed under there. She smiled dryly, suddenly remembering that Smoothtalk's real name was Judas. Was he about to play the turncoat—but to help her and Remy? "Why were you shooting at me in the French Quarter?" she demanded in a low tone.

"Speedo fired that shot, not me." Smoothtalk's arm slipped around her waist again, and at the same time he squeezed her hand, smiling pleasantly.

Jayne forced herself to smile back. Clearly her ex-client feared people were watching them. She tamped down her temper, reminding herself that she needed to pump Smoothtalk for information. Her eyes drifted toward the food table again, but Parker and the bewhiskered woman had vanished. As if sensing danger, Remy had set aside their drinks.

"You're in real trouble," Smoothtalk said. "But I've been keeping my ears open. The second you left town, Parker fired that assistant of yours and—"

"He fired Celeste?" Jayne was so shocked that she tripped over Smoothtalk's foot. He grabbed her elbow and steadied her. Yesterday Parker had lied. He'd said Celeste was at his house, helping him prepare the quarterly reports.

"I took it upon myself to call this Celeste. She wants her job back, so she's still snooping around, trying to find out—" Smoothtalk maneuvered them past a knot of dancers, then lowered his voice "—if Lynn has them."

Jayne's reeling mind simply couldn't keep up. "Lynn Seward?" she asked. "Parker's assistant?"

Smoothtalk nodded.

"What does Lynn have?" Jayne asked.

Smoothtalk's thin eyebrows drew together, creating one long, dark line above his sunglasses. "The books."

"The books?"

"The books. Everybody thinks you have them, including Parker. But Celeste thinks Lynn stole them."

This was very disjointed and hard to follow. The laughter, music and buzz of the crowd wasn't helping. Apparently Lynn Seward might be in possession of the books Parker had mentioned on the phone. "What exactly are you telling me?" Jayne urged.

"Don't you want to know *why* I'm telling you?"

Jayne wanted any information she could get. "Why?"

"Because you kept me out of jail," Smoothtalk said with gratitude, "that's why. Another trip to the joint, Jayne, and it would've broken my poor mama's heart. My boss told me to track you down in the Quarter, but when Speedo fired that shot, I called and said I don't do this kind of work anymore. And you know what?"

They were sure getting sidetracked. "What?"

"I got a legit job uptown."

Score one for the good guys. Jayne was glad to hear it. But she was in trouble—and she needed answers. A million questions were on the tip of her tongue. "What kind of books?" she asked insistently. "What's in them?"

"All I know is that it's got something to do with the Carrollton Riverside apartment complex."

That was the much-publicized landlord-tenant case that Parker had taken on free of charge. Jayne froze.

"Keep dancing," Smoothtalk said.

Somehow she managed to follow Smoothtalk's lead. Parker had worked so hard with the tenants of the Carrollton Riverside complex, fighting bad management. The civic-mindedness and community spirit he'd shown in taking the case had made him the perfect political candidate. That, and the fact that he was marrying her. Surely there was no fraud involved. *Don't even think it, Jayne.* "Smoothtalk, who's your boss?"

At the periphery of her vision, she suddenly saw Santa burst through a cluster of dancers.

"Gotta go," Smoothtalk said.

The man disappeared instantly, becoming nothing more than a swirl of white robes in the crowd. Jayne suddenly gasped. Was it her imagination, or was Santa following Smoothtalk?

Something snagged the bodice of her dress, diverting her attention. "Oh no!" she cried out, glancing down.

Sure enough, someone in the pressing crowd had dislodged her corsage.

Without thinking, she lunged for it, her arm outstretched. Right before she reached it, a lady's sandal kicked it a pace away. Before she thought it through, Jayne dropped to her knees and crawled forward. She lunged again. When she caught only a single fallen rose petal, a bittersweet sadness squeezed her heart. It was such a silly thing, but her eyes stung.

"Watch out, lady!" someone called.

"Get off the floor!"

Right before the rose was swept beneath the hard heel of a buccaneer's boot, a large, tanned hand with a ruffled cuff appeared, making a final sweep.

Jayne gasped, feeling a rush of hope. Remy had come to her rescue again.

But then he missed. And her lovely rose corsage—the one she'd wanted ever since the lonely night of the prom—tumbled away forever, leaving a trail of lost petals.

A millisecond later Remy's arms wrapped around her waist and pulled her from the floor. Hugging her against his chest, he gently assured, "There'll be a million other roses, Jayne."

The way he said it, Jayne almost believed it.

He smiled. "Who were you dancing with? I saw you talking."

Feeling guilty, Jayne stretched her gloved arms around Remy's neck and clung tight. He pulled his Cyrano nose downward, letting it hang around his neck, so that they could nuzzle cheek to cheek. Had she really been considering not telling Remy about the conversation? "Smoothtalk."

"Smoothtalk Sweeny?"

She nodded, wondering how much she should say. Remy didn't know she'd talked to Parker yet. And before Jayne got hysterical, she wanted an explanation. It made little sense for Parker to fire Celeste. Celeste was a great worker, and she was Jayne's assistant, not Parker's. If Celeste had been fired, as Smoothtalk had said, that meant Parker had lied. Was the woman at Parker's house really the surprise bride—and Catwoman? For the past two miserable days, Jayne had been wondering about those books....

Jayne realized Remy was scrutinizing her, and felt glad her feathered eyewear masked her features. "Smoothtalk says there're some kind of books missing," she finally said.

"Books?"

She forced herself to shrug. As guilty as she felt, she decided to withhold the information about the Carrollton Riverside case from Remy, at least for the moment. Maybe she hadn't been played for a fool—and maybe, if she had, Remy wouldn't need to know. "Someone thinks I have them, which is probably why my house was ransacked. They might be in Lynn Seward's possession."

Remy nodded, as if to say that pieces of the puzzle were falling into place. "I danced with Celeste."

Jayne's heart pounded. Maybe Smoothtalk was wrong. "Just now?" she asked, more quickly than she'd intended.

Remy was watching her closely. "That's how I got across the dance floor. She's dressed as a milkmaid."

Jayne exhaled a shaky breath. "And?"

"Parker fired her on Friday for some reason."

Jayne started to say, "I know." But the words didn't come out. She wasn't even sure why they didn't. Maybe because, if she admitted she'd known, it would mean admitting she'd withheld information from Remy. Or maybe it was because she'd trusted her fiancé too long to call him a liar without hard proof.

And if Parker was involved in something seriously shady, Jayne didn't even want to contemplate the consequences. Night would be day. North would be south. Everything would turn upside-down, and it would mean her whole life was a lie. It would mean she'd started a business with a man who wasn't to be trusted—and that she'd agreed to marry him, to let a liar become the father of her child.

Which he wasn't.

Remy was the baby's true father. There was no doubt about that now.

"I guess I could break into Lynn's place in the morning, when she leaves for work," Remy murmured.

When he smiled at her, Jayne melted. He swayed slowly to the music and drew her tightly against him, smoothing her hair until she pressed her cheek against his brocade jacket. He was so near, so male, that she could barely breathe. Through the tight breeches of his costume, she could feel the muscles of his thighs, the heat of his skin. Her gloved hands drifted from his neck and fanned across his back, until her palms cupped his shoulders. She stared deeply into his eyes again.

"Why so glum, *chère?*" he whispered. "We're getting closer to catching your bad guys."

But Remy Lafitte was the only bad guy she'd ever wanted, Jayne thought. Earlier tonight, he'd said she'd caught him. Had she?

Chapter Eleven

"There's an empty space at the other end of the block, Remy." Jayne pointed with a freshly manicured finger, the nail of which was no longer red, but a pretty pearl pink. "If it's still there," she added, as the driver in front of them stopped and prepared to park.

The green Buick was twice the size of the targeted parking area, so Remy readied himself for a long wait, casually stretching his arm along the back of the seat until he touched Jayne's shoulder.

She was really something—her smile as sunnily cheerful as the day, her lips pink-glossed and wet and kissable. Remy couldn't help but remember how they'd kissed at his bedroom door last night—their fingers twining, their tongues tussling, their thighs brushing. He'd barely been able to leave her, and the intensity of what he'd felt made this morning seem like the calm after a storm.

He'd never have guessed that domesticity might suit him. But he'd enjoyed the past few days—the easy silence when they'd cooked breakfast together, the casual flirtation when they'd gone clothes-shopping. When he asked her about her doctor, she'd realized she had an appointment early this morning. He'd taken her, waiting in the reception area with a few other soon-to-be dads.

Now Jayne shot him a quick glance. She was looking at him through clear, trusting eyes—no longer guiltily flushing or glancing away. They were sharing so much, and he was positive she was no longer holding anything back. Not that it would last.

She was marrying Parker Bradford tomorrow. And they were breaking into Lynn Seward's home today. Apparently Jayne meant to commit the crime wearing both her pearls and her heart-shaped beads, a floral-print Laura Ashley jumper and a fuzzy pastel blue mohair sweater. Her loose French twist left sexy wisps of hair curling around her forehead, and the red gloves she'd worn to the Venus ball were neatly folded in her lap.

Remy chuckled softly. "How many burglars do you suppose wear red opera-length gloves?"

"Oh, some." Jayne grinned. "Like the dress?"

Since he'd helped her choose the maternity jumper, she knew he did. He nodded. Violet pansies were printed on the fabric, making her eyes look more blue than blue gray. Wide straps hooked over the yellow top she wore beneath, and the dress hung free to her knees. He found himself imagining her fully showing, her rounded belly filling it out. She was going to be such a vision.

"I'm so sick of gray," she said, clearly fishing.

"Those gray suits of yours kind of turn me on." It was an understatement. Her prim business suits drove him wild.

Color rose on her cheeks. "Really?"

"Yeah." Remy wished he'd come to Lynn's alone. But the more time he spent with Jayne, the more likely she was to postpone her wedding. At least he hoped so. He glanced past the green Buick, scanning the house numbers and straining to get a look at Lynn's place. Behind him, the impatient driver of a compact car tooted his horn.

Remy sighed. What if he'd put Jayne in danger by bringing her here? If something happened to her, he'd never forgive himself. The information they had was so sketchy. He knew zilch about the books. Not what they contained, or who wanted them, or how desperately. He frowned. "I really shouldn't have let you come."

"*Let* me come?" Jayne unbuckled her seat belt and scooted across the seat toward him. "You're really hopeless, Remy."

"Seat belt," he reminded her for the umpteenth time that morning.

"I don't need it. We're not even moving."

Since it was true, Remy said nothing. He watched the Buick angle every which way, trying to fit into the parallel space. As he absently rubbed Jayne's arm, the mohair made him itch to touch her bare skin. "A few days with you sure makes one thing clear," he murmured.

Jayne snuggled against him. "Hmm?"

"You're in no shape to have this baby by your lonesome."

There was a long silence.

How could he have said something so stupid? Jayne had long been planning to parent the baby with Parker. How could he have forgotten?

Beside him, he heard a small choking sound. Then, in a stricken voice, Jayne said, "Don't you think I'll be a good enough mother?"

Her tone alone could have broken his heart. As the Buick in front of them finally slid into the parking spot, Remy wrapped both his arms around Jayne and squeezed tight. "You're gonna be just great."

"Are you sure?"

"Positive. That's not what I meant." The way Jayne clutched his arm took him by surprise, and the insistent pressure of her nails made him wince. Was this evidence that pregnant women had unruly moods? Jayne would kill him if he suggested that. So he merely hugged her to his chest while the driver in the car behind them laid on his horn.

She sniffed. "What *did* you mean?"

"You forget to take your vitamins, *chère,*" Remy said softly.

She squirmed away from him and crossed her arms defensively.

"It's okay, Jayne."

But it wasn't. She smiled wanly at him, as if to say he needn't bother to placate her. "I forgot my doctor's appointment, too."

"C'mere." He pulled her into his embrace again, so that her head curled in the crook of his arm and her cheek rested against his chest. "You would have remembered," he said.

But both of them knew it was a lie.

Remy never would have guessed Jayne could use someone to help her. She was such a competent professional. All sharp lines and efficient angles—no-nonsense. She was so independent and full of pride that leaning on someone else's shoulder didn't come easily to her. But details slipped her mind. She worked too hard, and she admitted to skipping meals and sleep. For all the baby clothes she'd bought, Remy discovered she hadn't remembered to get herself a single maternity outfit.

Brushing his lips across the top of her head, he thought back four and a half months. How long had she wandered through the French Quarter before she came to his office? It had been late, but she'd been wearing her work clothes. A weekend night, but she'd had no plans. Her birthday, but she'd had no date.

It must have been hard for a woman like Jayne to come to him and say the things she did the night they made their child. Feeling touched, Remy drew in a deep breath of her sweet-smelling hair and hugged her even tighter. Jayne felt something for him. At least she had that night. He was sure of it.

"I need to start Lamaze classes...." Her voice trailed off, and she lifted her gaze to his. Everything in her eyes said she knew she was all alone—and that Parker had done nothing to help her prepare for the baby. Even though her jaw set with fierce determination, tears suddenly shimmered in her eyes. "Remy, I'm doing the very best I can."

But sometimes she felt lonely and scared and wished she wasn't so damn independent, he thought. "Aw, *chère*, I can go to classes with you." He held her, swaying back and forth, forcing her to sink against the strength of his chest. "Things will be fine," he whispered, hoping it was true. "You'll see."

At that moment someone pounded on the car door. Remy glanced through the open window as a balding man in a blue hooded sweatsuit bellowed, "Get moving!"

Remy's temper flared. "She's pregnant," he said gruffly, by way of explanation.

Jayne lifted her head. "Mood swings, I guess," she said weakly.

"Sorry to interrupt," the man returned, now sounding nervous. "Terribly sorry." He backed away from the window, nearly on tiptoe.

Remy cupped Jayne's head gently, smoothing her hair. In the rearview mirror, he watched the man hop into his compact car, put it into reverse and back down the street. Within seconds, Jayne's good humor returned, as mysteriously as it had vanished—and Remy found himself angling into a space between a silver Jaguar and a gray VW Bug. He said, "My car sticks out like a sore thumb."

Jayne pushed her glasses firmly into place, frowned at the silver and gray cars, then stared through the windshield at the bright red hood of Remy's Cadillac. "Should we go get my Volvo? It's beige."

He shook his head. "Why not live dangerously?"

As soon as he got a good look at Lynn's house, he wanted to retract the words. "Just our luck," he drawled. "An old Creole cottage."

Green shutters bracketed both the barred windows and the front door of the two-story redbrick structure. Just looking at the precarious pitch of the steep, tar-blackened roof made Remy's head spin with vertigo.

In front, a single wrought-iron lamppost was rooted in the sliver of cement sidewalk. Along the walkway, weeds popped up between cracks like slender green periscopes that had risen from the earth's oceanic depths to look for spring. Beneath the lamppost, a kid had drawn a hopscotch board in chalk. To the right of Lynn's house was a connecting one-story garage with a flat roof. To the left, the adjacent apartment building loomed five stories high, throwing the small cottage into shadow.

"We can pull down the apartment building's fire-escape ladder," Jayne said. "Climb to the balcony and then—"

"*We're* not doing anything." Remy grabbed his work gloves from the seat, kissed Jayne quickly, then got out of the car. "Wait here, *chère.*"

She didn't. Remy hadn't even crossed the street before he heard her footsteps. As much as he wanted to keep Jayne safe, he felt powerless to deny her some small part in the adventure. Just as he pulled down the fire-escape ladder, she sidled up next to him.

"Ladies first," she reminded him, stepping regally past him and gripping both sides of the ladder. She'd already donned her gloves.

"Jayne..." he warned.

"Hmm?"

Remy sighed. To get inside Lynn's cottage, he was about to climb a metal ladder that looked unsafe. It would land him on a balcony that might well be occupied by inhabitants of the apartment building. If no one shot him or phoned the police by that time, Remy would then hop the balcony rail. He would roll onto Lynn's steeply pitched roof, whereupon he'd slowly inch his way across it on his belly. Maybe he'd arrive on the other side in one piece. If so, he'd leap onto the flat garage roof. With any luck, Lynn wouldn't have an alarm system. Because Remy would probably wind up breaking in her second-floor window with the heel of his boot.

He gazed deeply into Jayne's eyes. "Please," he said simply. She could call him whatever she wanted—chauvinistic, old-fashioned or just downright mean. No doubt he'd traversed more dangerous terrain in pursuit of the criminals he tracked, but this still wasn't exactly safe. The illegality of it bothered Remy, too. But he knew he'd break a thousand laws to protect Jayne.

"It's me they're after," she protested. "They think *I* have those books."

"Lynn's roof is dangerous...." He glanced upward, the sweep of his gaze emphasizing the truth of his words. Didn't the woman understand? "Jayne, you're pregnant."

She shifted her weight from one foot to the other, looking guilty. "I know that, Remy."

He started to explain how easily she could get hurt, but she didn't need his lectures. He glanced around. No one had noticed them. As respectable as Jayne looked, a passerby would think she was a tenant who'd locked herself out. He fixed his gaze on Jayne again and when he spoke again, his voice gentled. "I'm trying to take care of you."

She sighed and reached for her pearls and hearts. As she toyed with them, her glasses wiggled downward on the bridge of her nose. Pushing them into place, she said, "Okay, I'll stand lookout."

Remy shoved his gloves into a back pocket of his jeans, then leaned and lightly traced his fingers over Jayne's belly. All at once, his chest constricted, so tightly that he couldn't breathe. "Jayne," he said softly. "A part of me is growing inside you."

"I, er..." She cleared her throat. "I guess I usually think of it from my point of view. That *I'm* pregnant."

"We're pregnant," he drawled throatily.

"Like I said...I just haven't been thinking about it that way."

"Well..." He brushed his lips across hers. "That's the way it is."

"Why don't I just wait right here?" she said weakly.

Remy started climbing the fire escape ladder. Maybe Jayne was starting to truly understand. The child she'd been so intent on raising with Parker was going to be like Remy—with Remy's looks and traits and talents. Both the LeJeure and Lafitte families ran toward boys, so most likely the baby would be male....

Silently Remy landed on the balcony. With the quiet grace of a panther, he leaped over the wrought-iron rail and rolled onto Lynn's roof. His arms were outstretched, his splayed fingers seeking handholds. There weren't any.

With his washboard belly flat against the steep roof, Remy dug his boot heels into the tar, but they kept fighting for purchase, slipping precariously toward the eaves and the unsturdy gutter. He'd been so focused on making sure his and Jayne's baby didn't wind up motherless that a fatherless scenario hadn't occurred to him.

Until now.

"Great," Remy muttered. Then he started belly-crawling in the direction of the garage on the other side. From the ground, Jayne's worried eyes bored into him. He just hoped those books were inside. Whatever they contained, he needed to find them. Using the books as leverage, he could then convince Speedo, Smiley or Smoothtalk to put him in touch with whoever wanted Jayne. Even if she did marry Parker Bradford, at least Remy would know she was safe. Assuming that Parker himself wasn't involved in whatever was going on, of course.

"Made it," Remy murmured. He rolled again—this time landing flat-footed on the garage roof. He tugged his gloves from his back pocket and slipped them on. Luckily, Lynn's upstairs window was unlocked. He opened it, then cocked his head. Not a sound.

Stepping through the open window, he found himself in a bedroom. He headed downstairs, opened the front door and motioned to Jayne. Nervously she left her post next to the fire escape ladder and entered through the front door.

She glanced around. "Should we start upstairs or down?"

He nodded in the direction of the stairs. "With the bedroom. That's where people hide things fifty-eight percent of the time."

"Really?"

He shot her a quick smile. "Such are the statistics a man picks up in my line of work."

In the bedroom they found all kinds of books. Art volumes, novels and countless cookbooks—but nothing suspicious. "Given how many cookbooks she reads, let's try the kitchen next," Remy said.

"See anything?" Jayne asked five minutes later as she peered inside a kitchen cabinet.

Remy shook his head and opened the refrigerator door. "Darlin', doesn't it bother you that we're in someone's house?"

"Absolutely not," Jayne shot back with sudden venom. "We've been shot at, Remy. And that awful man destroyed the nursery."

"I just hope—" Remy cut himself off. "Got 'em."

It had to be them. The books were in the messy lower bin of the refrigerator, wedged between a head of cauliflower and a package of celery stalks. A thick rubber band held together the four small green cloth-covered volumes. Jayne hurried to his side and traced a finger over the cover of the top book.

Remy removed the rubber band, casually draped his arm around Jayne, then opened the first ledger.

"It's all numbers," she murmured. "Since everybody thinks we've got the books we might as well take them to your place and try to figure out what they mean."

What exactly had he been hoping for? Remy wondered, feeling his heart sink. *Simple solutions. Something in easy-to-read black and white that damned Parker Bradford.*

"ANY THUNDERBOLTS YET?" Jayne nestled into the crook of Remy's arm. She stared at the book in her lap, then at the others that were spread out around her and Remy on the sofa. Something that felt like the answer to a long-awaited question kept niggling at her brain.

Remy merely shook his head.

When he gently jostled Jayne and stood, she groaned in protest. He made an awfully comfortable pillow. In lieu of his broad, naked chest, she snuggled against a throw that wasn't nearly as nice. Then she watched Remy stretch, rolling his shoulders and flexing his biceps. Her eyes trailed over his pectorals, then down the whole length of his torso, following a vertical line of enticing black hair that vanished beneath the waistband of his pants.

Sighing, she glanced around the living room, taking in the digital clock radio on the desk in the corner. Soft music was playing. *And it's time to get busy.* She tightened her grip on the book in her lap and tucked her feet beneath her. At the movement, Scamper raised his head and shot her a pointed yellow-eyed glare from the other end of the sofa. Then the feline curled into another tight round ball of black and orange splotches.

"Be right back," Remy said.

"Where are you going?" Jayne asked. They couldn't afford to take a break, not that they weren't pleasant. She and Remy had chatted, as they often had over the weekend, nibbling snacks and comparing childhoods. They'd told their funniest stories and talked about the baby—about whether it was a boy or a girl, what to name it, who it would most look like.

Jayne forced her attention to the book again. Most of the numbers represented dollar amounts. Debit and credit columns weren't marked, but it seemed clear that money was being moved from place to place. How were the transfers of funds connected to the Carrollton Riverside apartment case?

Feeling as if she'd suddenly been caught red-handed, Jayne glanced up—and found herself staring at Remy's naked back. It was classic. The proverbial V. His skin was the color of honey and the texture of silk. One look at him, and guilt washed over her. Remy was so strong…and she was such a liar. He was here for her, but in her confusion, she didn't know what to tell him.

If she admitted she couldn't call off her wedding and ruin Parker's career, Remy would think she was spineless. But she couldn't bear to do it. Not unless she found proof of Parker's wrongdoing. The kind of hard evidence that would hold up in a court of law.

Feeling another rush of guilt, her lips parted. She started to tell Remy everything—that she'd talked to Parker, that he knew about the books, that Smoothtalk Sweeny had mentioned the Carrollton case—but Remy strode toward the doorway.

"If we don't get any flashes of insight tonight—" Remy's voice receded as he headed toward the sitting room "—we can figure it out tomorrow, *chère.*"

"No, we can't," Jayne whispered.

Because tomorrow was Mardi Gras. Fat Tuesday. And Jayne was scheduled to marry Parker at high noon. Just twelve hours later, the horn would blow at midnight, officially announcing the end of the carnival and the beginning of Lent.

Lent. That time of penance and atonement for one's sins.

Thinking of Remy's broad, strong muscular back, Jayne sighed wistfully.

But the fun and games were about to end, all right. Had Remy actually forgotten about her wedding tomorrow?

Every time Jayne shut her eyes, Saint Louis Cathedral loomed large in her mind. The round clock beneath the central spire was always fixed at two seconds before noon. She sighed shakily. Tomorrow morning, at exactly 9:00 a.m., the flight transporting her parents and her sisters and her sisters' husbands was scheduled to land at the New Orleans airport. The judge's huge, pawlike hand was going to swoop right down from the sky, literally. It would clamp around Jayne's shoulder, making the sleeve of her wedding dress bunch, and then he'd start calling her Robert.

Realizing her glasses had slid down to the tip of her nose, Jayne shoved them into place. "Do you think Lynn's discovered the books are missing?" she called out, trying to take her mind off her wedding.

Remy hadn't heard her. She twined her fingers thoughtfully around her pearls and plastic hearts and glanced through the window into the twilight. *Don't quit looking.* She sighed and stared at the book again. What did the numbers mean? All at once, her eye caught a particular sequence—and lingered. Why did she keep coming back to that nonsensical string of digits? This and one other set bothered her, somehow. "487-291-0008-7942-2," she whispered.

She riffled forward through the pages, then backward. She'd almost decided to practice tax law, because numerical analysis usually came easily to her. Why wouldn't it now?

None of it made any sense. Not unless— Her eyes narrowed, and she turned the pages more slowly. Then she gasped. It couldn't be true. But it was. Her eyes had found a third sequence of familiar numbers. "Oh, my word…"

"What?"

Jayne nearly jumped out of her skin. Pressing her hand to her heart, she said, "Remy, you scared me!" But he hadn't, not really. She was merely shocked, since he'd found her with her hand in the cookie jar.

"Sorry, *chère.*"

"You just—just surprised me," Jayne stammered. *Because I think I know what these books mean. Oh, what if I'm wrong?*

"I'll never do it again," Remy promised gravely.

His low, throaty voice sent a tingle through her. His fingers lightly grazed her cheeks as he removed her glasses. "What are you—"

Jayne stopped in midsentence when Remy seated himself next to her on the sofa. He was so close that she could feel his body heat, smell his spicy scent and touch his naked skin. How could the man take her glasses at a time like this? Only seventeen hours remained before her wedding. Without her glasses, the neat columns of numerical figures that had finally started to make sense became a mere blur again.

And she needed to see. How could she make once-in-a-lifetime decisions when things were so out of focus, when she wasn't positive of what she was up against? She had to know the truth before she told Remy.

When she glanced upward, she realized he'd been watching her. His slow smile was so infectious that she felt sure he'd removed her glasses to kiss her. Heaven knew, she wanted him to do so. She squinted. With one of the teensy screwdrivers from his toolbox, Remy was tightening the loose sidebars of her glasses.

The small, thoughtful gesture touched her even more than how he'd insisted they shop for maternity clothes. Remy slid the glasses onto her face again.

"How could you possibly be our brains, when your glasses are in such disrepair?" he asked in a teasing drawl.

Against all her better judgment, Jayne found herself huskily saying, "Hey, brawn, I thought you took off my glasses to kiss me."

"Anytime."

"What about now?"

In spite of her guilt, his soft chuckle warmed her to her very soul. One of his muscular forearms reached around her back. He crushed her against his chest and gently probed her mouth open with his. As Remy's large, splayed hand glided over her thigh, rounded to her hip and squeezed her waist, the ledger tumbled to the floor. The kiss was indulgent, slow and languorous, as if all eternity stretched before them.

But it didn't.

They had only seventeen hours. And Jayne was lying to him—even while she was reclining in his arms, even while she was sworn to marry another man. But how could she share her suspicions? If she was right, Parker would no longer be in her life.

She was giving Remy all the time she had, and the chance he'd asked for, so that they could know one another better. And yet she had to keep focusing on how things really were, not on how she wanted them to be. She had to quit taunting herself, pretending that Remy might commit to her. She knew better. Soon enough, Remy's feelings would untangle. He'd realize his supposed feelings for her were really for the baby.

Maybe Remy would realize she'd been played for a fool, too, and he'd know how stupidly she'd fallen for it. He'd feel sorry for her when he saw her wounded pride, and he'd probably say some kind words about how the right man would love her someday. But his glance would say that she should have known better.

But how could she? In the world of the illustrious Wright family, good girls just didn't get used.

And men like Parker Bradford were honest.

"Remy," she murmured. She gently backed away, masking both her guilt and her desire. At his surprised expression, she felt a twinge of pure sadness. She forced herself to retrieve the book from the floor.

"Sure you didn't find something?"

Everywhere his eyes fell on her heated skin, she felt naked. Didn't he know she wanted to forget this—to forget it all? To simply lean on him? To cling to him tightly, the way she had when they made love, as if it really meant something.

"Jayne?"

She shook her head. "Nothing."

He clearly didn't believe her.

The phone on the end table rang, jangling every bit as much as her nerves. Remy listened to a message from his answering service. Then he dialed Buddy Wyatt, who had left the message.

"Intricate system," she commented, taking in the relayed phone calls.

Remy shrugged, holding the receiver away from his lips. "I have to be careful about who gets my number."

He was just as circumspect about his address. Jayne wished she hadn't asked for the reminder that his was a dangerous occupation. *So's yours, Jayne.* Daily she dealt with the court system and accused criminals. *Not to mention a crooked fiancé.* Half listening to Remy's conversation, she scrutinized the neat rows of numbers again.

But it was right there in black and white.

487-291-0008-7942-2. One of the corporate account numbers for the law firm. The second series of digits she'd recognized was the number for Parker's Life-Ready savings account. She'd bet the remaining numerical sequences represented still more of Parker's accounts. She bit back a groan as a wiggling arrow of pain fishtailed from her left temple to her right. The last thing she needed right now was one of her headaches.

"Chère?"

Jayne had heard enough of the conversation to know that Remy had agreed to take one of Buddy's jobs, which meant he had to drive over and pick up the case file. The man Remy would be tracking had robbed a convenience store, then jumped bail. A sudden shiver shook Jayne's shoulders. She thought of the many things she'd seen Remy do—deliver Lisa Leigh, fix the baby's crib, play the piano. How could someone so sensitive and gentle do such dangerous work?

Gazing into Remy's beautiful silver eyes, Jayne felt suddenly empty. She wanted so much—to share her suspicions, to beg Remy to be careful, to ask him to find less dangerous work. Reaching out, she brushed her thumb over the bare skin next to his waistband with a touch that was more matter-of-fact than sensual. "What do you say you and I run away together forever?"

He shot her a grin. "You just say when."

But he didn't mean it. Remy was contemplating settling down with her. But what he wanted was the baby. Yes, the man was fooling himself. And Jayne wished with all her heart that she wasn't so very sure of it.

"WHERE ARE YOU, Remy?" Jayne whispered. She glanced nervously at the digital clock radio on the desk where she was seated, then reminded herself that he'd been gone only an hour.

During his absence, she'd called countless banks and tried to reach Celeste Beauregard. Now, on a hunch, she dialed the library. "Hattie Byrd, reference section," she said when the switchboard operator came on the line.

Moments later Hattie's grandmotherly voice gurgled over the wire. "Jayne, if you're still at that law office, Parker may not be the right fellow. And if you don't find one you're willing to go home to soon, I may start matchmaking."

I think I've put the man I want in danger, Hattie.

Jayne glanced at the clock again. Exactly four minutes had passed. Picturing Hattie Byrd made her feel better. The comforting seventy-year-old woman had white hair, coffee-colored skin and a mind as sharp as a tack. After forcing herself to chat for a moment, Jayne said, "I've got to find out who owns the Carrollton Riverside apartment complex, who's behind the management company and the board. I want to know who's—"

"In power?" Hattie queried.

Jayne's grip tightened around the phone receiver. "I need to know as soon as possible. I'm not sure, but I suspect you'll have to dig for the information."

Hattie laughed. "Excavation's my specialty, dear."

"Thanks, Hattie," Jayne said, feeling relieved. Hattie was well recognized in the New Orleans law-enforcement community for working wonders with a database.

Hattie said, "I'll call you back before closing time."

After a second's hesitation, Jayne gave Remy's unlisted phone number to Hattie.

Then Jayne bent over the books again, determined to decode every last line of numbers. She'd moved from the sofa to the desk, and she was now working with all four books at once. Since she'd turned off the radio, the room had become silent, save for Scamper's soft purring at her feet. Her shoulders ached, and in spite of Remy's herbal tea, which she'd reheated, her head was starting to pound. For some time, she completely lost herself, scribbling notes on a pad.

Hearing something, Jayne suddenly glanced up. Was it Remy? No, it was just the creaky building settling down for the night. Seeing the clock, she gasped. Another full hour had passed. "Oh, where are you, Remy?" she whispered.

With every row of figures she decoded, her level of panic rose. She lifted the phone receiver again. After she punched in a number, another bank service line put her on hold. "Remy, I really wish you'd come home," she murmured.

The herbal headache remedy had cooled, but she gulped down the dregs. No matter how she tried to stop them, her eyes kept darting to the clock. Every time a digital number clicked over, her pulse accelerated. *Just thank your lucky stars you've figured this out, Jayne. And quit torturing yourself.*

But she couldn't stop. Why hadn't she voiced her suspicions? And what if she'd just sent Remy into a trap? After all, it was Buddy Wyatt whom Parker had hired to follow her and Remy to Bayou Mystique. If Buddy was still in Parker's employ, maybe the man's earlier call to Remy had been a ruse. Maybe Parker knew that she and Remy had the books and had hired Buddy to lure Remy out into the open....

To kill him.

"Jayne!" she snapped in self-censure.

When she was taken off hold, Jayne blew out a sigh of relief. This evening was a nightmare, but at least the process of verifying her suspicions was helping her keep her mind off Remy's whereabouts.

The recording began, "If you are using a touch-tone phone, please press one now for easy-access account information."

Jayne used the PIN numbers for the Bradford and Wright accounts and followed the series of prompts, leaving a check mark in the margin of a ledger when she'd verified the account name.

Sure enough, it was the escrow account that held the rent money for the Carrollton Riverside apartment complex. For the past year, while the case was pending, the tenants of the huge, sprawling multiplex hadn't been paying their rent.

Instead, they'd entrusted their money to Bradford and Wright, and the firm had placed it in an escrow account. Because the complex was comprised of six high-rise buildings, each of which contained more than one hundred separate apartments, Jayne had estimated that the rent for the entire complex per month was nearly a quarter of a million dollars.

Since the case began, funds in excess of two million dollars had become available to Parker—and Parker was using every last red cent for his personal use. He'd even used stolen money to run his campaign for the election this Wednesday. The ledger books showed that he and at least one partner had been systematically stealing clients' money. And not just from the Carrollton accounts.

Judging from the trail of money transfers, Jayne guessed that Parker had been investing the stolen funds, but that he'd lost all the money from the Carrollton accounts in a bad investment. Some of the client accounts were empty. Since Celeste helped with the quarterly reports, she was the one person besides Jayne who might recognize the account numbers. Which was probably why she'd been fired.

"Historic Creole cottages don't come cheap," Jayne muttered, thinking of Lynn Seward. Jayne had no idea why Lynn had taken the books. Maybe she'd been in cahoots with Parker—and was now trying to save her hide or blackmail him.

Who knows? Jayne thought. *And who cares?* The threads of the case were so tangled that it would take months to unravel them. The main point was that people at Jayne's firm were stealing money from clients.

Not only had Parker betrayed Jayne's trust, he'd ruined the business they shared. Instead of marrying the man, she was going to have to put him behind bars. *Too bad I'm a defense attorney, not a prosecutor.*

But she still couldn't quite believe it.

And who else—other than Lynn Seward—was involved?

Glancing at the clock again, Jayne felt sick. She never should have let Remy leave, not given what she'd suspected. At least two million dollars in cash was missing from the bank. Parker and his cohorts were probably scrambling to replace the money before they were caught. And if no one found out, then all would proceed as planned.

There would be a wedding, a honeymoon, an election that would send Parker to the Louisiana House of Representatives and eventually to Washington. But that bright future would end if the authorities were given the books.

People had killed for less.

When the phone rang, Jayne yelped. Snatching the receiver, she said, "Remy?"

"No, this is Hattie. I found out who owns the Carrollton Riverside complex."

As pleased as she was at the news, Jayne's heart sank. Where was Remy? "Who?" she managed to ask.

"Hal Knowles," Hattie said.

Jayne could almost hear Remy saying, "I told you so." *If he's still alive.*

REMY KNEW something was wrong. The second he opened the door, he saw Jayne perched right on the edge of a chair in front of the desk. One hand clutched Scamper, who was in her lap. The other rested on the telephone.

Something's happened to the baby.

That was his first thought. He was hardly proud of it, but a craving hit the back of his throat and he reached into his empty jacket pocket for a cigarette.

"Jayne?" he said.

She merely stared at him as if she'd seen a ghost.

When he stepped across the threshold, her eyes widened. Then, sending Scamper flying, Jayne lunged across the room—and right into Remy's arms. He instinctively hugged her, and she clung to him as if she never meant to let him go.

"Where have you been?" she wailed.

He glanced at the top of her head in surprise. *Jayne's just worried because I was late.* A slow, dawning smile lifted his lips. Her hair was still in a sexy, loose French twist, and he began removing the pins, tossing them on an end table. A second later, he was fluffing her hair around her shoulders. "Buddy's wife, Myra, asked me if I'd have a cup of coffee," he drawled gently. "And then Buddy couldn't find the case file, and . . ."

Remy swallowed hard. All at once, he became conscious of Jayne's body—her breasts pressing insistently against his chest, her hair whispering through his fingertips, her back arching in response to where his palm had landed at the small of her spine.

"You should have called," she whimpered.

He couldn't help it. Her possessiveness excited him every bit as much as the honesty they'd begun to share. She'd been watching and waiting for him, hoping he'd call. Nuzzling his face against her silken hair, her soft cheek, he murmured, "Miss me, *chère?*"

"You've been gone for hours."

"Just three," he returned huskily. And three hours wasn't long at all—not to a man who was often gone for days. Suddenly his breath caught with emotion; he was unable to believe she was really this upset. Everything in her tone said that her marriage tomorrow to Parker was the last thing on her mind.

"Remy, I've got to tell you something. I . . ."

"When I came through that door," Remy whispered hoarsely, "you told me everything I ever wanted to know." He could still hear her pounding footsteps as she'd bolted across the room and into his embrace. Each step had said she loved him.

"But, Remy, I—"

Feeling sure she didn't love Parker, he tightened his arms around her waist and silenced her with a kiss, driving his tongue deep between her lips. He'd never tell her how to live her life, but he'd give her a reminder of what his loving was like.

His mouth never leaving hers, he half carried, half walked her down the hallway. His hands sought her everywhere at once. Gliding effortlessly over her shoulders and hips and behind, they lifted her jumper, dipped over her silken thighs and teased her through her panties—only to reappear, sliding beneath the straps of her modest jumper, brushing over her breasts.

He backed her right to the edge of his bed—until her knees buckled and she wound up seated on the mattress. In a swift motion, he tugged off his T-shirt and tossed it on the floor. Then he kicked off his boots. When he flicked on the low-wattage bedside lamp, her lips parted in an unspoken protest.

"Carnival's over, *chère,*" he whispered, gazing into her eyes. Tomorrow was Mardi Gras morning, but their own private carnival had ended when he came inside tonight . . . when he heard her voice catch with the panic of a woman in love. Four and a half months ago, he'd made love to her in the heat of the night. But now it wasn't right for them to hide, masked by the darkness. They'd made a baby together. And it was time to quit pretending. Time to admit that what was happening between them was real. Softly he said, "This time I want to see every inch of you."

"All right, Remy," she whispered.

She made a concerted effort to try to steady her breath, but he wanted to hear her pant for him, too. To see her expression when she lost control. She was so prim, so proper. Her face, with its ivory skin and clear eyes, was so honest. No outfit could ever be more chaste than that maternity jumper strewn with violets, but it was the most provocative thing Remy had ever seen. His chest constricted with longing, his jeans tightened with desire.

And his soft groan was irrepressible. He leaned forward and released it against Jayne's lips, kissing her more deeply than he ever had. As he lowered himself on top of her, he slid her dress upward on her creamy thighs. Through his well-worn jeans, he felt her bare legs shaking with need.

Gently wedging a muscular thigh between them, he whispered, "Let me inside you, Jayne."

She gasped. Beneath him, her muscles twitched involuntarily, and then her quivering knees started to part. On his naked shoulders, her fingertips trembled. "It's been so long, Remy," she whispered.

At the words, he began to move on top of her—kissing her, forgetting the barrier of their remaining clothes, willing her to feel how ready for her he was. Her hands, so gentle before, now clutched his back, her nails pricking his skin.

"Ah, Jayne..." he murmured brokenly. Lifting his body a fraction, he rid her of the jumper and pulled off his jeans. He was so close to being inside her that all rational thought was leaving his mind. But tonight he had to love her so hard and good that she'd admit she wanted to belong to him. He had to make her see that the three of them—him, her, the baby—belonged together. As he lowered his weight again, he felt every nuance of her body—the soft, open cleft beneath her high-waisted white panties, her bare silken legs that dangled down the sides of his.

When she squirmed against the intensity of his touch, Remy held her firmly, licking languid kisses from her ears down her neck, then back again as his hands found her breasts and cupped them.

"Remy, please..." Her voice had become nothing more than a soft pant. "I've got to tell you..."

Whatever it was, she didn't have a chance. Because he was kissing the tips of her breasts, blowing on them, brushing them with his work-roughened thumbs.

She whispered, "Oh, please..."

But this time, there was nothing she wanted to tell him in words. One of her damp, trembling hands slid between their bodies, groping uncertainly, daring to touch him intimately. The way he'd loved her four and a half months ago came racing back to him, strengthening his desire. But there was so much more between them now. Thinking of the baby, he lowered himself, rained kisses over her belly, then moved lower still.

"Oh no..." She gasped. "No, please..."

He drank her in, until she arched toward him, her every movement a plea and a cry for the touch of his lips. And only after she'd received her pleasure did he glide upward again.

He lifted her then, driving deep inside her with a slow solid thrust that threatened to shatter him. The way she looked at him alone was enough to make him lose control—her eyes shining with desire, her expression so open and honest and vulnerable.

He'd sworn he wouldn't ask again. But he found himself raggedly saying, "Tell me you don't love Parker."

"You know I don't." The words were barely audible; her voice was a simpering cry.

"Do you love me?"

"I do, Remy."

"I love you, too." Yes, he'd sworn he wouldn't ask, but he had. And he'd gotten the answer he wanted. Jayne loved him. And Remy was going to become the father he'd never had—for their baby. Over and over, he lifted her—until she rocked against him uncontrollably, until his backside clenched with tension and he exploded. After a moment, she haltingly whispered, "I love you so much, Remy."

He didn't have the breath to respond. But he smiled, knowing he'd make love to her all night. Jayne wasn't going anywhere—least of all to her wedding. She was staying right here. With him. And tonight, he was going to make her his forever.

Chapter Twelve

Mardi Gras
Tuesday, February 20

"*Chère*, it's Mardi Gras mornin'." Ten minutes ago, Remy had lazily rolled his head on the pillow, only to find that Jayne was gone.

Smiling, he'd glanced at the clock. The wedding was less than an hour away, but Jayne wouldn't be getting married. Not today. Later she would. To him. Not that he'd asked her yet. But during the night Parker's engagement ring had been removed; it was long forgotten on the bedside table. Still smiling, Remy had shut his eyes again and listened—for Jayne's soft humming, the gently playing radio, a clatter of silverware and breakfast plates.

Nothing.

"Not even coffee?" Then he realized—with the highly honed tracking skills of his profession—that Jayne was no longer in his apartment.

Because he was a bounty hunter, his first thought had been that she was in extreme danger. His second had been that she was pregnant, which decreased the likelihood of someone's harming her by twenty-eight percent. His third had been that she'd changed her mind and decided to marry Parker.

That had been ten minutes ago.

Now Remy clutched the steering wheel of his car, his feelings of deep, raw-boned fear rising to the surface, masked as anger. He sped alongside Lake Pontchartrain, driving faster than any man had a legal right to, having no clue what he'd do to Jayne when he found her. Maybe he'd take her in his arms. Or maybe he'd kill her.

"As if she might not be in enough danger already," he muttered, telling himself to cool his jets. Still, his pulse was racing. Lord knew he could handle tough situations. But this was different. Jayne was involved, and she was pregnant.

She'd taken the books, too. By punching the redial button on his telephone, Remy had found out Jayne had called a cab. Seconds later, the cab company had traced the car. She was en route to her town house.

The notepad on the desk had contained a wealth of information. There had been enough bank names written in Jayne's neat cursive that Remy realized the books contained account numbers. The word *Parker* was both circled and underlined, and Celeste Beauregard's phone number was jotted in a margin.

So was Hattie Byrd's. As far as Remy was concerned, Hattie was one of the best bounty hunters around, even if she surfed through cyberspace, tracking her quarry on the Internet instead of on the pavement. But Remy had no way of finding out what information Jayne had requested. Hattie wasn't home and wasn't expected at the library until noon.

Noon.

The hour Jayne would march down the aisle with Parker Bradford. Remy guessed it was about eleven-thirty now. Maybe closer to twelve. If Jayne had decided to marry the man, should he charge in and stop the wedding?

And had Jayne really been playing him for a fool? Had she decoded the books while he was gone last night—and withheld her findings from him? Just how long had she been stringing him along?

There has to be some explanation. Jayne couldn't have hidden information from him again. Not when she'd lain beneath him throughout the night—so naked, so open and vulnerable, sharing so much.

"Unless she's been trying to protect Parker all along," Remy whispered.

He swerved into her driveway—then stopped before he reached the carport. Her Volvo was gone. Remy's eyes narrowed, and he stared through the windshield at the dusty, gravel-strewn cement—until the faint patterns of swirling gravel convinced him she'd backed out and then headed west.

The clue was something. But then, *west* was a big place. He had to find something else. And quick. He drove beneath the carport, got out and slammed the car door.

As he jogged through Jayne's yard, Remy dislodged a brick from the landscaped circle around her willow tree. When he found the front door locked, he eyed one of her living room windows, weighed the brick in his hand, then tossed it through. Glass shattered, then tinkled into her flower boxes.

Remy waited to see if the irate neighbor would appear, hardly feeling guilty. Why should he? The notepad Jayne had left behind indicated that Parker was neck-deep in trouble. And rather than tell Remy last night, Jayne had flung herself into his arms—seducing him, touching him, loving him.

And now she'd left him.

Damn. She'd taken the evidence that her fiancé was a dirty rotten scoundrel, too. Remy thrust his hand through the jagged glass, unlatched the window and slid it upward. Then he leaped inside—and headed straight for Jayne's bedroom.

Her wedding dress was gone.

He shook his head. "How could you do this to me, Jayne?" *To us. And to the baby.* For the first time in years, maybe in his life, tears stung Remy's eyes, making them feel gritty.

Don't give up. He turned abruptly and headed for the kitchen phone. The redial button gave him local information. Whose number or address had she been trying to get? He glanced at the pad next to the phone, then grabbed a pencil and gently rubbed it across the paper. A second later, words appeared, fuzzily white against the sketchy graphite. "Bingo," Remy whispered, feeling none too happy about it.

In Jayne's neat cursive handwriting were the words *Sugarcane Lane.*

And only one residence was there. An isolated French villa that belonged to Hal Knowles.

"SWEET LITTLE JAYNE."

As Remy silently crossed the flagstone patio outside the villa, Hal Knowles's voice traveled outward on the midday breeze—from inside a light, airy room, through an open set of French doors, and then to Remy's ears.

Inside, fans attached to the high ceiling turned lazily. Knowles was seated on a fluffy chintz sofa with his back to the doors. Because the fiftyish businessman faced a mirrored wall, Remy could see every nuance of his cruel face. Jayne stood between the mirrored wall and the sofa, facing the French doors and Remy.

Not that she saw him. A potted palm just inside the doors shielded Remy from view. As much as he wanted to enter the room and take a stand beside Jayne, he couldn't. She'd deceived him. If he went inside now, he might never believe whatever explanation she gave him. And if there wasn't one, Remy's heart was going to break.

Knowles threaded his fingers through his silver hair, then draped an arm over the sofa back. In the mirror, Remy watched the man's other hand slip between the sofa side cushions.

"Sweet Jayne," Knowles crooned, "I knew you had the books all along, and I do hope you've come to offer to sell them to me."

"I only got them yesterday, Hal," Jayne snapped. "They were in Lynn Seward's vegetable bin."

Knowles chuckled, but the sound wasn't pleasant. "Lynn had them?"

Jayne planted her hands on her hips. "Isn't that what I just said?"

Knowles's mouth set in a thin, bloodless line, but he waved a hand in the air nonchalantly. "Well, my dear, what matters is that you have them now."

"So you really are behind this?"

"Obviously."

"You're the one who broke into my home, Hal?" Jayne crossed her arms, her voice rising to a near shriek. "You're the one who—"

When she stopped in midsentence, Remy felt as if a knife twisted in his gut. No doubt she was remembering how callously Knowles had destroyed the nursery.

Remy's eyes narrowed. Because of the light, Knowles seemed sharper in the mirror than in person—as if he were more an illusion than flesh and blood. Now the man caught his own reflection in the mirror. His eyes flicked over his own outfit—cream slacks and sweater, shiny black shoes, a panama hat with a black brim. He looked as if he owned a banana republic instead of half of New Orleans, Remy thought.

"Why don't you be a good girl," Knowles continued, "and tell me where you've put my books?"

"I wouldn't let you have them for a million dollars," Jayne pronounced regally.

"Too bad," Knowles shot back, "because that's about what I'd offer you for them. A small price to pay for my reputation as one of New Orleans most-loved native sons. Don't you think?"

The lethal calm in Knowles's tone made Remy glad he'd called Buddy Wyatt and Dan Stanley. Not that his friends would necessarily get the messages in time. Remy glanced over his shoulder, scanning the property for any sign of movement.

The villa sure was creepy. It was completely isolated, surrounded by a privacy wall and overgrown with moss-draped oaks, pecan trees and palmettos. Remy felt the hairs at his nape rise.

"You know, Jayne," Knowles went on in a smug, self-satisfied tone, "I could have had Smoothtalk, Speedo and Smiley just kill you in the French Quarter."

"Smoothtalk wouldn't harm a hair on my head," Jayne returned coolly. "It was Smoothtalk who told me this mess involved the Carrollton Riverside case." She raised her finger and pointed at Knowles. "You're the owner. You quit providing services to tenants. And when they took you to court, Parker started collecting their rent and—"

"Smoothtalk told you all that?"

Jayne started toying with the pearls and plastic hearts that circled her neck. "I deduced some of it myself."

Remy's body went rigid. Not only had Jayne definitely withheld information from him last night, she'd been deceiving him even longer. She'd had strong reason to suspect that Parker was involved in illegal activities since the night they'd attended the Venus ball.

This mess. That was what Jayne had just called it. As far as Remy was concerned, fraud was a crime.

Suddenly his mind ran wild. All along, maybe Jayne had just needed a tough guy to help her find and decode those books. Maybe the baby wasn't even really his. Maybe she'd just used it as a ruse, so that she could stay with him over these last days—seducing him, sleeping with him, making him fall crazy in love with her....

And all so that she could protect Parker.

Knowles's soft, persuasive chuckle brought Remy back to his senses.

"Jayne, what business is it of yours if Parker and I borrowed a few measly dollars from the Carrollton escrow accounts?" Knowles said.

So it all boiled down to the most mundane of things, Remy thought as he leaned in the doorway, right out of sight. Just another crooked lawyer and another crooked businessman working in collusion to get rich quick and rip off the general public.

Jayne said, "But Carrollton was just one case."

"Heavens, Jayne," Knowles drawled, "have you got a tape recorder in your pocket or something?"

Surely Jayne wouldn't be that foolish, Remy thought. Taped information would never be admissible in court. On the other hand, the woman had been shortsighted enough to come here alone. And she might well be a woman driven by love, who'd come here to risk her life to try to save Parker Bradford's reputation.

The mere thought nearly did Remy in.

Jayne backed up and leaned against the mirrored wall behind her, as if for support. "Parker wasn't providing legal advice for your sugarcane refineries, Hal, he was helping you steal from employee funds... payrolls, pensions, credit unions—"

Knowles's fist slammed down on the back of the sofa. "Suffice it to say that Parker and I have broken a thousand laws. What is your point, Jayne?"

Jayne stomped her foot. "How did you force Parker to do this?"

Even now, Jayne was trying to give Parker an out. Remy heard a rustling sound and glanced over his shoulder. Buddy Wyatt and Dan Stanley waved from behind a pecan tree. Seeing them, Remy felt sorely tempted to just leave. Let *them* save Jayne's darn life.

"What are you going to do with my books, Jayne?" Knowles demanded again.

"I'm going to go find Parker and ask him what—"

Knowles's evil chuckle cut her off. "Parker shouldn't be too hard to find." Knowles jerked his head in the direction of the clock. "He's at Saint Louis Cathedral, getting married."

"Impossible," Jayne returned levelly. "I'm here."

"Oh, but, my dear, he's not marrying you. I believe he's marrying, er . . ." Knowles casually lifted his panama hat from his head. Turning it one way, then another, he surveyed the band. When he tired of toying with Jayne, he emitted a bored sigh, and replaced the hat on his head. "I believe the *Times-Picayune* identified the woman as the surprise bride." At that, Knowles slapped his knee. "I suppose she's truly a surprise bride now."

Jayne gasped.

Knowles bellowed once more, "What are you going to do with my books?"

"I don't know!"

Remy had heard enough. He slipped around the French doors, his eyes intent on Knowles's back. Crouching down, he crept silently forward.

"I'll tell you exactly what you're going to do with those books." Knowles disengaged his hand from between the sofa cushions. When it swung upward, he was pointing a gun right at Jayne.

Her hands shot to her abdomen.

Knowles rose slowly to his feet. "You're going to give those books to me."

Remy cleared his throat.

The second Knowles turned, Remy lunged over the sofa back, his weight hitting Knowles full force. Taking a swipe at the man's arm, Remy sent the gun scuttling across the floor. Just as Remy pulled out his handcuffs, Buddy Wyatt and Dan Stanley charged through the French doors.

Remy rose to his feet and backed away from Knowles. Buddy and Dan could wrap up the case now. Remy just wanted to get as far away from here—and Jayne—as possible.

Buddy started to read Knowles his rights.

"You can't arrest me!" Knowles exclaimed.

"Sure we can." Dan scooped up the gun. "On attempted murder. Speedo finally talked and we found the casing to the bullet he fired in the French Quarter. He said he was in your employ at the time."

"I've never heard of anyone named Speedo," Knowles said. "I deny all charges."

"While you're denying them," Buddy said, "don't forget fraud."

Remy knew they'd never make the fraud charge stick—not without the books, which were in Jayne's possession. He nodded at Buddy and Dan. "Thanks, guys," he murmured.

Then Remy turned on his heel and strode through the French doors. Cutting across the villa's lawn, he hopped the privacy wall. His Cadillac was parked right behind Jayne's Volvo. Just as he opened the door, he heard Jayne's footsteps pounding behind him.

"Where are you going?" she called.

He turned and leaned in the open door of his car. Automatically his hand reached for the dashboard. Then he remembered that he'd quit smoking and his cigarettes weren't there.

Jayne hadn't even guessed anything was wrong. She probably thought he'd come out to get something from his car. She was wearing another of the maternity jumpers they'd bought, waving at him with one hand, hugging her fuzzy pale blue sweater around herself with the other. Just watching her run toward him made his heart feel heavy. How was he going to leave her?

She ran right into him, sliding her hands around his waist and pressing her cheek against his chest. He wanted to hold her more than life, to forget what had just transpired and wrap her in his embrace. Instead, he forced himself to merely stand there.

"We've got to get to the church, Remy!" she exclaimed breathlessly, gazing up at him.

Inwardly he flinched. "You really expect me to go to your wedding?"

She nodded, as if to say the case wasn't completely solved yet. "And thank you for saving my life," she added with a grin. "I was so scared when Hal pulled that gun that I nearly fainted. If you hadn't been there, I just don't know what I would have done...."

As she rambled, he merely stared at her, so long that her grin started to fade by degrees. How could she be so blissfully unaware of his feelings? And didn't she know when to quit playing with fire?

Jayne's words finally ground to a halt. She gulped. "I really do appreciate your saving my life," she repeated.

"I saved our baby's life," he shot back, emotion getting the best of him and turning his voice hard.

She gaped at him in puzzlement, so shocked by his tone that she clearly couldn't yet believe she'd heard it. "Remy, of course you were saving our baby."

"So, it *is* mine?"

He felt her knees buckle against his. Felt her catch herself just as quickly and tighten her grip on his waist. And then he watched all the color drain from her face.

"What did you just say?" she asked in a choked voice.

"You heard me right."

Her head shook, as if in denial.

"All along," he said, "you suspected Parker and didn't tell me. So why should I believe that the baby you're carrying is really mine?"

"This *is* your baby, Remy."

He glared at her. Her eyes were wide with shock, and tears shimmered in them. All right, he conceded, she hadn't been lying about that. "I suppose you're going to hide those books, so that Parker'll get off scot-free?"

She gasped. Color flooded her cheeks again, turning them scarlet. "Oh, Remy..." she began in a pleading tone.

His jaw set. "What?"

"Of course I'm not. I..." Jayne's eyes darted to the road, as if she were panicking.

In spite of the fact that he didn't want to hear her excuses, he said, "You?"

"I—I didn't want you to know how Parker fooled me, Remy. I couldn't let you think I'd been taken in like an idiot, that I was stupid. I was going to figure it all out and then tell you...."

She was leaning harder against him, as if her sheer body weight could hold him there. He let her cling to his waist while he reached into one of his jeans pockets and withdrew his keys.

Jayne's pleading voice became a near cry. "Can't you understand, Remy? Doesn't loyalty mean anything to you?"

"Loyalty to what, *chère?* To a criminal like Parker? You sure haven't been loyal to me."

She looked so miserable that Remy almost gave in and drew her against him. Why did she have to be so damn pretty? So vulnerable-looking? When she blinked, the tears that had been gathering in her eyelashes started to fall.

"I've known Parker so many years," she continued, her eyes begging his. "We went to school together, started a business—"

Remy's chuckle carried a warning. He reminded himself that he'd long held Jayne up as a standard—and that he'd held her up too high. "Jayne, the man is marrying another woman. Right now. At this very moment. Where the hell is his loyalty to you?"

"I know, but you've got to under—"

"I understand that you'll stop at nothing to exonerate him."

"But, Remy, he was the first man who ever said he loved me . . ."

Remy's throat closed like a trap and he couldn't breathe. "Any man can say that, Jayne," he said hoarsely. "But never forget I was the first man fool enough to mean it."

"You're not a fool." She hugged him fiercely. "I love you. Oh, Remy, we can't start fighting. Not now. Not when everything's over and we can be together."

"The fight was between you and Parker." As Remy tried to lean away from Jayne, her hold on him tightened. "I'm just some guy who got stuck in the middle."

But it wasn't exactly true. There was plenty of fight between them. And a lot of love. It was in her falling tears, in the baby she was carrying, and in the way she'd made love to him throughout the night. They couldn't be together, though. Not when she kept secrets and deceived him. Not when she wouldn't share her whole self.

"I'm going to turn Parker in," Jayne pleaded, lifting a hand long enough to swipe at her damp cheeks. "You'll see. You have to believe me, Remy. And the books are right in my car. I'm going to give them to Dan. I'm going to—"

In midsentence, Jayne choked back a sob, and Remy's heart lurched. Involuntarily he reached for her, but he stopped his hand in midair.

"I swear I was going to tell you everything!"

"The same way you were going to tell me about my baby?" he returned with lethal calm.

The words sent her staggering backward. When she was clear of him, she leaned forward and clutched a handful of his shirt.

"I have to go," he said simply.

His shirt slipped through her fingers, and she stumbled. Her voice catching with emotion, she said, "Where are you going?"

"Out of your life," he returned.

And with that, Remy got in his car, shut the door and drove away.

JAYNE HEADED straight for the church.

For one long, stunned second, she had stood in the empty parking spot where Remy's car had been. Now she laid on the horn of her Volvo and pressed the gas pedal all the way to the floor. Not that it mattered. Remy was so long gone that she wouldn't even pass him on the road. Setting her face in a fierce expression, she ignored the tears that leaked beneath the frames of her glasses.

The glasses Remy had fixed.

The thought made her want to pull over to the side of the road, curl into a ball in the car and weep. Instead, she sobbed loudly, but kept driving.

Oh, she *had* been protecting Parker. She knew that now. Still, that didn't mean she wasn't in love with Remy.

Sure, she'd wanted to give Parker the benefit of the doubt because of their seven-year association. But was that such a crime? She would do that a million times over for Remy.

"Pride goeth before a fall," she said in a tremulous voice, thinking of her mother's favorite axiom. Oh, how could she have withheld so much from the man she loved? Last night proved Remy truly wanted her, didn't it? That was why he'd made love to her under the glow of soft lights. In lovers' whispers, they'd vowed never to keep secrets or hide things from each other. They were supposed to share everything now. To never worry about feeling exposed . . .

But she loved Remy almost too much. So much that she kept fearing his rejection. That was why she hadn't told him about the baby, and why she'd foolishly wanted to solve this problem with Parker herself. Jayne tried to steady her shoulders, but they kept shaking with her sobs.

We could have been a family. Me, Remy and the baby. But I blew it. Oh, damnation, I blew it.

"Don't worry, Jayne," she croaked in a broken voice. "He'll come crawling back."

But he wouldn't.

Remy was never coming back at all—much less crawling.

It was all up to her now. First, she had to send Parker to prison. Then she'd find Remy. She'd go to any lengths to get him back, too. And if she did, two things were certain. She would never lie again. And she would never let him go.

Jayne careened in front of Saint Louis Cathedral, her damp eyes leaping to the clock under the middle spire. *Was it really 12:45?* It couldn't be! Was her wedding over? From beneath the seat, she grabbed the ledger books.

Wiping away her tears, she jumped out of the car, bolted up the cathedral steps and burst through the central door.

Then she stopped in her tracks.

Far away, at the other end of the long white runner in the aisle, a tuxedo-clad Parker was standing at the altar. The woman who clung to his arm was wearing Jayne's missing wedding dress with the long, heavy veil. Just seeing the couple made Jayne's tears dry and her heart harden.

Parker, she thought with venom. The bastard—and there was just no other word for him—was trying to fool everyone. But she wasn't going to let him. It would be a cold day in the deepest depths of hell before he got away with this. Jayne would make sure of that. She narrowed her eyes and saw, with satisfaction, that the media had turned out in full force for her society wedding. Reporters crowded the side aisles, and cameramen hunkered down next to the bridesmaids.

The bridesmaids. Jayne realized that her six pregnant sisters formed a neat line behind the proxy bride. Standing regally along the altar rail, they wore pretty peach dresses and clutched bright bouquets of spring flowers. Jayne's brothers-in-law had dutifully filed behind Parker.

Not a soul noticed Jayne. All eyes were fixed on the bride and groom.

For the briefest instant, Jayne felt like a complete outsider. Everything was so incredibly lovely that her heart wrenched and fresh tears wet her eyelashes. Her gaze darted to the first pew, where her mother and father were standing. They looked so proud that Jayne turned tail to run. But then she forced herself to face the altar again, blinking her stinging eyelids and staying her ground.

It could be worse, she told herself firmly. *You could have actually been in love with Parker.* Swallowing her pride, Jayne squared her shoulders and started marching right down the center aisle, feeling her fury rise with every step. Her misplaced loyalty to Parker Bradford had cost her Remy. *The father of my baby. The man I want to marry. The only man I can ever love.*

Before Jayne could reach the altar, the minister said, "I now pronounce you man and wife. You may kiss the bride."

She watched in mortification as Parker gingerly tilted the veil of the wedding dress. It was a smooth move, all right. He turned the mystery bride's shoulders toward the altar, so that she faced away from the congregation, and then he ducked beneath her veil for the kiss. No doubt he meant to lift the woman into a cradling embrace, too—and then carry her from the church before anyone could get a look at her.

It was sheer lunacy.

It was the kind of thing that happened in cartoons.

Or during Mardi Gras…when nothing was as it seemed.

But, for Jayne, Mardi Gras no longer meant the season for costumes, pretending and revelry. From now on, it could only mean one thing. The time when she'd fallen in love with Remy Lafitte—only to lose him.

Don't think about Remy, or you'll cry again, Jayne.

No, she definitely couldn't let Parker see her cry. Especially not when the man was pretending to marry her. He probably thought the chances of the scandal breaking over the next twenty-four hours were slim. By tomorrow night, of course, the election would be over and he'd be a member of the state House of Representatives. *And in an even better position to rob trusting citizens.* Within a week, Jayne was sure, he'd have had his supposed marriage to her annulled.

But none of that was going to happen. Because she was going to expose her fiancé as a fraud.

A soft cry suddenly rose from the congregation.

"That's Jayne Wright!" someone said in a shocked tone.

"My heavens!" exclaimed a hushed voice. "Who did Parker just marry, then?"

The low murmur of joined voices sounded in sighs and gasps. A light flashed as one lone cameraman snapped a photograph. Then many lights, as the others followed suit.

From the corner of her eye, Jayne saw her parents wrench around and gape at her. Her sister Charlotte lost her hold on her bouquet, and it tumbled to the floor. Jayne forced herself to keep walking. Whatever the reaction of her family, she meant to deal with Parker first.

"Heavens to Betsy," Helen Wright murmured as she passed.

"Jayne?" Antonia gasped, just as Jayne reached Parker.

"If that's Jayne," Paula said, "then who is—"

"The bride?" Edwina finished.

Beneath the veil, the mystery woman yelped, as if only now realizing she'd been caught. As Jayne advanced, the woman groped for the train of the wedding dress and tried to edge backward.

"Oh, no, you don't," Jayne said in a lethal tone. With lightning speed, she grasped the veil and, with one quick tug, pulled it off and tossed it onto the white runner.

"Lynn Seward," Jayne pronounced loudly, not the least bit surprised. She held up the ledgers and waved them in the air. "While you two were getting married, I've been busy tracking down these."

"You broke into my house!" Lynn shrieked.

Parker gasped. "You had them, Lynn?"

Pure fury coursed through Jayne's veins. Books in hand, she whirled toward the congregation. She waved her arm over the crowd—as if everyone had fallen under a spell and she was wielding the magic wand that could turn illusion into reality again. "Parker's been stealing money from the Carrollton Riverside apartment escrow funds," Jayne called out. "He and Hal Knowles have been robbing employee funds at Hal's sugarcane refineries, too."

Everyone in the congregation gasped in unison.

Parker groaned. "Jayne, how could you!"

Her heart pounding with anger, Jayne pivoted and faced Parker again. "How could *you?*" Her eyes trailed over him, taking in how possessively Lynn clung to him. No doubt, Lynn Seward and Parker Bradford were lovers. Lynn had begun to treat Jayne kindly only after the wedding plans were announced—probably hoping to encourage Jayne's prenuptial jitters. Parker wasn't such an old-fashioned Southern gentleman, after all.

"He never loved you!" Lynn spat. "He loved me. He's always loved me. But he needed a wife from an old political family like yours to help him get elected. I took the books out of his safe the other night. I was going to give them back if he called off his wedding to you."

"Lynn," Parker said, clearly in shock, "you mean you had the books the whole time? You could have gotten Jayne killed!"

Jayne fought the urge to simply reach out and slap her ex-fiancé. "You didn't exactly come forward to save me," Jayne said, trying not to think of the man who had. She glanced toward the aisle and realized that the reporters were writing down her every word. She glared at Lynn. "Guess your little plan backfired, didn't it, Lynn? When Hal Knowles assumed I had the books, he sent thugs after me. And when they actually fired a shot at me in the French Quarter, you got scared and didn't tell Parker what you'd done."

"Parker was just marrying you to win the election!" Lynn wailed.

For the first time, Jayne heard her own heart thudding dully. Blood whirred loudly in her ears. "Or in case he got arrested for any of his crimes," she managed to add. "Maybe he didn't think I'd testify against him if I was his wife."

"I was trying to help you, Jayne!" Parker shouted the words in the general direction of the congregation.

"Help me?" Jayne echoed in a venomous tone.

"Jayne's pregnant," Parker called out.

At the words, a whoosh of air left her lungs.

Then more hushed whispers sounded from the congregation. Jayne's eyes slid past Lynn to her siblings. She glanced at them in turn, her gaze finally settling on Edwina, who was first in line.

"Lord knows, we'll all help you with the baby, Jayne." Edwina shot Parker a murderous stare, before smiling at Jayne. "We're just thanking our lucky stars that you didn't marry this...*man.*" Edwina spat out the word *man* as if it were a curse.

"That's right, honey," Helen Wright called out.

Recognizing her mother's voice, feeling the support emanating from her siblings at the altar, Jayne felt tears sting her eyes again. She glanced over her shoulder. Her mother smiled bravely at her. Jayne's throat tightened, but she forced herself to meet her father's gaze. He looked absolutely livid.

"I know every judge in this country," Judge Wright said to Parker, "and I hope whichever one sits on your case sends you away for a long, long time." He glanced at Jayne. "You all right, Robert?"

At that, a tear did slide down her cheeks. This was her family. No matter what, they'd always love her. "Yeah, Dad," she managed to say.

And then she turned to Parker a final time.

As if he only now realized what he'd lost—his career, his freedom, his bride—Parker's voice rose to a wail. "You people can't do this to me! You need me, Jayne. We're partners! No one's going to marry you, and you're all alone!"

The words were so terrible that utter silence fell over the congregation. Jayne bit back a sob.

"There's not even a daddy to claim your baby now!" Parker shouted.

"Oh, yes, there is."

And there really was.

When Jayne whirled around, she saw Remy standing in the center aisle of the cathedral. She'd never been so glad to see anyone in her life. Buddy Wyatt and Dan Stanley flanked him. They'd probably come for the books—and to lock away Lynn and Parker. Remy might not have forgiven her, but he'd come. And he'd publicly claimed their baby.

Parker gasped. "Lafitte's the father of the baby?"

"Yes—" Jayne's eyes never left Remy's "—he most certainly is."

Suddenly, unexpectedly, from behind his back, Remy withdrew one long-stemmed rose.

There'll be a million more roses, Jayne.

She could hear the words as surely as if Remy had spoken them aloud.

And this particular rose meant he hadn't come for the baby alone. He'd come for her. Slowly Remy spread his arms open wide.

Jayne bolted for his loving embrace, salty tears making her eyes feel gritty. "Forgive me?" she whispered as he caught her and hugged her close.

"Of course I do," Remy murmured, nuzzling his cheek against hers. "I got halfway down the road and knew I could never live without you or the baby. And I know you love me, too."

"Oh, I really do," Jayne said on a tearful sigh.

"Ah, *chère*," Remy whispered simply, before his lips captured hers in a kiss that spoke louder than words—saying that in a world where things were sometimes not what they seemed, their love, so genuine and real and true, would always endure.

Epilogue

July 4

"Pant, *chère,*" Remy said.

For the past few hours, Remy had done nothing but call her *chère,* sugar and darlin'. Of course, Jayne now knew her husband meant every last one of those endearments. She dutifully exhaled a long series of quick pants. *Just thank your lucky stars this can't last forever,* she thought. Or maybe it could. Her due date had been June 23, and here it was the Fourth of July.

"I said pant."

Jayne exhaled another grouping of the darn pants until her glasses fogged. All at once, she yelped. Two tears dislodged from her eyes and rolled down her cheeks.

No big deal. She'd been crying off and on for hours. That was how bad the pain could get. Next time she saw Belle Burdette, she might just tell the little girl to stick to her guns—and forget about having babies.

Now, Jayne, you don't really mean that.

But labor could sure make a woman testy. She twisted her wedding band on her swollen pinkie—it was the only finger the ring would fit nowadays—then reached for the pearls and heart-shaped Mardi Gras beads that graced her neck. "Remy!" she suddenly wailed.

"Nice deep breaths now, *chère.*"

Feeling Remy's hands on her knees, Jayne looked wildly around her and Remy's new house on Dauphine Street. It was large enough to accommodate both his need for chaos and hers for empty space. But why had she agreed to have the baby at home? Maybe she wouldn't be cramping so badly if she were in a nice utilitarian hospital. Especially since she'd fought so hard to make the city buy more ambulances. All she and Remy had to do was call 911 and—

She moaned.

"Think about something pleasant, Jayne."

"What?" she shrieked.

"Anything, sweetheart."

A sharp pang of pain brought her nearly to a sitting position. *Think about something, Jayne.* But what? Her life? She'd never known anyone's could change so much in a mere few months, that was for sure.

Hal Knowles, Parker Bradford and Jason Moody, alias Speedo, had gone to prison, of course. Lynn Seward had received a probationary sentence, as had Smiley. Smoothtalk was still keeping to the straight and narrow.

Because of the media presence at the wedding on Mardi Gras Day, news of Parker's and Hal Knowles's fraud scheme had instantly hit the papers. And, to Jayne's complete amazement, she'd found herself the winner of the election the following day. Impressed by her honesty, the tenants of the Carrollton Riverside apartments, as well as the general public, had written her in, and she'd won by a landslide.

Fortunately, her new husband had a flexible schedule and could take care of the new baby when the House of Representatives was in session. Meantime, Celeste was back at her job and keeping the newly founded Wright Legal Services office running like clockwork.

As for the illustrious Wright family? Well, they were making their adjustments. Six little girl babies had recently been born, and all were happily awaiting the entrance of their new cousin into the world. While Jayne's sisters all conceded that Remy probably wouldn't become the next president, they all thought he was the best-looking of the husbands—and a fine catch.

Predictably, Helen Wright had merely smiled when Jayne's marriage to Remy was announced and said, "Nothing more surprising than a surprise!" Shortly thereafter, feeling absolutely convinced that Remy must be related to the infamous pirate Lafitte, Helen Wright had begun to work on Remy's genealogy.

The judge had accepted Remy with open arms the instant he heard that the LaJeure and Lafitte families ran to boys.

Not that Remy couldn't hold his own with the elder Robert. As a man who'd long worked in the New Orleans law-enforcement community, Remy knew his way around politics.

Not to mention makeshift delivery rooms.

"Are you with me, Jayne?"

Barely.

"Push, *chère*," he said. "You can do it."

Feeling Remy's hands press harder on her knees, Jayne clenched her teeth against the pain and pushed.

And pushed.

And pushed.

And then it happened.

Jayne was sure her whole body had just turned inside out. Had something gone wrong? No...no, it hadn't.

The tiny, damp, squawking mass of their child was suddenly wiggling wildly in Remy's hands. A moment later, he held up the baby so that she could see.

"He's fine," Remy assured gently, placing the infant into Jayne's arms. "He's just a little messy."

He? It's a boy?

Jayne was too stunned to speak. All at once, she realized she was crying and her cheeks were wet with tears. She sniffed loudly and stared down at her son. Next to her, Remy dabbed the baby gently with a damp cloth, bathing him. Not that the baby noticed. He was letting out long, piercing cries—filling his lungs over and over again.

"Oh, Remy..." Jayne said on a sigh.

Sliding next to her, Remy's arms slipped beneath hers so that they could both hold their son. After a long moment, he said, "I think there are some folks outside clamoring to come in."

The illustrious Wright family, and Jenny Lafitte.

"Let's wait," Jayne whispered, gazing down at their little baby boy. "Just for another minute."

Remy nodded.

Outside, night had fallen. Through the window, the sky suddenly lit up with the beginnings of the Fourth of July fireworks. Jayne glanced between the window, the baby and Remy. And then her eyes landed on the roses in the room. She hadn't seen them before. A dozen or so, in a clear vase. She looked at Remy and the baby again.

"There's a million more roses in the other room," Remy said with a slow smile.

Unable to take her eyes from her husband and son, Jayne shakily whispered, ''Everything I've ever wanted is right in here.''

Remy's smile deepened then—and he leaned past their newborn, his lips feathering across hers. The kiss was lighter than the air, but Jayne knew it was still the most substantial thing in the world.